YA Anstey, Cindy
ANS

Carols and chaos

NC

CINDY ANSTEY

Swoon Reads | New York

A Swoon Reads Book
An imprint of Feiwel and Friends and Macmillan Publishing Group, LLC
175 Fifth Avenue, New York, NY 10010

Carols and Chaos. Copyright © 2018 by Cynthia Ann Anstey.
All rights reserved. Printed in the United States of America.

Our books may be purchased in bulk for promotional, educational, or business use. Please contact your local bookseller or the Macmillan Corporate and Premium Sales Department at (800) 221-7945 ext. 5442 or by email at MacmillanSpecialMarkets@macmillan.com.

Library of Congress Cataloging-in-Publication Data

Names: Anstey, Cindy, author.
Title: Carols and chaos / by Cindy Anstey.
Description: First edition. | New York, N.Y. : Swoon Reads, 2018. | Sequel to: Suitors and sabotage. | Summary: Kate Darby, a lady's maid, and Matt Harlow, a valet, become entangled in a yuletide counterfeiting scheme at Christmas time, 1817, as they try to stave off their feelings for one another.
Identifiers: LCCN 2018003012 | ISBN 9781250174871 (pbk.) | ISBN 9781250174864 (ebook)
Subjects: | CYAC: Love—Fiction. | Household employees—Fiction. | Counterfeits and counterfeiting—Fiction. | Christmas—Fiction. | Great Britain—History—George III, 1760-1820—Fiction.
Classification: LCC PZ7.1.A59 Car 2018 | DDC [Fic]—dc23
LC record available at https://lccn.loc.gov/2018003012

Book design by Sophie Erb

First edition, 2018

1 3 5 7 9 10 8 6 4 2

swoonreads.com

As always, for my family—especially,
Mike, Christine, Deb, and Dan

chapter 1

In which there is a bullish meeting

FRIDAY, DECEMBER 12, 1817

Miss Kate Darby of Shackleford Park scowled, and yet the recipient of her dark looks was not in the least intimidated. She snorted in vexation—very quietly, of course, just a whisper of warm breath drifted into the afternoon chill. She tried to exude strength, calm, and dominance in this staring contest: to look away would be perceived as weakness . . . at her peril.

"Nothing to worry about, my friend," she said, her words barely audible. "I will be out of your way momentarily."

The beneficiary of this bravado was a big fellow with a broad forehead, prominent eyes, and curly black hair. He wore a look of irritation that was growing more passionate with each passing moment. The threat that his mood would escalate into fury, and the dire consequences that would accompany this rage, was all too real.

Standing some twenty feet apart, Kate knew that the distance was too close for comfort—for both of them. The bull could cross that divide very quickly despite his size and weight; there would be no outrunning this huge battering ram. And so she stared, willing the behemoth to stay just where he was, shoulders hunched, pawing the ground.

Slowly, in small moves, Kate inched backward. The gate leading to Wattage Lane was behind her . . . somewhere. If only she had been paying better attention.

So intent on correcting a mistake, she had slipped through a narrow opening on the east side of the field, leaving Marie by the road. Distracted by eager anticipation, Kate had not assessed her surroundings properly. There had been no animal in sight when she had glanced around the large enclosure. She had seen, but not signified, the large hoofprints in the hardened mud.

Foolish and foolhardy, she had skipped across the meadow, loudly calling to the cart rolling past the far side of the enclosure. Perhaps if she had moved with deliberation, quietly with stealth, she might have made it across the wide expanse without incident.

It was a moot point.

The rightful occupant of the pasture had heard her halloos and drawn near, likely to investigate first, and then, having found an interloper, to challenge. If Kate did not find her way out of the enclosure fast, she would suffer the consequences of her imprudent distraction.

"This is a rather sticky situation," a familiar deep, melodic voice said softly. It wasn't a whisper, but the statement was spoken in a gentle tone in recognition of her precarious position in the standoff.

Keeping her expression passive, Kate fought the urge to turn. "Ah, Mr. Harlow. You heard me call."

"Indeed, Miss Darby. I believe they heard you all the way back to Tishdale. I'm sure every hen in the neighborhood just stopped laying."

Kate almost laughed—almost. "Please, Mr. Harlow, do not be amusing. It would be to my detriment."

"Oh, I do apologize. The hens are likely fine. You, on the other hand . . . well, definitely sticky."

"I've dealt with worse."

"Really?"

"I have three older brothers."

"Yes, indeed. Far more dangerous than a raging bull."

"I've always thought so. This is merely a modest predicament," she said airily, and then swallowed with difficulty when the bull snorted. "How far am I from the gate?"

"Not far. Shift a little to your left—yes, exactly. And now, straight back ten feet or so."

There was a squeal of metal on metal behind her—hinges.

"What are you doing?" Kate asked, though she had a fairly good idea.

"It might be easier to slip out of an open gate than to barrel through."

"Excellent idea."

"I thought so."

"You'll close it after me?"

"Should I? I thought the big fellow might want to gad about . . . looking for cows."

"What he might want to do, and what is best for everyone in the area, might not be the same thing. He should probably stay in the field."

"In that case, I will swing the gate closed behind you."

"Excellent. Are you ready? I will count to three—oh. Oh no."

Lowering his head, the bull snorted again. It was the final warning, and Kate knew it. The standoff was over.

Pivoting, Kate ran. She could hear the pounding hooves advancing on her. A scream built in her throat, and she tensed, readying for the blow. Suddenly, a shriek split the air and the pounding halted abruptly.

Surprised, Kate glanced over her shoulder and blindly careened into Matt Harlow. Momentum propelled them awkwardly through the gate, but Matt quickly regained his footing. They stuttered to a stop a few feet from the enclosure, still standing but with Matt's arms wrapped around Kate. Then, seeing the bull turn his head in their direction, Matt leapt forward. He slammed the gate shut, knocking his cap to the ground in the process. Both stared across the field to the figure that was standing on the far wall, shrieking and flapping her burgundy cloak.

Kate giggled, a little longer than warranted. There was a touch of mania to the sound. "That's Mary . . . I mean, Marie," she said quietly, looking up at Mr. Harlow. Realizing that he was much too close for propriety, Kate shifted away and turned back to the far side of the field, lifting her arm in a large swooping wave.

"Thank you, Marie! I'm fine now," she shouted. "All is well!"

Seeing her friend jump down from the stone wall, Kate dropped her voice. "Thank you," she said again, directing her comment this time to Mr. Matt Harlow.

"Most welcome," he said with a broad smile. "Wouldn't want to see you laid up this close to Christmas."

"Or laid out."

They stared at each other for some minutes. "That, too," he said quietly, ignoring her teasing tone.

Kate smiled, strangely pleased by his brief frown.

Her memory had not played her wrong, not embellished the appealing aspect that was the Steeple valet. Matt Harlow was indeed the handsome young man with broad shoulders, medium brown hair, and hazel eyes that she remembered. He did dress impeccably and yet have a slightly disheveled look about his hair. More important, his impish yet charming smile had been reaffixed.

While Matt bent to retrieve his cap, Kate set about

straightening her cloak as it had twisted to the side. Once completed, she tugged her mittens back into place. Then they turned in unison to greet each other properly—civil expressions on their faces as were dictated for persons of such a short acquaintance.

"Good afternoon, Miss Darby," he said formally, nodding his head in a respectful bow.

"Good afternoon, Mr. Harlow." Kate bobbed a curtsy.

"Fine day for a stroll," he said with a raised brow.

"Indeed. And a drive from the coast. Did you have a pleasant journey?" Kate asked.

"Well, the trip was far less eventful than the last few minutes."

He seemed to wait for Kate to explain . . . which she didn't do. It was far more fun keeping him wondering. "Yes, I can imagine that's true."

"Oh, for heaven's sake, Miss Darby. Why were you shouting across the pasture? And why were you giving that poor bull a hard time? Invading his territory and all that. You could have been killed."

"Yes, that was a mistake . . . though an honest one. Farmer Gibbs took his animals off the field some weeks ago. He must have thought the day too fine to waste and put them, or at least him, back on."

"Which still doesn't explain why you felt the need to cross the field in the first place. There is a perfectly good road on either side."

Kate laughed. Now they were at the heart of the matter.

"Yes, however, the road *I* was on leads to Shackleford Park. The road *you* were traveling leads to Wattage."

"I beg your pardon? We were on the wrong road?"

"Yes. I was in Tishdale with Marie." Kate turned, looking over her shoulder to see the top half of Marie Whynaught standing behind the stone wall. The hood of her cloak had fallen back to reveal dark blond curls and a furrowed brow, conflicting with her pert features.

Facing Matt once more, Kate used her chin to point toward the opposite road. "You missed the turn. We were on our way back to Shackleford Park when I saw your cart across the pasture. You would have realized your mistake at Wattage, but it would have taken you three-quarters of an hour out of your way and then again to return. It seemed reasonable to save you from traveling hither and yon on a deplorable road for nothing. Hence the shouting for your attention . . . and thereby gaining the bull's interest."

"Thank you for putting your life in danger to save me from an hour and a half of pointless travel."

Kate laughed. "Yes, well, it was quite unintentional—the danger part, not the helping part."

"I should hope so."

"So what's all this, then?" a new voice called from farther down Wattage Lane.

Matt winked at Kate and then turned his head. "You were taking us down the wrong road, Johnny. You've never been good with directions."

"Me? *You* was the one here in the summer."

Kate shifted so that she might see Johnny—last name unknown. Wearing the green Steeple livery, he was about Matt's age—nineteen or so—tall and lanky, as most footmen tended to be, with a striking countenance if not handsome. His eyes were a trifle too deep-set to complement his thin lips, and yet there was an appealing hint of mischief about him.

"Had you been attending properly, I wouldna made the mistake, now would I?" the footman said. "You were too busy waxing on about the charms of—"

"Shall I introduce you?" Matt interrupted with a glare.

Johnny laughed, not in the least slighted. He stepped forward and doffed his hat. "Johnny Grinstead, third footman to the Steeples of Musson House . . . for near on three months."

"Kate Darby, lady's maid at Shackleford Park. It's a pleasure."

"Indeed it is, Miss Darby," he said, stepping closer still and dropping his voice to an intimate whisper before reaching out to take her hand. "Lovely country you have here," he crooned.

With a smile, Kate agreed and glanced at Matt to see him shaking his head. She grinned as he shouldered Johnny out of the way, pulling her hand free from the grasp of his companion and tucking it into the crook of his elbow.

"You can show us the way to Shackleford Park," Matt said, leading her down the lane to where the cart waited.

"It is simple enough," she said as she minced through a patch of mud. "Turn around, and take the first left off the main road."

"Simple enough for someone who has lived in this area of Kent all her life, but for us poor coastal souls . . . well, we would appreciate your guidance."

Kate didn't argue further. After all, spending a few minutes with Matt Harlow in the intimacy of a pony cart before being inundated with people and duties was a rather pleasant notion.

The pony cart, tied to a gorse bush by the side of the road, was of a good size, though not quite a wagon. Packed to a level above the rails, the cargo was hidden and held in place by canvas tied in the corners. The cloth was heavily soiled, likely in an attempt to demean the contents. The road from the coast was not known for highwaymen, but it would be beetle-headed to take a chance with the precious foodstuffs being sent ahead by the Steeple family.

Glancing up the road, Kate congratulated herself on her quick thinking—willfully ignoring her close encounter with the Gibbses' bull. The road to Wattage was a disaster at the best of times—with the surveyor of that parish paying little heed to its ruts and crumbling bridges—but it was doubly so in the winter.

Yes, there were plenty of reasons for her impulsive sprint across the pasture. It had nothing to do with Kate's enthusiasm to see Matt. They barely knew each other; they had shared a few significant looks in the summer but not much more than that. She was drawn to him as *anyone* might be. A handsome stranger with an infectious smile was a rare commodity at Shackleford.

"—Bailey."

Kate jerked out of her reverie. "I beg your pardon?"

"If you could hold Bailey," Matt said, passing her the reins to the pony, who was now unhitched from the bush as well as the cart. Kate nodded, leading the large pony—almost horse-sized—farther down the narrow road out of the way.

Matt and Johnny soon had the cart facing the right direction and Bailey reattached. Kate was handed up to the driver's bench and they were off. Squished between the young men, Kate was acutely aware of Matt's leg pressed against hers—Johnny's was as well, but it wasn't as distracting.

"How was your journey thus far?" Kate asked Johnny.

Johnny proceeded to describe the lengthy, though uneventful, trip in such harrowing terms that he had her smiling all the way back to the main road. He turned left at her direction, and they pulled up along the east side of the Gibbses' pasture, where Marie waited . . . looking none too pleased.

"You ought not to have run across the field," Marie said without preamble as they pulled up before her. She had pulled her hood back over her head and was partially hidden in its shadows. Her mittened hands were tucked under her crossed arms. They were held tightly against the front of her burgundy cloak as she leaned against the wall in a half-standing, half-sitting posture.

"I said much the same, miss." Matt nodded as he helped Kate alight. "Though I have it on good authority that we were destined to a miserable hour and a half journey had she not done so."

"Exactly. Hardly worth the eff—"

"Thank you for distracting the bull, Mary—"

"Marie. You keep forgetting; it's Marie now."

"Oh yes . . . You are right. I must be more flustered than I realized." Kate lifted her cheeks, hoping to appease her companion, who was a gem at the best of times—and a bitter pill at the worst. "It's only been a few weeks."

"Nearly a month now," Marie huffed.

Similarly to the way Kate had been elevated in the spring, Marie had been raised from her former position as a housemaid to lady's maid; Mrs. Beeswanger's previous maid had left service to be married in November. However, when Mary had stepped across the divide into the domain of the upper servants, she had shaken the detritus of her previous duties behind her, raised her chin in the air, and adopted a French pronunciation to her name. Marie no longer wished to associate with those at the lower table, did not want to laugh and chat as Kate still did.

It was a rather rigid approach to the social hierarchy below stairs that Kate hoped would soften over time. She quickly introduced Marie Whynaught to the travelers.

"Hang on, now," Johnny said, still sitting on the cart's bench. "I thought Darby, here, was the lady's maid."

Kate's smile was genuine this time. "There are ladies aplenty at Shackleford Park," she explained. "Marie's duties are to Mrs. Beeswanger, while I care for Miss Beeswanger and Miss Chively." She caught the shared look between the two young men. Imogene Chively was betrothed to their Ben Steeple of Musson House . . . though it was unlikely that Johnny had met Mr. Ben, as the young gentleman had been apprenticing in Canterbury since September. "The two youngest daughters are not yet out."

Johnny looked confused. "Are there no gentlemen?"

"Of course, Mr. Beeswanger . . . and Jasper. Though one can hardly call him a gentleman, as he is a dog."

"But an important part of the family," Matt said with a laugh. He offered Marie a hand.

She looked at it as if it were a rotting fish. "Yes?"

"Would you like some assistance, Miss Whynaught? Onto the cart? We are going the same direction. It will give you a nice respite."

"We don't need a nice respite, do we, Kate?"

"Yes, that would be lovely, thank you," Kate said even as Marie bristled. She reached for the parcel sitting at Marie's feet and passed it to Johnny to set under the bench.

"It is to your benefit that Mrs. Beeswanger thought that the girls will need warmer shawls this evening," Marie said as she hiked up her skirts and used the wheel hub as a step.

"Otherwise, we would not have been coming back from Tishdale and seen you go past on the wrong road!"

Kate cringed. Marie's tone was decidedly caustic.

"There's no room up here," Marie continued. "There is barely room for two, let alone three. I don't know how you did it, Kate."

"It was a mite tight," Matt said, offering Kate a grin. "Perhaps we will make ourselves comfortable in the back."

Johnny leaned forward so that he might see past Marie. "Not sure you'll fit there, either." He had a mischievous smile.

At the back of the cart, Kate let down the tailboard, eyeing the space speculatively. The box was, indeed, filled to capacity with little room to sit. Only the edge offered any possibility of a perch. To stay aboard, they would have to cling to the sides, leaning into each other. Such a shame!

Matt helped Kate aboard with a flourish more befitting a great lady. She settled her cloak and skirts out of Matt's way and he jumped up, trying not to jostle her. Their feet swung with the cart's motion, and they shared a smile whenever they bumped persons . . . which was not a rare occurrence. Kate might have exaggerated the motion a little, but she was fairly certain Matt did as well. Flirting was a most marvelous invention.

"I was rather surprised when Mrs. Lundy told me that you were coming ahead of the family," Kate said, staring at the view behind the cart. It was a quiet stretch of the road with no farms or cottages for another quarter mile. The fields broke through the trees at irregular intervals, affording a pretty sight of the surrounding countryside.

"Mrs. Lundy?"

"Shackleford Park's housekeeper. You would have met her in the summer."

"Ah yes, I remember. Very short, rather stern-looking woman."

Kate laughed at the erroneous description. "No, indeed, that would be Cook. I'm referring to a tall, affable woman who jangles as she walks."

"Ah yes, I remember her well."

"Clearly." Kate shook her head with a giggle—a tiny one. "I would have thought that Mr. Ernest would have need of you . . . that you would have come later with the Steeples."

"Ah yes, but Mr. Ben has need of me more, or so Mr. Ernest thought might be the case. Mr. Ben is arriving from Canterbury tomorrow. He wants to see Miss Imogene as much as possible before returning to his duties in the new year."

Kate looked up to see Matt waggle his brows at her, and she laughed again.

"As to coming early, someone had to accompany Johnny to prevent him from gorging on these preserves."

"I heard that!" Johnny called from the front of the cart.

"Mrs. Lundy will be happy for the goods and the extra hands," Kate said, grinning. "She has been running around since Stir-up Day, making sure the puddings were made, the rooms spotlessly clean, and the decorations ready to go up.

Now that there are only twelve days until Christmas Eve, she is in a tizzy."

"Tizzy?"

"Yes, most definitely. This will be the first occasion with both families together—"

"Of many."

"Yes, exactly. And Mrs. Lundy, being rather old-fashioned—of a superstitious bend, if you know what I mean—she feels *this* Yuletide season, more than any other, must flow smoothly. A good omen for the future."

"Really?"

"Well, that is Mrs. Lundy's belief."

"And Cook's," Marie added from the front of the cart, half turned in her seat. "She wants everything done according to custom to ensure that 1818 is a prosperous year." Her harrumph left Kate wondering if Marie had the same conviction.

"It seems we are here, my good fellows," Johnny said.

Kate glanced over her shoulder and waved to the gardener as he pointed Johnny toward the service drive; the large manor was visible through the trees. Shackleford Park was not an ancient building. The original fifteenth-century house, a shoddy place with uneven floors and chimneys that smoked, had been torn down ten years earlier. A new, chateau-style manor with a mansard roof had been erected in its place.

Kate had no recollection of the old house. There had been no purpose to visit before, having been hired on as a scullery maid at the age of fourteen. When, at sixteen, she had taken on the duties of a housemaid, she had enjoyed the benefit of cleaning a house without the rot of age and layers of ash from years of fires. Positions at Shackleford Park were the envy of the neighborhood.

Upon arriving in the stable yard, Kate slid from her perch, dropping a full six inches to the cobbles. As she turned to untie the ropes, she was surprised to see Mrs. Lundy, wearing neither a cloak nor a shawl, rushing toward them from the service entrance of the manor. A boy of ten followed in her wake. The patched coat and dirty face identified him as a village child—Kate knew him as the boy hired for outside work at her mother's cottage.

"There you are," Mrs. Lundy said, looking at Kate. "Colby has just this minute arrived. Your mother has urgent need of you. You must away immediately."

Kate, stunned and silent, blinked at Colby.

The towheaded boy blinked back. "There were an accident, miss."

"Quickly, my girl, quickly." Mrs. Lundy waved her hands as if to shoo her off.

Kate nodded, pivoted, and then glanced over her shoulder. "Might I cut through the deer park, Mrs. Lundy? It will save me a full ten minutes."

"Of course, of course. Mr. Beeswanger will not mind. You must see to your mother."

Kate nodded again and without another word lifted her skirts and raced back down the drive.

chapter 2

In which a porker, an ewer, and a dirt floor suffer the ravages of a helpful neighbor

Kate was across the road and into the Shackleford deer park within minutes. But there she paused, waiting for Colby Jordan.

"Colby! Please hurry, or I will have to leave you behind." The boy wasn't dawdling but neither was he rushing.

Though spurred by her words, Colby shouted for her to go ahead. "Don't worry about me, miss!"

"All right. I'll run ahead . . ." Kate's frown deepened. "What happened, Colby?"

"A fire, miss," the boy said, panting with the effort of his newfound haste. He must have seen Kate's start, for he quickly added, "Out, it's out. Not too much damage, but Dame Darby were burnt."

With those ominous words, Kate whirled around and raced down the path that led deep into the woods. She had no cause to worry about mantraps, as all knew of Mr. Beeswanger's abhorrence of the contraptions, but there were plenty of other obstacles to avoid. Fallen branches, mud holes, icy puddles, and even a few snowy patches forced Kate to dodge and watch her footing.

Within ten or so minutes skirting the south side of the park, the blue skies were once again visible through the trees as they thinned out. Soon the hedge-groves that lined the Vyse-on-Hill fields were visible and the path widened to the south lane. Kate grabbed the marker post for a moment to catch her breath, ignoring the stitch in her side as best she could. Colby was far enough behind that she could no longer see him.

With a great gulp of air, Kate set off again. The way was clearer from here on, as the lane ran up the hill between the hedges. At the crest, she could see her mother's cottage nestled below among the yews, looking unscathed and quite normal. It was a great relief.

The ivy-covered stone wall that edged the yard was too high to vault, but the white gate was near enough and led directly to the kitchen from the garden. Stooping to avoid knocking her head on the low entrance, Kate rushed in. "Mam," she called before coming to a halt just inside the door.

It wasn't a large room, but it was comfortable and held the necessities. With a low-beamed ceiling, the old wooden table took up much of one end and the huge fireplace dominated the other. Wooden chairs and a bench sat on the near side of the fire and a door to the sleeping chamber on the other.

A short, plump woman standing next to a cast-iron pot in the fire smiled. Her graying hair spilled out from under her cap in a haphazard cascade, and she squealed with delight. "Katey!"

Panting and frowning, Kate held her hands pressed into her sides. "Mam. Colby. Said. You. Were. Hurt. An. Emergency."

"So glad he found ya, Katey-bird. I be in great need of your help."

Glancing around, Kate noted a pile of mending on the table, new blackened soot on the wall behind the chair, a puddle on the stone below it, and a collection of broken pottery piled next to the door. All seemed to be under control. And then her mother reached over to stir the boiling pot with a wooden spoon, exposing a coiled bandage that covered her arm from her wrist to her elbow.

Kate threw her mitts on the table and rushed over. "Mam, what have you done?"

"This? Oh, this is nothin'." She waved her daughter away. "Bit of a burn, nothin' to be concerned about."

Taking the spoon, Kate shuffled her mother away from the fire. Then, holding back the flaps of her cloak with one hand, she stirred the pot with the other. Her mother shifted to the nearest chair, groaning as she did so.

"Why didn't you ask Colby to send his mother over?" Kate asked. "I'm sure Mrs. Jordan wouldn't have minded helping you."

Mam clucked and then sighed. "She was here." She shook her head and gave Kate a significant look. "Not in Tobarton anymore."

Kate turned her frown back to the pot. She knew the direction of the conversation; it was a well-worn path. Her mother was not happy in Vyse-on-Hill.

"Agnes came over as soon as she saw the smoke—the porker was fattier than I thought an' it spilled out somethin' fierce. Splashed across the wall an' caught. It were a mess, but I was handlin' it just fine when she storms in here. Knocks over me clay ewer that were sittin' on the table, an' throws water against the wall. Bossy woman, made me sit and wrapped up me arm so tight I can hardly move me wrist. How'm I to sew without me wrist?

"Then she tells me to not worry about the soup, that she'll bring over supper. But the woman cuts her carrots sideways. How's a person to eat a carrot cut up all wrong? An' she doesn't use enough potatoes. She brought over a rabbit stew last week that was all turnip and onion. I ask you, what is that?"

"Kindness?"

"Kindness! No siree. Agnes is puttin' on airs. Like I'm a charity case now that me sons want no part o' me."

Kate banged the spoon on the side of the pot, then set

the utensil on the shelf above the mantel and placed a lid over the bubbling concoction. She turned and squatted in front of her mother, who glanced at the floor rather than meet Kate's gaze.

Taking her mother's undamaged hand in her own, Kate waited until she looked up. "The boys care a great deal about you, as you know very well. Are they not paying for this fine establishment? Do they not drop by to see you two or three times a week? You know they would have had you in the village if there had been a cottage to rent there. It is not their fault that this was the only place available on Lady Day. Perhaps next March there will be something closer—but Tobarton is only a twenty-minute walk."

"Not goin' ta move around like a vagabond. I shoulda been able ta stay in *my* cottage where *I* raised up my babies. That were *my* place—not Peggy's. Moved in there when your pap and I married—kept it after he passed away. Always made rent. There was no need for me ta go."

"We have been through this before, Mam. It was the only cottage big enough for Henry and his family, what with three little ones and another on the way. It made the most sense."

"I coulda slept by the fire."

"No, you could not have, Mam. You know that." Kate did not have to say anything about Peggy, her oldest brother's wife. They did not get along at all. It was Peggy more than the overcrowding that had the Darby boys looking for a place for their mother. The bickering had been getting to everyone. Her two other brothers, Merle and Ross, often took the children to their place next door to get away from the constant battle of wills.

The Vyse-on-Hill cottage had seemed like an excellent solution—quite roomy for one. But her mother was lonely no matter how often the boys and Kate visited. She said it wasn't the same.

"You know this is only temporary. We'll be out of here soon enough. Into Tishdale."

"Not soon enough for me," her mother grumbled, looking both angry and hurt at the same time. "Ten years don't be very temporary. You'll work at the big house while I twiddle me thumbs waiting to open our dressmaking shop. An' I know one day you'll decide to stay on at Shackleford, leaving me high and dry. I'll 'ave waited for nothin'. Ten years is a long wait for nothin'."

"It might be sooner, Mam," Kate said, ignoring her mother's pessimism. Kate had no intention of working for others all her life; she looked forward to her own place in town with great eagerness. Something her mother had yet to understand. "It all depends on how much I can save . . ." Kate glanced out the window to see the shadow of the leafless apple tree stretching across the yard. Sundown came early at this time of year. "And I have to keep my job in order to save. I have to be getting back. The misses will be needing me to get ready for dinner. What can I help you with before I go? Why did you send Colby after me?"

"That." Mam pointed at the table.

"Your mending?"

"Told Mrs. Lundy that I would have the linens ready by Monday. Not going to make it now. I needs you ta help."

Kate stood for a moment, fighting the sharp retort that wanted to launch from her tongue. This was not the first time that her mother had claimed an emergency that had sent her on a panicked rush to the cottage for nothing.

"You know I cannot sit here and do your mending, Mam. I have to be at the Park, should the girls need me."

"But it won't get done for Christmas day, Katey-bird, if you don't help me. What with so much company comin'—Mrs. Lundy needs her linens."

"That's true, Mam. But I have to get back. I'll ask Mrs. Jordan if she might help, and tell Mrs. Lundy that they will be a little late. Will that work?" They would have to be laundered as well—the whole room reeked of smoke. The linen would have sopped up the odor.

"It will have ta, won't it? If that's the best ya can do." She did not look mollified.

With a quick peck on her mother's cheek, Kate grabbed up her mitts and opened the door. "I'll see you next week? At the big house?"

"Thought that they was holdin' the open house in the

barn this year. Too many workers ta feed in the servants' hall now."

"Yes, indeed. You're right. Mr. Snowdon has the tables ready to set up, and Cook has picked out the geese and started the mincemeat tarts. It'll be grand."

"Will your brothers be there?"

Kate huffed—ever so quietly; her mother was trying to demonstrate how little she saw of her children, and therefore knew nothing of their plans. It was far from the truth.

"Of course. You know Merle would not miss roast goose!" Waving over her shoulder, Kate crossed the threshold and closed the door. She thought she heard a murmur as she did so . . . It sounded as if her mother had said *I might see you sooner*, but that didn't make sense. If her mother thought she could entice Kate back to Vyse before the new year, she had another think coming.

Rather than turn back toward the deer park, Kate headed into the hamlet and crossed the road to the Jordan cottage, Mam's closest neighbor. The good woman must have been watching for her, as Kate had barely stepped onto the walk when Mrs. Jordan came to the door—wiping her hands on a cloth. She was a thin, tired-looking woman with a sour expression when her face was at rest. However, whenever her eyes came in contact with any other human soul, Mrs. Jordan stood straighter and smiled; it changed her entire countenance.

"Beggin' yer pardon, Miss Darby." Mrs. Jordan addressed

Kate as a lady's maid of the great house, not as a neighbor's daughter. "Had I known she sent Colby for ya, I woulda put a stop to it. I know yer busy what with the fine company comin' for the season an' all."

"Not to worry, Mrs. Jordan. But I must get back. Mam is concerned about the linens."

"They'll be done by Monday, miss. Already told 'er I would help."

"Thank you, Mrs. Jordan. You are very kind. I will let Mrs. Lundy know." Kate returned to the road and waved her good-byes to both Mrs. Jordan and her mother, who was peeking out of the cottage window as Kate passed.

MATT FROWNED, staring after Kate as she rushed away. He felt ineffectual, wishing he could do something. Glancing up at the housekeeper, who was staring after Kate as well, he was bewildered by the woman's expression; it was resigned rather than anxious.

"Would the cart be faster?" he asked, stepping toward the vehicle.

Mrs. Lundy turned toward him with a quizzical expression. "Faster?"

"Than running across the park."

"Oh. Oh no. Very kind of you to offer. No need. The roads being what they are at this time of year, walking—or rather running—is much quicker. Though I imagine it is a tempest in a teapot. Usually is . . . but one must act accordingly. Not assume. You know how it is. As soon as you assume . . ." She paused and then gave her head a slight shake. She must have seen the confusion on Matt's face at her rather disjointed conversation. "Let's get you inside and warmed up, Mr. Harlow. No need to stand in the cold." And in so saying, Mrs. Lundy turned, taking herself out of the cold.

Matt looked up the drive again. Kate was now a mere speck; she would soon be lost behind the curve of the road. He stared for some minutes more and then straightened his shoulders and pivoted. Johnny had unfastened the ropes holding the canvas and was passing various foodstuffs to the Shackleford Park footmen.

Cook from Musson House had sent all of Sir Andrew's favorites, not wanting the old gentleman to do without the special treats as *she* made them. Mincemeat, plum pudding, shortbread, and marzipan were all staples of the season, but Cook believed hers to be the best. After all, Sir Andrew had been saying so for years. Add to that a haunch of pork, a basket of sole, and an array of jams and preserves, and the Steeple contribution to the celebration of Yuletide was rather substantial.

Matt reached over the rail and retrieved his bags, nodding to Johnny as he did so. Then, rather than follow the food through the kitchen court, he made his way to the service entrance in Mrs. Lundy's footsteps. Once inside the long narrow corridor, he headed to the far end, where he knew the servants' hall to be. While he could easily find his way up to the guest wing without guidance, he knew better than to assume that Mr. Ernest and Mr. Ben would be in the same rooms as they had been in the summer.

The servants' hall was well occupied. Two maids sat on a bench at the long table playing cards; one looked up at him with a huge smile and elbowed her seatmate as she did so. Another woman sat by the window mending, and a young, somewhat disheveled boy with dirty nails played jacks by the fire. Next to him, a man with his back turned to the door stared at an unlit candle on the mantel. Matt had arrived during that brief hour when duties were at a minimum—just before the staff entered the hectic confusion of dinner and then labored into the night.

"Excuse me, does anyone know the room assignments?" Matt asked the room at large.

All looked toward the fireplace where the man with his back to the door stiffened. With an audible harrumph, he turned. In his middle years with a sharp chin and curled lip, the man arched his left brow and tendered Matt a sardonic appraisal before speaking. "Ah, you have returned, Mr. Heathrow. Welcome," he said in a tone that held no warmth.

Matt nodded, not bothering with a correction of his name. "Thank you, Walker." The Beeswanger butler did not intimidate Matt. He knew from what kind of cloth the man was cut. The only time Walker smiled or even chuckled was in the presence of the Beeswangers or their guests; to the staff he was a terror. "Same rooms as before?"

"Indeed." Walker turned back to the fascinating unlit candle.

With a shrug toward the gawking maids, Matt reentered the corridor, bypassing the narrow spiral stairs that led to the front of the guest wing. He chose, instead, to make his way to the far end of the house and up the back stairs nearest the room he would be using during the Steeples' stay.

Glancing into the hallway first, to verify that none of the family was in the vicinity, Matt sauntered down the carpeted corridor, admiring the paneled walls that had sent Mr. Ben into raptures when they had visited in the summer. Mr. Ben, as an architect's apprentice, saw much value in such embellishments. There was no doubt that the house was both well designed and well appointed. Matt was quite certain that Sir Andrew and Lady Margaret would be impressed. It *would* be worth the effort of bestirring their weary selves away from the warmth and comfort of their own hearth—a sentiment Matt had overheard when Sir Andrew had complained of the need to travel.

Between the doors, partway down the main hall, Matt stopped. He had counted three doors and therefore . . . He reached into the paneling and pulled at a hidden handle. A section of the wall swung forward, revealing a small but cozy room sandwiched between the two guest rooms that had been assigned to Mr. Ernest and Mr. Ben.

Stepping through, Matt quickly closed the door lest a member of the family catch sight of him. As a gentleman's gentleman, Matt was not under the same rules of invisibility as the lower staff, but being as unobtrusive as possible was always good practice.

The room had been nicely prepared. The narrow bed sported not one but two rough blankets, and a fresh rushlight had been placed on the diminutive table under the window. A wardrobe of adequate portions sat opposite a small fireplace—which waited at the ready. Indeed, it was to Matt's relief that Mrs. Lundy, not Walker, was in charge of the manor's guests and their servants.

Rubbing his hands together for warmth, Matt considered lighting the fire but decided to wait until later. There was enough coal to see him through the night if he did not start it too early. So instead, he set about unpacking. It was a rather odd happenstance to be sent ahead of the family. But Mr. Ben would arrive on the morrow, and Matt could go about his usual duties. Until then, he was at loose ends. Though organizing his brushes and polishes took a fair amount of time.

As the sun started to go down, Matt dug into his supplies and pulled out a candle, setting aside the rushlight in case he needed it in the middle of the night. Having just stacked his books on the table and pulled down his waistcoat in an all-done manner, there was a quiet knock on the hallway panel.

"Mr. Harlow? Are you there?"

Recognizing the voice, Matt rushed to the door, opening it to the smiling countenance of Miss Darby. "I am indeed. Is your mother well?" he asked, keeping his relief hidden. He doubted Kate would be smiling in such a lively manner had there been a problem at home, but it seemed politic to ask.

"Yes, indeed. A small fire that was already out by the time I got there. Tempest in a teapot," she said, likely unaware that she was repeating Mrs. Lundy's words.

Unfortunately, she instantly wiped the smile from her face, setting it to a serious expression. Matt much preferred to see her elven features full of merriment.

"Miss Imogene would like to speak with you."

"With me? Really? Do you know what it is about?" Imogene Chively, a close friend of the Beeswanger family, was staying at Shackleford Park.

"No, I'm afraid I don't. Miss Imogene has been pacing about her room for a quarter hour with two letters in her hand. Going back and forth between the two. I hope nothing dire has occurred . . . but no, I know not. She simply stopped in the center of the floor, nodded, and then sent me to fetch you."

Matt frowned. A young lady rarely, if ever, requested to speak with her future husband's valet . . . though in truth, Matt was more Mr. Ernest's man now. Still, two different worlds—never the twain should meet. "I'll come right away," he said, blowing out his candle and giving his room a quick glance to make sure everything was in place.

He followed Kate down the corridor, trying to ignore the enticing sway of her hips and focus on why Miss Imogene might need to speak with him . . . to no avail.

chapter 3

In which there is an embarrassing set-to regarding mistletoe

Matt entered a good-sized room with a generous window overlooking . . . well, it was too dark to see, but he believed it to be the side garden. A glowing fire provided ample warmth, and Miss Imogene Chively sat in a chair next to it, using the lighted candles on the mantel to read a letter in her hand. She was a pretty young lady, with blond hair and blue eyes and a reserved manner about her. A black dog lay curled up on the floor beside her.

Standing by the door, Matt glanced at Kate while they waited to be noticed. She bobbed her brows in his direction; he smiled, and they both started when Miss Chively cleared her throat to get their attention.

"Thank you for coming, Mr. Harlow. I do so appreciate it." She gestured him closer and picked up another letter that had been sitting on her lap. She waved them both in the air. "I have news," she said, and then dropped her volume to a near whisper. "And a request."

"Yes, indeed." Matt waited and waited. "Yes, Miss Chively," he prodded.

Imogene Chively produced such a heavy sigh that Matt was fairly certain that he knew the news before she announced it.

"There has been a delay, I'm afraid. Mr. Ben will not be arriving until Monday now. You will be footloose and fancy-free for two days, Mr. Harlow."

Ah, he had been right. "That is a shame, miss."

"You don't want to be at loose ends for two days?"

Matt chuckled. "A shame that Mr. Ben has been delayed, miss."

Miss Chively sighed again, her eyes glazing over with a faraway look.

"And the request?"

The young lady frowned as if confused momentarily and then gave her head a little shake. "Oh yes. It is a great favor I must ask of you, Mr. Harlow, as it will require you to go out of your way."

"Indeed?" Matt could say no more as he really did not know where this was heading.

"Yes. Did you pack for Mr. Ben when he left for Canterbury?"

"Of course, miss." Now Matt was thoroughly bewildered,

but he did not say so. He wanted to look toward Kate, see if she could elucidate by way of an expression. Or she might mouth an explanation. Or perhaps he merely wanted to see that he was not the only confused person in the room. He stared at the edge of Miss Chively's chair instead.

"Excellent. Did he take any books with him?"

"Yes, architectural books, of course." Mr. Ben was not a great novel reader, as Mr. Ernest was, but he did appreciate the dusty tomes from the Musson House library about old buildings and foundations and the like. Not to Matt's taste but—

"Oh, wonderful. Then you *can* advise me after all. Excellent, most excellent." With a grin, Miss Chively bounced out of her chair, fairly dancing. "I was afraid that I would get it wrong."

This time Matt did glance toward Kate. She lifted her shoulders in a very unhelpful shrug.

"Being my first gift, I so want to get it right," Miss Chively continued, as if she were making sense. Finally, she looked up to meet Matt's eyes. "Oh, I should probably explain."

"That would be appreciated, miss."

"Yes, of course. Well, I have decided on the perfect gift for Mr. Ben. A book about architecture—well, some aspect of it, at least. I wrote to Mr. Gupta—he is the bookseller in Tishdale—and he has just informed me that he has over ten books on the subject. Which is a marvel and a dilemma at the same time. I do not want to present my beloved with a gift on Christmas day, only to discover he already has it.

Would it be too much of an imposition to ask you to look at those books? To ride into Tishdale tomorrow, see if you recognize any? Perhaps hone the number to three or four. I will, of course, make the final choice, but . . . well, is it too much to ask?"

Matt smiled, relieved that the request was of such a benign nature. No snipping a lock of hair or stealing a waistcoat to find a matching neckcloth. "Not at all. I can walk there in the morning."

"Or hitch a ride. I believe Mrs. Beeswanger said something about the mistletoe coming in on the stagecoach."

"Yes, one way or another I will visit the bookstore. But I should probably point out that I do not know all the books that Mr. Ben has read on architecture, and that he might have acquired one or two while in Canterbury."

Miss Chively nodded. "There is that . . . Well, we can only try our best." She pursed her lips and snorted. "Try *my* best," she clarified, sitting back down. She lifted one of the letters closer, rereading it yet again with a smile playing at the corners of her mouth. It had a small sketch on the bottom.

Matt felt a soft touch on his elbow and realized that the interview was over. He turned, exited, and discovered that Kate had followed him.

"I'm afraid you missed tea, and supper is not until eight thirty, after the family has their dinner. Are you hungry?" she asked, one hand on the partially closed door. She was standing across the threshold.

"Not at all. Johnny and I stopped at an inn along the way." He *was* a bit peckish, but not enough to put anyone out. Always best to stay on a cook's good side; requesting an unscheduled bite would not be appreciated.

"Excellent." Kate leaned as if she were about to go inside the room and then shifted back. "Do you know your way to the servants' hall from here?" she asked.

Matt smiled. Was Kate prolonging their conversation intentionally? He set a serious expression on his face. Frowning, he nodded. "I believe I shall retrace my steps." He made a show of looking around and then pointed in the wrong direction.

Kate grinned, no doubt remembering that this wasn't his first time at Shackleford Park, even if he had not had cause to be in the family wing before. "Right at the bottom of the corridor," she said, pointing left.

Matt nodded, maintaining his frown.

"Kate?" Miss Chively's call interrupted their nonsense, and they turned immediately, Kate into the warmth of Miss Chively's room, and Matt to wend his way back from whence he came.

"THAT WAS VERY kind of him," Miss Imogene said without looking up from her letter. "He need not have agreed. It's not part of his duties."

"I believe Mr. Harlow likes to be helpful . . . at least that has been my impression thus far." Kate sauntered across to the wardrobe, trying to exude a calm she did not feel. Matt Harlow's presence was proving to be a most excellent diversion, offering her ample opportunity to flirt. It was an art Kate greatly enjoyed and yet could seldom practice.

"And quite personable."

Kate glanced over her shoulder and met Miss Imogene's sparkling eyes. "Indeed," she said, instilling the ambiguous word with a great deal of warmth.

"One might even say handsome."

"Yes, one might say so . . . if one paid mind to such things." Kate's casual reply was . . . too casual.

"One? One such as a young lady's maid?"

Kate reached into the wardrobe, putting her hand on a soft purple dinner gown. "Not sure Marie noticed, miss. The lilac for tonight?"

"No, I'll save that one for Monday. Not the rose dress, either . . . Let's go with the Pomona green."

"Very good, miss." Kate pulled the gown out of the wardrobe, careful not to catch the lace at the neck or the tucks around the sleeves. It was a lovely, though lightweight, gown that had been sent over from Gracebridge Manor. "You'll need your new shawl, for certain, with this one."

"Yes, I think you might be right." Miss Imogene's voice sounded distant, as if she was lost in thought again. "Yes, it was very kind of Mr. Harlow," Miss Imogene repeated, but in a different tone. Almost questioning.

Kate frowned. She turned back to find the young lady fixing her with a worried stare. "Miss?"

"Be careful, Kate, please. Don't give the Beeswangers cause to notice."

Kate shook her head as if confused, when in fact she knew exactly to what Miss Imogene referred.

"Mrs. Beeswanger is a gem. Look how she has taken me in and treated me like a daughter—better than, in my case. A marvelous, generous person to be sure, but she will not be comfortable—well, she likes a smooth-running household and—well, a dalliance would be disruptive in so many different ways."

"It would, miss. And I would never do anything to put my future in jeopardy. Saving up for a dress shop with me mam. You need not worry. I might flirt a bit, but I know where the future lies."

Miss Imogene sighed, looking relieved. "Excellent," she said in a lackluster tone.

SATURDAY, DECEMBER 13, 1817

"NO! I SAID so before and I say so again and there's an end to it."

Walker stabbed at his breakfast plate without looking up. It afforded the others at the housekeeper's table the opportunity to exchange glances without arousing his disapproval. Kate met Matt's questioning frown and shook her head. She hoped it conveyed an *I'll explain later* message. His answering shrug was equally ambiguous.

Kate dropped her eyes to her plate and grimaced. It would have been lovely, and unusual, to start the day without a set-to between Mrs. Lundy and Walker. Days such as those were few and far between, but given the benevolence of the season, Kate had been hopeful. And yet here they were, arguing about authority—authority over Johnny, the Musson House footman. He had been sent to assist with the Yuletide preparations, but did he fall under Walker's direction—being that he was a footman—or Mrs. Lundy's, since she had the lion's share of the extra duties brought on by the season? Cook didn't step into the fray whatsoever, despite the fact that Johnny had delivered foodstuffs and could be seen as an addition to the kitchen.

Really, it was most uncomfortable . . . and embarrassing.

Kate swallowed and turned her eyes toward the busy wallpaper festooned with cheerful spring flowers. It was just as well that the upper and lower servants ate their meals separately—except the midday dinner, of course. It would have been difficult for the female staff to offer the butler the dignity his position demanded if they witnessed this constant petulance every day. Rumors, of course, were rife. But Mrs. Lundy countered Walker's demands regularly and protected her girls with the tenacity of a mastiff. Though the men knew Walker's temperament rightly enough; they experienced it firsthand.

"It is a shame that you feel so strongly about the matter, Mr. Walker," Mrs. Lundy said, not sounding in the least apologetic. "As Johnny has already agreed."

"I am going to send Bernie this afternoon. That will be soon enough."

"No, it will not. My girls need to sort through the mistletoe and start the kissing boughs in between their other duties. The stagecoach from the midlands is due within the hour; Johnny will be there to meet it." Mrs. Lundy smiled as she spoke, clearly not indisposed by Walker's mood. She lifted the pot beside her and turned to Marie. "More tea, my dear?"

Startled by the sudden attention, Marie dropped the tiny spoon that she had been about to use and the salt on it sprayed across the tablecloth. In no more than a blink, Mrs. Lundy and Cook reached across, grabbed a pinch from the table, and tossed it over their respective shoulders.

"Can't be too careful at this time of year," Mrs. Lundy said to the amusement of the younger staff. Cook nodded emphatically.

"Well," Mrs. Lundy said, pouring out the last of the tea to Norbert, Mr. Beeswanger's valet. "I'd best make haste." She pushed away from the table. "Please excuse me, I have to speak with the mistress." She nodded to all but Walker and left.

Silence flooded the room, filling her void. It lasted for ten minutes or so, becoming increasingly awkward until they all rose at once to vacate. Livy, the scullery maid, stepped through the door to begin clearing and Kate pulled Matt aside in the corridor . . . after watching Walker march toward the front of the house.

"Please, pay no attention to their bickering, Mr. Harlow. Walker and Mrs. Lundy have very different approaches in caring for the family and the house. I'm sure it was thus when you were here in the summer."

"Yes, I believe so. Though there seems to be more tension than there was before. Has something occurred?"

"No, not really. Though Mr. Walker does seem to become testier during Christmastide. It might be the added chores, or he looks at the more relaxed atmosphere of the season as an abomination." Kate laughed, trying to hide her discomfort. She remembered Musson House being in possession of a much more congenial atmosphere below stairs.

"Ah, there you are," Mrs. Lundy said, coming back down the corridor toward them, her keys making a distinct jingle as she walked. "So glad I caught you." She frowned marginally as she glanced from Matt to Kate and back again. "I beg your pardon, but I must ask a favor."

"Of course," Matt replied before even learning what was involved.

Kate smiled. Kind and helpful. Very impressive.

"Mrs. Beeswanger has handed me a list of wines she wishes to have available over the holidays. As I understand that you are going into town with Johnny, might I imposition you to visit the wine merchant on Mrs. Beeswanger's behalf?"

"Of course, easily done." Matt nodded. "Not an imposition at all . . . if you give me the direction."

Mrs. Lundy smiled. "Fortunately, Tishdale is not overly large; most shops and places of business are on the main road. Mr. Niven will deliver, so there is no need to wait."

"Not a problem, Mrs. Lundy. Think on it no more." He took the list and then turned to face Kate as Mrs. Lundy wheeled around and headed toward the kitchen. "Might you need a jaunt into town, too, to pick up . . . something? There is a possibility that we will lose our bearings yet again and be destined to appalling winter horrors. We will need the guidance of one who knows the area well." His impish expression indicated that he knew very well that she would not be able to do so. "We could end up wandering the woods in the cold, hiding from bears intent on doing us terrible harm."

"You need not fear . . . at least not of bears, Mr. Harlow. Though I do recommend staying out of Farmer Gibbs's field. His bull is rather tetchy."

Matt Harlow grinned in a thoroughly charming manner. "Yes. So I have heard."

"THERE BE NO shortage of pretty girls at Shackleford Park," Johnny said much too casually, as he slapped the reins against Bailey's rump. The pony ignored him, plodding along the road to Tishdale at his own comfortable pace.

"Indeed." Sitting on the cart's bench beside his friend, Matt shrugged. The winsome personage of Kate Darby came entirely unbidden to his mind, and he turned his head slightly to hide any betraying glint in his eyes.

"Yup, yup. Pippa has been makin' sheep's eyes at ya since we got there."

"Which one is Pippa?" Matt asked, playing the game.

"The redheaded housemaid, cute little thin' with lots o' curls an' a pert nose. Saucy as all get out." He glanced over at Matt and smiled. "You could chat her up an' see how it goes."

"I could, indeed," Matt said, being excessively agreeable.

"Maud might be a little long in the tooth for ya, but what about Gwen?"

"Gwen is?" Matt's mind was still focused on Kate—her trim figure, thick dark hair, lively smile. "Hmmm? Pardon me, I was thinking of something else."

"Or some*one* else?"

"One never knows." Matt turned back in time to see Johnny shake his head. He was clearly trying to goad Matt into revealing a leaning, a preference . . . anything that could be fodder for teasing.

"Thought that Miss Darby mighta caught yer eye. She be quite fetchin'."

"No more than the others," Matt said too quickly and then tipped his head side to side, nonchalantly stretching his neck. "Nothing to make the blood stir," he lied.

Johnny laughed and turned his eyes back to the road. It

took Matt a few minutes to realize that Johnny was still talking.

"I did so want to give 'em something. A token . . . you know."

Matt frowned. "Them?"

"Camille's little sisters. Thought a box o' candy or a pretty ribbon might do it up proper." He snapped his tongue and then heaved a deep sigh. "But I'm cleaned out."

Matt shook his head, understanding all too well. "Good fortune abandon you again?"

Johnny was an uncomplicated soul but for two weaknesses: love and cards. Unrequited love and unlucky cards, to be exact.

Johnny was smitten with Camille LaPierre, Lady Margaret's personal maid. A pretty French girl with fine manners and dainty ways, she was appreciated by the entire male staff of Musson House—young and old. Fighting to be noticed in the crowd of admirers, Johnny had played the clown, but Camille had not been impressed. He had treated her like a lady, helping her down from the carriage whenever she accompanied Lady Margaret and wiping the bench before she sat for dinner. Camille was indifferent. He lent her a book of poetry—the flowery, useless, romantic sort—and offered to explain it to her. Camille denied him the pleasure.

So now Johnny had decided to play the benefactor. Gifts. But it would be unseemly to bestow a gift on a young woman who was not a sweetheart. It created an obligation; however, a gift to a child brought with it no expectation and was, therefore, quite acceptable.

Unfortunately, Johnny's appreciation of luck, especially as it pertained to cards, was nearly as strong as his attraction to Camille. He invariably lost in that arena as well.

"You know, Johnny, you are going to have to choose," Matt said. "Miss LaPierre will never look at a penniless footman."

"Won't look at a footman, penniless or otherwise. The only way I got her talkin' to me was to say I was gonna be an under-butler soon."

"Well, that was a little foolhardy. You've only been at Musson House three months."

"*Soon* is a relative kinda word. Could be next year."

"Or the one after that?"

"Exactly. See. One day it'll 'appen. And that'll be soon enough." He smiled brightly, clearly pleased with his own cleverness.

"I'm not sure Miss LaPierre will see it the same way."

"Sure she will. *Soon* as she sees what a fine fellow I can be—givin' little gifties to her sisters an' all."

"Well, I suppose a flawed plan is better than no plan at all."

"Flawed?" Johnny looked genuinely puzzled.

"Didn't you say that you were tapped out?"

"Oh. Yes. That's right." He frowned fiercely at Bailey's swishing tail.

Passing Farmer Gibbs's field, Matt craned his neck to stare beyond the wall, but the bull was nowhere to be seen. He smiled, recalling the sight of Kate Darby taking on a bull four, if not five, times her size. He almost chuckled but glanced toward Johnny and swallowed his mirth.

They approached Tishdale at the leisurely pace required by a deplorable road pocked by frozen puddles and the occasional hollow of snow. The Gambling Goat sat on the edge of town, just off the main thoroughfare. As they pulled into the yard of the post inn, Matt could see a number of people milling about in clutches of two or three. When he inquired within, he was not surprised to learn that the coach was late.

"I'll walk to the booksellers," Matt told Johnny, joining his friend outside again. Matt patted his coat to ensure that he had the wine list. "Mr. Gupta can direct me to the wine merchant. If I don't see you on the street, then I'll meet you back here."

Johnny nodded halfheartedly. He was staring at a dark-haired young lady across the yard waiting with an older version—likely her mother.

"Thought you were taken, Johnny boy. Devoted to Camille."

"Hmm, what?" His friend turned back, grinning sheepishly. "Right. Books, wine, meet here."

Mr. Gupta's bookstore was in the second block of the rowed redbrick shops with black doors and large mullioned windows with white shutters. Flower boxes, devoid of flowers, sported sprigs of holly leaves with cheerful red berries. It was a picturesque market town, with plenty of hustle and bustle despite the cold weather.

The bell jangled with a discordant clang when Matt entered, and a large mustached gentleman from India stepped through the back curtain to greet him. The store was lined with bookshelves, and the wares looked dusty and disorganized. However, looks can be deceiving, for no sooner had Matt explained his purpose than Mr. Gupta led him to a particular shelf where Matt could browse. There was a larger selection of architectural books than Matt expected, and it took some time to whittle the choices down to three. In fact, he decided on four that might suit Miss Imogene's purpose—but it was all a guess.

The wine merchant was a mere two shops farther down the main road, where the overly affable Mr. Niven looked at Mrs. Beeswanger's order and declared her an aficionado of wines. Matt found this amusing since the listed selections in the man's store were not diverse. There was little doubt that the Beeswangers were aware of what was available and ordered accordingly.

By the time Matt returned to the Gambling Goat, Johnny was tying up the tailboard of the cart, and a large crate marked with the Beeswanger name sat in the back. The coach had finally arrived.

"Can't believe my luck," Johnny said as Matt approached. He waggled his shoulders, his eyes alive with excitement.

Matt glanced around for the dark-haired young lady but only met the glare of an old codger standing by the inn's door. "Oh?" he said in a noncommittal way.

"Get in, get in. I'll tell ya on the way. Walker is gonna be right put out that we've been gone this long. I've got ta polish the dining room candlesticks when I get back."

It would seem that the struggle about authority over Johnny had been resolved, and Walker had taken the upper hand.

"I can buy something for the little ones after all," Johnny said as soon as Matt had pulled himself up on the bench beside his friend.

"How did that come about?" Matt asked. He held on to the side of the cart as it started to move.

"Sold me ring. You know, the one from the harvest fair. Not worth a penny. But this here fella paid me a full shilling for it."

"What? The tin one with the stag's head stamped on it?"

"Yup, that's the one. I were leanin' on the rain barrel, gettin' more than a little tired o' waitin', when this here red-headed fella comes over an' stands right next ta me. Seemed right put out. He bleats about waitin' for the coach an' how cold it is. Went on an' on somethin' awful. I were just about to move off when he looks over at me and says, 'It's Yuletide, ya know,' as if I were arguin' with him. A bit dicked in the nob." Johnny tapped at his temple with his index finger.

"What has this to do with your ring?"

"I'm gettin' there; don't rush me." He flicked the reins, only to be ignored by Bailey yet again. "'I should get somethin' for my hard work,' this here fool says, as if all folks got gifts for Christmas."

"Something for himself?"

"Yup. Like I said: dicked in the nob. Anyways, I asked if he fancied me ring, 'cause I were lookin' for some funds. Well, wouldn't ya know, the feller offers ta buy it . . . This road?" Johnny pointed.

"Yes, that's the one. Don't want to miss it again."

Johnny grinned, directing the pony toward Shackleford Park. "So I starts to dicker, askin' high—*a shilling*, says I. This here fella frowns at me an' then pulls one outta his coat pocket—no bargainin', nothin'." With a sharp jerk of his head, Johnny straightened his shoulders. "Yup, I'll be able ta get the little ones somethin' worthwhile now."

Matt smiled, caught up in Johnny's euphoria. For once, Lady Luck had offered his friend a boon. Though it did seem a waste, for Matt was fairly certain that a box of candy for Camille's sisters would do nothing to sweeten her resolve toward Johnny's awkward attempts to woo.

chapter 4

In which cold ears bring out the woodland fairies

Sunday, December 14, 1817—St. Thomas Day

"It was an eloquent sermon this morning," Kate told Reverend Comstock as she pulled on her mitts, standing in the vestibule of St. Bartholomew Church. In truth, she had hardly heard a word; she had been too aware of the presence of one Matt Harlow seated not two pews ahead on the other side of the center aisle, partially hidden behind a post. And, of course, there was the weighty matter of not letting anyone else know that she was aware of Matt—she had decided to call the handsome valet by his given name . . . in her mind. "Yes, very thought-provoking," she added.

"I'm glad to have provided some inspiration on such an auspicious day. Which aspect of my sermon spoke to you the most?" The gray-haired minister beamed and reached out to tap her hand.

Frowning slightly, Kate tried to recall the gist of the homily. Unlike most towns, Tishdale celebrated St. Thomas Day a week earlier than the rest of the county—though no one knew why, it remained thus for near on three decades. It was a day devoted to the elderly and poor widows of the parish; it was likely that the sermon had to do with charity. "Charity—" she started to say.

"Indeed," Marie, standing by her elbow, interrupted. She gave Kate a significant look. "Charity would have been the obvious choice, but to center your lesson on doubt, that it could provide a pathway and then a foundation to faith . . . well, truly inspired." And with those words of praise, Marie pulled Kate out the door and into the cold. She laughed and shook her head as they wended their way through the chatting congregation. "You weren't paying the least bit of attention."

"I was, too," Kate argued and then smiled.

"I stand corrected," Marie said, widening her eyes and fixing Kate with a mock glare. "You were not paying attention to the *sermon*."

"There is that." Kate stopped herself from giggling just in time. Marie continued to tug her forward until Kate planted her feet. "Why are we in a hurry?" she asked, turning slightly so that she could watch those leaving the church. She made a show of tying her scarf around the hood of her cloak but left the cowl draped down her back so that she could still see, still watch for Matt.

Fat, fluffy flakes wafted gently on the breeze, melting as soon as they touched skin or the ground. It would make a picturesque background as they walked back to the manor . . . as long as the wind didn't pick up. She had arrived at St. Bartholomew Church with Marie, sitting on the driver's bench of the family coach, but she had declined a return ride. Kate was hoping a certain someone would be interested in walking back with her. Unfortunately, Marie had followed her lead.

"Come on, Kate." Marie tugged again. "I promised Mrs. Beeswanger that I would help distribute the alms. She is going to give me a pouch of coins for the widows while Mrs. Lundy will dole out the cooked wheat."

"Then there is absolutely no need to rush; the family has not yet come out of the church, let alone hopped into the coach. And as to the *mumpers*, the numbers are not so vast that they will be lined up along the drive waiting on you. I don't imagine any of the poor women will arrive looking for their charity until this afternoon."

Marie didn't answer, but looked beyond Kate and then pursed her pretty mouth.

"Mornin', ladies," Johnny said, joining them. He squinted toward Marie and then quickly back to Kate.

She glanced over his shoulder and smiled; Matt was in his wake—looking ever so dapper in his tweed frock coat and matching cap. His unruly hair, curling up over the edge of the cap, softened the attire's crispness.

"Good morning," Kate replied, still watching Matt.

He winked.

Kate grinned and they stared at each other for a moment until Marie bumped Kate to get her attention. "Let's go. The family has just come out and will be riding past us in no time."

Forcing her gaze back to the church, Kate saw that the Beeswangers were, indeed, making their way toward the waiting coach. Her eyes met those of Miss Imogene and she half smiled. Miss Emily glanced at Kate, as well, before the two girls spoke to each other and then hurried after the family.

Kate swallowed and chewed at her lip for a moment. Were the girls uncomfortable about her friendship with the boys from Musson House? They had kept her so busy yesterday that Kate and Matt had barely had enough time to nod or smile at each other—Kate nodded, Matt smiled. Had that been intentional? Had there been disapproval in their myriad of requests? Kate huffed through her nose.

No. That was foolish. Miss Imogene and Miss Emily had been greatly concerned about the particulars of their gowns because the guests of the evening had been titled strangers. There was no hidden cause behind a last-minute request to press a piece of lace—the lace had been wrinkled. Miss Emily's favorite fichu was dirty and in need of an extra wash, and their hair *did* require more time as they had chosen laborious upsweeps meant to impress. Indeed, she need not be concerned—overly.

Turning, Kate took Marie's arm and tugged her toward the road. She was fairly certain that Matt and Johnny would follow but ensured that they would by specifically offering to lead. "This way," she said, glancing over her shoulder. She felt Marie trip, but Kate tightened her grip to prevent her friend from falling. "Don't want you to take the wrong road and head back to the coast unintentionally. Wolves and bears abound in the woods, you know," she exaggerated.

"We'd best stay close, then." Matt stepped to Kate's side. They ignored Marie's sniff of disapproval.

They walked for a few minutes in companionable silence—well, three persons were companionable—nodding and hallooing to many of the townsfolk. It wasn't until they were out of Tishdale proper and sauntering down the main road that the Beeswanger coach rumbled past and they all relaxed. Critical eyes were now few and far between.

"I been hoping ta get some girl advice," Johnny said, nodding at both Marie and Kate. He was walking on the far side while Matt walked next to Kate. Frowning, Kate glanced at Marie and saw a reflected expression of confusion. "Girl advice?"

"Yup. What do ya think a pair o' girls—bein' nine or ten or thereabouts—what do ya think might make 'em happy? A gift that might impress 'em."

"Impress their older sister, is more to the point," Matt added in his deep, melodious baritone.

Johnny grinned.

"Well." Marie snapped her tongue. "Unless you know these girls well, you will be wasting your money. Girls are as different as boys in their likes and dislikes. There is no one gift that will fit any girl . . . Really! Some girls like dolls, some like horse figurines, some like bright scarves, some like muffs . . . I could go on."

"A special food might be appreciated," Kate said, trying to be more helpful. "One of those rare sweet oranges or a box of fudge. Or something for warmth, like a woolen hat or mitts. Perhaps something everyone needs, like a handkerchief. In fact, there are an infinite number of gifts that would be suitable."

"Really?"

"Indeed." Marie sniffed with great superiority. "A stroll down Main Street, looking in the store windows, would provide you with any number of possibilities."

"True enough, true enough. Finding the time ta shop, though, that might be a problem."

"Your problem, not—" Marie began.

"Christmas Day is not until a week from Thursday; still plenty of time," Kate talked over Marie's peevish rejoinder. "And we still have one more market day before Christmas."

Marie grumbled, Johnny sighed, and Matt shrugged with one shoulder while Kate observed the day.

The walk back to Shackleford Park was exceptionally pleasant—not for the conversation, as Johnny took over and proceeded to discuss all manner of things that pertained to

Musson House, with very little relevance to Tishdale. And it could *not* be said that the general mood of the group was agreeable, as Marie continued to huff and scowl. Nor did the weather contribute to the enjoyment, as the wind *had* picked up and the temperature started to drop. Kate's toes were frigid and the tips of her ears were starting to hurt . . . until Matt grabbed her hood and yanked it up over her head.

Yes, perhaps that was the moment when Kate decided that it was a wonderful day. The wind was more of a blow than a howl, Marie didn't look quite as disgruntled . . . well, she did, but somehow Kate could ignore it without distress. And Johnny seemed more obtuse than self-serving.

And Matt? Well, he said little, but his smiles and sparkling eyes spoke volumes. There was an otherworld sense to the woods and fields, as if friendly fairies or tree elves watched from the shadows. Yes, an exceptionally pleasant walk.

Kate grinned and decided that this might well be her favorite time of year.

Unfortunately, Shackleford Park came into view, looming large and important, bringing reality back to the fore. As the group turned down the service road, they saw two figures approaching. Kate knew them to be Pippa and one of the laundry maids, Gwen, on their half day. Mrs. Lundy often let the girls leave a little early on such occasions.

The two had their heads together; their giggles carried on the wind, rushing ahead of them. But when they looked up, spotting the returning churchgoers, they stilled. Laughter died and silence reigned as the group approached. The girls' lips were curled, but their smiles were wooden.

"Have a good afternoon," Kate called as they passed. She was puzzled by the awkwardness in the girls' stance. Her confusion heightened when the giggles continued behind their backs. Glancing at Marie, Kate looked for an explanation.

Marie lifted her shoulders, not in nonchalance but in an *I have no idea* gesture.

Leading the way, Matt opened and held the service door as they slipped inside. While the hall offered no warmth, no longer having to contend with the wind brought great relief. Kate knew that by the time she gained her own little room, her toes would no longer be stiff and frozen.

Pushing the hood off her head, Kate's boots clicked across the tiled floors as she walked toward the back stairs with the others in her wake. A familiar laugh echoed down the corridor from the servants' hall and hit Kate full in the face. She blinked in horror and felt a rush of blood to her cheeks. No. It couldn't be.

Redirecting her steps, aware that the others hesitated to follow, Kate marched into the large, mostly empty room. In a space meant to house the entire staff for their early afternoon dinner, two women sat on a bench nearest the fire, chatting in easy conversation.

It was a scene that should *not* have caused Kate acute embarrassment, but it did. It most certainly did! Mrs. Lundy was entertaining Kate's mother . . . which was not in itself a disaster. But there was a familiar two-handled pot sitting at her mother's elbow. She had come to Shackleford Park on St. Thomas Day looking for cooked wheat—as if she were a poor widow in need of charity! Kate was ready to melt into the floor. This was an insult to her brothers, who took care of all her mother's material needs. In her loneliness and looking for sympathy, her mother had brought shame with her to the manor.

Kate must have made a sound of some sort—likely a squeak of dismay—for both women suddenly turned.

"Katey-bird!" Mam jumped to her feet and rushed around the table to where Kate stood, unable to move.

"Mam, what are you doing here?" Kate swallowed the lump in her throat and realized that her mother had been planning this all along. Her parting comment two days ago now made sense.

"I brought over one o' them pilla covers that I was workin' on. Wanted Mrs. Lundy to know they was done. She's goin' to send someone over ta pick the other linens up."

Without saying anything, Kate turned her gaze to the pot.

"Oh, an' I thought I might have some wheat while I was here. Been thinkin' of makin' a pudding or two."

"You could have asked Ross, Mam. There was no need to disturb Mrs. Lundy. Ross would have brought you some wheat if you needed it."

"Not to worry, Kate my dear. There is enough for everyone. Mrs. Beeswanger will not mind in the least." Mrs. Lundy had crossed to her side of the room and clearly understood the source of Kate's distress.

"O' course she wouldna mind. It be St. Thomas Day." Kate's mother wore a defiant expression. "An' I be a widow."

"I'll take your pot in to Cook, shall I, Dame Darby? Give you a chance to have a quick word with Kate before she has to rush upstairs and help the misses out of their church clothes." And so saying, Mrs. Lundy squeezed Kate's arm and left the room—pot in hand.

Kate turned to see that the corridor was empty behind her. Marie and Johnny and, thankfully, Matt had melted away. No one wanted to witness her humiliation.

"In all the years that I have worked here, Mam, you have never come to the manor looking for charity. Not when I was a scullery maid and not when I was a housemaid . . . and now, you chose *now* to come begging. I am a lady's maid, an upper servant. I have a position of prestige and you have just brought me down, brought me low, in the eyes of each and every person below stairs! And for what?"

"But, Katey, I just wanted to make a puddin' or two."

"Ross could have brought you the wheat you needed, you know that! You have three strapping sons, all proud tenant farmers. They have provided for you ever since Da died. We love you; we visit you; we take care of you. I have spent every half day, every holiday with you. But I cannot be with you all the time. I have already imposed on Mrs. Lundy's goodwill three times in as many months. Dropped everything to rush to you, only to find that your urgent need is not at all urgent. If I lose this position, we won't be able to buy a dress shop."

"We can work from the cottage, Katey-bird, in Vyse."

"No, no, and no. We have gone over this time and time again. A shop in town can bring in a living—mending while sitting at the table in Vyse cannot."

"But it's takin' too long, Katey-bird. I'm lonely."

"I am sorry that you are lonely, Mam. But this . . . this bid to mortify me will do nothing other than harden my resolve. I will not quit. I will not lose my dream because you don't like the cozy little house Henry found you. Your claim that no one visits you rings hollow, when not a day goes by without company; I am heartily disappointed, Mam, that you would seek to embarrass me, embarrass the family."

"That not be my intent." Kate's mother lifted her chin, looking defiant. "I just wanted to—"

"Make a puddin' or two. Yes, so you said. Ah, and here is Mrs. Lundy with your wheat."

Kate curled her lips up as she thanked the housekeeper for the generosity; she even managed to not grimace when Mrs. Lundy reminded her mother about the Staff Day open house in the barn. However, it was near impossible for her to offer an affectionate kiss on her mother's upturned cheek; it was a dutiful kiss and nothing more. She did not walk her mother to the door but hurried away—to hide her shame.

The general perception would be either that poor Dame

Darby was neglected—how could Kate be so heartless! Or Dame Darby was as dotty as they come—poor Kate, what a trial. Yes, her mother would have all the sympathy and attention she desired, at Kate's expense.

It would take some time before the giggles behind her back subsided.

"Dear, dear." Cook tsked and shook her head as she reached for the ham platter. She served herself a generous second helping. "It's an omen, for certain."

Norbert nodded emphatically. "Exactly what I said. There is no clearer sign of bad luck than a wild bird fluttering around the house—"

"Or a black cat crossing your path," Cook pointed out. "Or a horseshoe hanging upside down or—"

"Indeed." Norbert frowned, interrupting to regain control of the conversation. "It flew right in the front door of Hendred Manor. The poor squire. Who knows what terrible incident is coming his way."

"It was cold today," Matt said reasonably, settling back in his chair. "The bird might simply have been looking for a little warmth—not a harbinger of disaster at all." He glanced in Kate's direction, a small smile playing at the corner of his mouth.

Kate inwardly sighed in relief; she could discern no change in Matt's attitude toward her . . . unlike the others.

At tea, Walker had clicked his tongue in disgust when

he looked down his nose at Kate, which was not, in fact, a change, but he added a snort and a grin to get his message across. A successful attempt to deride her—Kate shrugged for anyone watching. Cook's attitude was unintentionally worse. She took Kate's hands, gave them a squeeze, and asked if there was anything she could do to help with the difficult family situation. Kate assured her all was well.

Bernie and Charles, the footmen, had danced a circle around her just before supper, chanting, "Wheat, wheat, give me wheat." Kate joined them but changed the words to "treat, treat, Christmas treat" and led them into the kitchen. Cook smacked their fingers as they reached for the marzipan cookies heading for the servants' hall.

But with Matt there seemed to be no change. He did not look askance at her, and more important, there was no pity in his gaze.

"Can never be too careful at this time of year," Mrs. Lundy said.

Kate looked to the head of the table with a frown. She had forgotten the topic of conversation.

"Yes, *especially* now," Cook agreed. "The least little thin' could start up the bad luck. We need ta be careful and watchful. Nip it in the bud."

"Mrs. Lundy," a small voice broke into the conversation. Little Livy, the scullery maid, had been clearing the housekeeper's plate. "I saw Pippa sweepin' dirt out the front door after the sun be down yesterday."

Cook gasped.

"No, no, I'm sure it will be fine," Mrs. Lundy reassured Livy and the older retainers.

Matt, Marie, and Kate wore matching skeptical expressions—not for the reassurance but for the concern.

"I'll have Pippa walk backward through the front door tomorrow. That sort of damage is easily fixed. Yes, yes, nothing to worry about, child."

"Jane cracked her looking glass this mornin'." Livy seemed determined to see trouble brewing.

Again, Cook gasped.

"Really?" Mrs. Lundy swallowed, starting to look uncomfortable.

"Who is Jane?" Matt asked, likely trying to redirect the conversation rather than suffering from a need to know who had been so foolish as to crack her mirror just before the change of the year.

"Our dairy maid," Kate explained.

"Well, I won't worry." Mrs. Lundy stared at the far wall. "Dust, a looking glass. No . . . all should be well. If there were a third, though . . ."

"The salt spilled yesterday," Cook reminded the housekeeper.

"Yes, but we cast it over our shoulders immediately; bad luck had no time to form."

"Of course." Cook looked relieved. She sat back, nodding, and allowed Livy to take her plate as well.

"I don't know if I should mention it, but I placed my bonnet on the bed before I put it on for church this morning." Marie's eyes sparkled with mischief and she studiously ignored Kate's warning stare. "I didn't mean to attract bad luck."

"Your bonnet?" Cook remarked. "Nothing to worry about—if it had been a hat . . . well, that would be an entirely different manner."

"I may have laid my hat on the bed," Walker added in a deceptively reasonable tone.

There was a sudden silence as those dictated by the Fates blinked fearfully.

"When would that have been, Mr. Walker? You have not been out of doors this entire week," Kate reminded him and all those taken in by the butler's sudden sociability. She ignored his glare.

"Oh my, yes," laughed Cook. "You had me goin' there for a minute, Mr. Walker." She batted her hand in the air. "You be funnin'." So good-natured, Cook never heard the barbs in Mr. Walker's words.

"Still . . ." Mrs. Lundy paused for thought before continuing. "Let's send Teddy out to the stables and have him check on the cats. Make sure they are behaving as they ought to. Cats are particularly sensitive to the exceptional forces around us." She glanced toward the dark window where most of the upper servants were reflected back at her. "In the morning—it's too late to see anything now."

"Teddy will be busy with the master's boots first thing in—" Walker began.

"Just after he has set the kitchen fire, Mr. Walker." Mrs. Lundy's tone brooked no argument.

"Of course." Mr. Walker shrugged—acquiescing much too easily.

Kate wondered if Teddy would be directed to *see* odd cat behavior, no matter what the truth. It would be a subtle but effective way to put Mrs. Lundy in a heightened state of anxiety.

With a sigh that brought Matt's eyes in her direction, Kate shook her head. If nothing else, this nonsense was a welcome distraction from her mother's antics. She looked to the foot of the table and found Walker staring back. The curl of his mouth made it clear that he did not appreciate her earlier interference.

"How did your mother like her wheat?" the butler asked in a light, breezy tone that was undercut with ice.

chapter 5

In which Matt consigns the person responsible for Mr. Ben's packing to the fiery pits of the underworld

MONDAY, DECEMBER 15, 1817

Matt sat in his room by the window, waiting on the narrow chair with an uninteresting book in hand—some sort of poetry that Mr. Ernest had thought worthy of high praise . . . but it was a little too florid for Matt's taste. He had been waiting most of the morning, only showing his face at the breakfast table. The difficulty was that Miss Imogene had not specified when Mr. Ben was due to arrive from Canterbury, and Matt wanted to be at the ready.

Not only would he have to unpack Mr. Ben's luggage, Matt would have to assess the damage—he was certain there would be damage—to Mr. Ben's various coats, waistcoats, boots . . . and likely his neckcloths. Yes, there was much to do in order to have Mr. Ben in top order by the time he went down to dinner this evening.

Matt wanted to show Mr. Ben off to his best advantage . . . though, if he were to admit it, there was some doubt as to whether or not Miss Imogene would notice. But Matt would! Matt would see wrinkles and cringe. No, Matt would not let Mr. Ben step foot outside his room in a wrinkled coat. Therefore . . . yes, he had to add pressing to his list of immediate duties. The sooner Mr. Ben arrived, the more likely Matt would get all that was absolutely *necessary* complete on time.

Being in a constant state of preparedness meant that Matt had rushed into Mr. Ben's room twice when sounds indicated that there was something about next door. Teddy, plunking the coalscuttle down noisily beside the fireplace, had caused the first thump. The young lad had looked up in shock at Matt's hurried entrance but answered with a grin when Matt inquired about skittish cats. He could think of little else to say.

"Nothin' odd that I could see, Mr. Harlow. Though Mr. Walker thought that jumpin' at one another was worrisome. I told him cats do that all the time, pouncin' and playin'. No . . . the cats be just fine. No odd goings-on."

"I'm sure Mr. Walker was pleased to hear that."

"He didna seem to be—though, Mrs. Lundy thanked me right enough."

Matt smiled, nodded, and returned to his room, and his seat, and his uninteresting book.

Pippa, the saucy red-haired maid, caused the next foray when she brought up an extra blanket to place at the foot of Mr. Ben's bed. Matt backed out as quietly as he could, not wanting to disturb her. He had almost made it back to his room when she ran into the hall and asked if there was anything that she could get him—tea, coffee, small beer. He thought not . . . nor did he need a new towel or new set of sheets. Yes, his coat was made of a fine material. No, he had no sweetheart waiting for him in Chotsdown. Matt closed his door with, perhaps, a little more force than was called for. He reopened it, leaving it slightly ajar, when he was certain Pippa had gone.

And yet, Pippa's words had provided a distraction. While he had truthfully addressed her query—he had no sweetheart in Chotsdown—Matt's *thoughts* were quite firmly fixed on a girl at Shackleford Park, one Miss Kate Darby. He enjoyed Kate's company to such a degree that he was even now listening for her footsteps. She had a light, almost skipping gait, lithe and full of energy . . . well, that would be whenever Mrs. Darby—Dame Darby as everyone was disposed to call her at the Park—was not causing some sort of to-do.

Matt didn't know what to think of Mrs. Darby; he had little experience with mothers. His own had died bringing him into the world. Papa rarely mentioned her and they had functioned quite well with just the two of them. The Harlow Tailor Shop and their apartment above had been run with efficiency, though, lacking any feminine touch. Matt had learned the tailoring trade at his father's side until he was almost thirteen. They had shared in the household duties at night while tending to their gentlemen customers during the day. Sir Andrew Steeple had been a regular patron . . . until Matt had walked into the shop one day to find his father clutching at his chest and turning a ghastly color.

The shop and all its wares were sold after Papa's death. Papa's sister, Aunt Doris, claimed the money and Matt, and brought him to live with her, her six children, and Uncle Reg in the fishing village of Worlop. Again Matt was without motherly company, as Uncle Reg kept him busy on the boat; Matt was obligated to work from before sunrise until after sundown repairing nets, laying line, and hauling up fish. Matt knew it was not the life for him before a week had passed, but it took him three weeks to build up the courage to say so.

Uncle Reg and Aunt Doris had scoffed at his idea of a position at Musson House, accused him of giving himself airs. But Matt proved them wrong; he walked up to the manor on a Thursday—the Steeples always went into town on Thursdays—and waited in the shadows until the good man came out with Lady Margaret. Sir Andrew remembered him very well and immediately took him on as a boot boy. Within two years he was a footman, and then last year, when Mr. Ernest and Mr. Ben were going into London for the Season, Matt's knowledge of tailoring secured him the prestigious position of valet. His papa would be proud . . . Perhaps his mother might be, too, but . . . well, he knew little of mothers.

Which brought him back full circle; Matt didn't know what to make of Mrs. Darby or how she affected Kate. Although the good woman did seem, perhaps, somewhat . . . well, odd.

It was at this juncture that Matt heard a sound, a lithe skipping sort of step that seemed to be approaching. He was suddenly alert, tipping his head toward the door in order to hear better.

"Mr. Harlow?" Kate called.

Matt was at his door immediately, though he pushed it open slowly, casually. "Yes, Miss Darby?"

"Oh, I am so pleased to know that I guessed right. I thought you might be anticipating the arrival of Mr. Ben, and I know your window to be facing the back garden." She paused as if waiting for a reaction.

Matt nodded, looking into her lovely brown eyes, wondering why he would describe them as full of merriment, sparkling even, when in truth they were normal eyes. He noted, too, that his heart hammered against his chest, and he felt inclined, very inclined, to step closer. He had enjoyed a flirtation or two—appreciating light banter and stolen kisses—but nothing had truly engaged his heart. Other than dreaming about his own tailor shop, nothing had filled him with eager anticipation . . . until now.

Still, Matt remained at a respectful distance, though he did lean slightly forward, and observed that Kate did as well.

"Mr. Ben has just arrived. Miss Imogene is with him in the drawing room at present, but I imagine you will see him fairly soon as he didn't hire a carriage—apparently they are hard to come by at this time of year—and as a result he is *thoroughly rumpled*." Kate smiled in such a manner that Matt was certain the description was not hers.

"Excellent, Miss Darby—"

"Pardon me for interrupting, Mr. Harlow, but I was wondering if you would be comfortable dispensing with some formality in regard to address? Perhaps when no one else is about?"

"Are you suggesting . . . that we use first names, Miss Darby?"

"I am, indeed. However, I understand if you prefer—"

This time Matt interrupted. "I think it a fine suggestion, Kate, for I will admit that I think of you as such already."

"Do you?" Kate lifted an eyebrow at him and tilted her head slightly. Then she grinned, and Matt found that he could not look away from her mouth, her lips and the way they curved up to form a bright smile. "Matt?"

"Umm. Yes?" Matt lifted his gaze back to those sparkling eyes. "Yes, Kate?"

"You were going to say something in regard to Mr. Ben's arrival."

"Oh. Oh Lud! Yes, I was going to thank you for your trouble and set to work . . . So, thank you for—"

"My trouble?"

"Yes, exactly. But now I must—"

"Set to work?"

Matt chuckled. "Indeed." And so saying, he stepped into the corridor with her and closed his bedroom door. It blended into the wall panel once again.

"I'll show you the way," Kate offered, crooking her elbow in his arm.

They walked six steps and then stopped in front of the next door.

"Thank you for the escort, Kate. I would have been entirely lost without your help . . . ," Matt began but turned at the sound of footsteps.

Even though the echo emanated from the back stairs, Kate immediately dropped his arm, nodded, and then scooted back down the hallway. Bernie—or was it Charles?—entered the corridor with several satchels in arm and turned toward Matt, missing the retreating figure behind him.

The footman passed Matt, depositing Mr. Ben's bags in his room with only a brief comment about Cook baking Christmas pudding—the mouthwatering smell was wafting through the house—before leaving Matt to his work and thoughts.

"DEPLORABLE ROADS." Mr. Ben laughed when Matt greeted him with raised brows. "Not really my fault." The tall, young gentleman was covered in mud splatters. It was even encrusted in his dark brown hair and smeared across his chin. He did *not* look suitable for company.

"Are you certain you did not ride cross-country?" Matt asked, helping Mr. Ben out of his coat and placing it gingerly across the back of a chair, trying not to knock off the mud until he could get the thing out of doors.

Mr. Ben laughed again. "Well, perhaps I took one or two fields when the road veered out of the way. I did want to get here as quickly as possible. I was meant to be here Saturday. The delay was most irritating and entirely unnecessary. I'm sure you understand."

Matt did understand; there was no bigger draw than anticipating the company of one's fiancée. But to sacrifice a coat to secure an extra hour—well, that might be going a bit far . . . But then he thought of Kate and decided that the coat would be fine.

"Miss Chively did not say what caused your delay."

"No, I'm certain she did not. Miss Chively likely did not want to besmirch the good name of Theodore Perkins, but I have no such qualm, as his stupidity cost me precious hours—forty-eight hours that could have been spent with my dear Miss Chively. I was, instead, required to clear the buffoon's name. If my mentor had not asked it of me, I would not have gone in search of a magistrate. Perkins got himself into the fool's basket; he ought to have got himself out."

Matt merely nodded, more confused than ever.

"I would have checked. Would you not have done likewise?" Mr. Ben continued his enigmatic conversation.

"I might have . . . if I knew what I was checking?"

The young gentleman paused as Matt passed him a tepid pitcher of water. Burbling, splashing, and huffing replaced words for several minutes, and then he continued.

"The carver—he was working on a chimneypiece for one of the houses we have been redesigning—well, the man accused Perkins of cheating him and thereby sullying Lord Penton's good name. Perkins is, after all, one of the apprentices. Can you imagine? A simple job; all Perkins had to do was pay the man. Trying to settle up before Christmas—with fake coins."

"What?" Matt stopped and blinked. This was not good. The authorities took counterfeits quite seriously. It was at best a transporting offense, at worst a hanging. "He hadn't minted them, had he? The coins?"

"No," Mr. Ben said with a sigh. "No. Got them in exchange somewhere along the way and did not check. Who doesn't scrape at the silver or try to bend a coin that's been tossed to you? Even a babe would check!" He shook his head as Matt offered him the least wrinkled waistcoat he could find in Mr. Ben's luggage. It was a sturdy gray twill.

"Is the yellow silk, cut with a sapphire stripe, not in good shape?"

Matt held up a sorry rag of wrinkles, usually called a yellow waistcoat. "I *can* return it to its former glory, Mr. Ben, but it will take a fair amount of time and pressing."

"Hmmm, yes, that might not have been folded properly."

"No," Matt said icily, consigning whoever had done Mr. Ben's packing to the fiery pits of the underworld—until he saw Mr. Ben's sheepish grin and realized that the young gentleman was the guilty party. "You might think of hiring yourself a valet, Mr. Ben. Your clothes will be all the happier for the intervention."

The chuckle and smile Mr. Ben offered Matt did not make him feel any more kindly disposed, whatsoever.

"Naturally, the magistrate," Mr. Ben continued his story, "saw the right of it. Cleared Perkins's name and, more important, Lord Penton's reputation. The fine old gentleman could have been brought up on charges, too, being that he houses and trains Perkins . . . as he does me. Really, what a mess that would have been!"

"Indeed," Matt said, barely heeding the cause of all the huffing and puffing. He had other concerns—grave concerns—having just pulled off Mr. Ben's mud-caked riding boots, and was fighting the urge to groan. With a noble effort, he changed the sound into a sigh and turned to pull a pair of Hessians from the larger of the satchels deposited by the bed.

Shoving his feet into the boots with undue haste, Mr. Ben stood and glanced in the looking glass. He pulled down the corners of his waistcoat, checked the length of his watch fob and straightened his shoulders. "Don't worry, Matt, I'll be back to change for dinner. You can do me up proud then." And so saying, the young gentleman quit the room, looking far from the perfection Matt had envisioned a mere twenty minutes earlier.

KATE STARED INTO the wardrobe, her hand touching the soft silk of Miss Imogene's lilac dinner gown, lost in thought. In her mind she returned to the hallway and her short conversation with Matt. She allowed excitement free rein for a few moments before frowning and shaking her head.

What was she thinking? What was she doing? She should *never* have suggested that they call each other by their first names. It was offering an intimacy that could never be realized. Impetuous, yet again. When would she learn to think before she acted? Really!

Footsteps, mere footsteps echoing up the back stairs had shouted a warning and brought with it a flood of anxiety and guilt. Matt and she might have been discovered having a conversation in a deserted hallway. Heavens!

Kate was certain that the clicking heels on the wooden treads were those of Bernie or Charles. Neither of the footmen was a threat to her position, but gossip most definitely was. And a lady's maid's conduct *had* to be beyond reproach. She had direct access to the family; she had private knowledge. She should not, could not, be caught flirting with a handsome valet in a quiet corridor . . . no matter how much she was taken with him.

And she did fancy him.

In all her eighteen years, she had yet to encounter a young man who made her want to bask in his presence. She wanted to reach out and touch him, to feel the press of his lips on hers, to—

"Oh, excellent. I'm so glad you are here," Miss Imogene said as she rushed into the room closing the door behind her—well, behind Jasper, who followed at her heels.

Kate grimaced. One look at Miss Imogene's dress made it clear why the young lady would seek assistance in the middle of the day. The bottom of her lovely cream gown was flounced with lace, ribbon, and muddy paw prints.

"Jasper was very enthused to see Ben," Miss Imogene said, as she grinned at the St. John's water dog. "Weren't we all!" She sighed and then turned back toward Kate. "But he was covered in mud, and Jasper, in his excitement, transferred some of the muck to me. I hope you can get it out."

"Not a problem, miss. I'll let it dry and try brushing it first." Kate smiled as Miss Imogene reached behind her back, trying pointlessly to undo her buttons.

Without saying anything, Kate turned Miss Imogene around, untied her waist ribbon, and then set to work on the twenty or so pearl buttons running down the young lady's back.

Soon the soiled dress was in a puddle on the floor and a fresh gown—light blue with a square neck and puff sleeves—was partially on. "It must have been grand to see Mr. Ben again," Kate said more as a statement than a query. She could tell Miss Imogene was all atwitter as she readied the sleeves for the young lady to slip on.

"Grand isn't the half of it."

A quick knock on the door interrupted their proceedings and Miss Emily slipped into the room. "Oh, Kate, I might have known you would come to Imogene's rescue. I thought I might help, but I see that I am not needed."

"You are always needed," Miss Imogene corrected her friend with a broad smile. "Are they here yet? Do I have to hurry?"

With a frown, Kate lifted her eyes to meet Miss Imogene's in the looking glass. "They?"

Had Kate missed a conversation? The rest of the Steeples were due to arrive the day after tomorrow. Who was coming today? Mr. and Mrs. Chively? Were Miss Imogene's parents coming to visit? Miss Imogene had not seen them since September because of an estrangement. Were they finally going to let bygones be bygones? Christmas was a perfect time to mend fences.

"Yes," Miss Imogene said, not knowing where Kate's thoughts had taken her. "I am quite looking forward to the occasion. There was no ceremony at Gracebridge Manor when the Yule log was brought in—no choosing, no celebration. Father was . . . is not a great believer in merriment."

Ah yes, the Yule log. Kate had quite forgotten—distracted as she had been.

"But this year is different," Miss Emily said, giving her friend a quick squeeze, interfering briefly with the donning of the new gown. She walked over to the window, leaning into the glass. "Not here yet," she said as she squinted up the drive. "The tenant farmers usually bring them right to the front door. Farmer Tanner's log will be declared the best; it's his turn this year—although they will make a show of trying to decide which one is best suited to stay lit all Christmas Day."

"And smolder until Twelfth Night—that is the tricky part," Kate added. It was an important tradition that brought prosperity and protected the house from evil. She smiled. At least, that was what Mrs. Lundy had said when she had announced the coming of the logs at breakfast.

"Oh . . . oh, I think I see something." Miss Emily pushed her brown curls away from her face, trying to see farther. "Yes, they are coming. One, two, and yes, there is the third team." She turned back to the room. "Are you ready?"

"Done," Kate answered as she stepped away from Miss Imogene, hands raised.

"Thank you, Kate. You are a marvel." Miss Imogene giggled with excitement.

"Shawls," Kate called as the girls hurried to the door. She grabbed not one but two from a chest of drawers.

Miss Imogene skipped across the floor and pulled out a third. "Here, Kate. Come with us."

Kate started and then took the offered shawl with a grin. She had planned to run to her room for her cloak; now there was no need. She wouldn't miss any of the merriment.

By the time they arrived at the front of the manor, Walker was ushering the family out the wide, arched door. He glared at Kate as she slipped through with them, but she ignored the butler as best she could . . . Well, actually she offered him a one-shouldered shrug and brazenly tendered her thanks. His curled lip spoke of how much he appreciated her efforts.

Outside, three broad-shouldered, substantial men had pulled their teams into a line, dragging the potential Yule logs in as close as possible while leaving room for the family and the staff. Given the crowding, it would seem that everyone was eager to witness one of the first ceremonies of the season.

Mr. and Mrs. Beeswanger initially greeted Farmer Gibbs, as he had won the previous year. Then proceeded to shake hands with Farmer Rundell and, finally, Farmer Tanner. They circled behind the teams of horses, nodding to the laborers and looking thoroughly engrossed in the enterprise. The bark was examined, knuckles rapped against the wood, and Mr. Beeswanger took a deep sniff. Though what the gentleman could learn from such procedures was a mystery to Kate; she thought it had more to do with theatrics and custom.

Kate joined Marie, shuffling aside to allow the family room to participate. Mr. Ben, looking devoid of mud, made his way directly to Miss Imogene.

"I wish Ernest were here to see this," he said as they paraded forward to join in the all-important discussion about which log would burn the longest.

Kate glanced around, looking for a tall, handsome valet, and tried not to huff her disappointment too loudly when she could not spot Matt.

"Marie . . . ?" Kate began, turning her head toward her friend as she spoke. She didn't finish her question; Matt had slipped in beside them. He made a show of being surprised to see *her*.

"Yes?" Marie said, not really paying mind; her gaze was focused on Mrs. Lundy, who stood nearby with a tray of oil, salt, and wine. They would be used to anoint the chosen log before it was unhitched and the farmhands carried it into the manor. While coal was used to heat the rest of the Park, the large hearth in the grand hall entrance had been built for this express purpose. Mrs. Beeswanger said that sentiment and prudence insisted on a place suitable for the luck-bearing Yule log. An instrument that consumed mistakes and bad choices could not be overlooked.

Then, finally, it was declared. Farmer Tanner's log looked

to be the best candidate to be lit Christmas Eve by a remnant of last year's log and last until the end of Christmas Day. It might even smolder until Twelfth Night and offer them all great fortune.

With a pat on the back, the company congratulated Farmer Tanner, and Mrs. Beeswanger anointed the log. Bernie and Charles carried out a wassail bowl to be served to everyone present. Each member of the family offered a toast to the log, the season, the future, and the company—including Miss Imogene and Mr. Ben. There were peals of laughter, loud voices, and even a chorus of "Here We Come a-Wassailing." Just before the nip in the air sent all inside to the warmth, Cook arrived with baskets of goodies for all three farmers to share with their families and laborers.

"Puts our Yule log ceremony to great shame," Matt said to Kate through the noise of the gathering. "At Musson House, Sir Andrew offers a prayer but not much else."

"Well, I could use a prayer right now," Johnny said, coming up behind them and draping his arm across Matt's shoulder—until a look from his friend suggested that he remove it. "Two days. They be here in two days an' I have yet to find somethin' for Camille's sisters."

"I thought I saw a peddler on the drive today. A substantial cart with a black-hoofed pony." Kate frowned, recalling the sight when she had glanced out the window earlier.

"A tinker. An' of great worth had I been lookin' for pots or pans, perhaps a knife or two."

Kate laughed, looking at the bottom of her wassail cup, disappointed to see that the hot cider was gone. "Worry not, a week is a week. There will be others looking to make a sale before Yuletide." She was too busy enjoying the warmth of Matt's gaze to be overly concerned about Johnny's dilemma. It seemed a harmless enough quest.

chapter 6

In which Kate is burdened with being sensible

TUESDAY, DECEMBER 16, 1817

The next morning, after setting up Miss Emily and Miss Imogene with cups of steaming hot chocolate, plumped pillows, and a book for one, paper and graphite stick for the other, Kate stepped down the stairs into a beehive of activity. She was on her way to the housekeeper's room to break her fast at the usual time, but there was not the usual amount of hustle and bustle—there was far more.

Pippa busily swept twigs and needles down the narrow hall toward the door while Livy scooted around her with a tray of toast and bacon—ignoring Pippa's shout of indignation when her refuse pile was scattered by Livy's skirts. Clearly, the evergreens had been delivered, and a quick peek into the servants' hall as she passed proved her theory to be true. A good third of the large table was piled high with boughs and branches as well as ribbons and dried fruit; the crate of mistletoe sat on the floor beside them.

Cassie, one of the housemaids, jostled Kate in her rush through the doorway to join the other members of the lower staff, who were waiting impatiently. The aroma of their first meal of the day wafted from the sideboard, reminding Kate that her belly was empty. She nodded her acceptance of Cassie's apology and then hurried to Mrs. Lundy's private sitting room, where the rest of the upper servants gathered.

"Where is Norbert?" Mrs. Lundy asked, frustration evident in her tone. "Everything is topsy-turvy this morning."

Kate smiled. "'Tis the season."

"Exactly." Mrs. Lundy batted at the air. "Never mind. Sit. We will start. Livy, pass the dishes." And so saying, the girl did just that.

Soon a silence of busy minds and mouths permeated the room, disrupted only by the clinking of cutlery and, eventually, Mr. Norbert's entrance.

"Pardon me, one and all. Glad you went ahead . . . Had a devil of a time rising this morning."

Kate nodded in sympathy; the family had stayed up late—no doubt to celebrate and enjoy Mr. Ben's arrival—but it meant that Norbert, Matt, Marie, and Kate had had to do so as well. Morning had, indeed, come too quickly.

Casting her eyes to the other end of the table, Kate found Matt staring back. They grinned at each other. Focusing again on her plate, Kate enjoyed the scrutiny, using her peripheral vision and that innate sense of being watched to verify that Matt was as aware of her presence as she was of his. She smiled at her fried tomatoes and spread a generous amount of Cook's fine blackberry jam on her toast before lifting her eyes again. Purposely, she turned her head in the other direction first—practicing a little coquetry.

Mrs. Lundy was watching her. The housekeeper's expression was neither tolerant nor relaxed; it could have been a reflection of the anticipated hectic day, or it could have been a reaction to Kate's subtle flirting. Either way, it was a splash of icy water.

Kate spent the rest of the meal with her gaze firmly fixed on her plate. When the upper servants rose en masse to vacate, Mrs. Lundy put a hand on Kate's arm as she stood to go.

"Might I speak with you, my dear?" Mrs. Lundy's tone was puzzling.

Kate waited, doing her best not to look up at Matt as he passed through the door. Rather than delay Livy's clearing, Mrs. Lundy motioned Kate to follow her into the stillroom next door. There the housekeeper closed the door and stood looking at Kate for several minutes before sighing.

She did not mince her words but went straight to the point. "Kate, dear, there is no doubt that Mr. Harlow is a handsome young man with charming manners, but . . ."

Kate waited; she knew what was coming. Mrs. Lundy had

no authority over her anymore. Only Mrs. Beeswanger—and, of course, the young ladies—could call her to task now. Still, some habits die hard, and Kate was certain she was in for a terrible set-down. She clenched her jaw and readied for the onslaught.

But it never came.

Instead, Mrs. Lundy started to smile. It was a sad sort of smile, but a smile nonetheless. "Nothing like a charmer to turn a girl's head," she said.

"I have said as much to Miss Imogene." Kate flashed a grin and then set her mouth back to its serious expression.

"Yes, I imagine you have." Mrs. Lundy sighed again. "Well, I have something to say as well, my dear, and I hope you will listen. I know it's not for me to ask anything of you, but you have been under my care for several years, and I am quite fond of you . . . and I wish only the best for you."

Kate had never seen Mrs. Lundy look so uncomfortable. "Are you going to suggest that I keep my distance from Mr. Harlow?" she asked, unnerved by the housekeeper's hesitance.

With a slight chuckle, Mrs. Lundy shook her head. "No, indeed not. If you were Pippa or Gwen, I would rail for several minutes about bad behavior and address the dangers of a dalliance, but you, my dear, have a good—if somewhat rash—head on your shoulders. No, but I *would* recommend caution. I can see that Mr. Harlow and you are interested in each other, and as heady and marvelous as that feels right now, I might remind you of a few things.

"You know nothing of Mr. Harlow or his people—truly, your acquaintance is of a very short duration. While I would say that his interest is sincere, we . . . you do not know that as a certainty. And you would not be the first girl to be deceived. But even if his interest is genuine, how far does that go? You cannot ascertain his purpose in the time that he will be here. When the Steeples leave in the new year, he will be going with them. Back to the coast—back to his people, hours away. He has an excellent position, as do you, but those positions will keep you from seeing each other except for occasional family gatherings. I know not *his* plans—but *you* have dreams. You have a future in mind that does not involve a young man visiting from the coast."

"Mrs. Lundy, you are so very kind, and I appreciate your concern, but you need not worry. I am well aware of my responsibilities." Kate gulped, disheartened by reality. "Perhaps I should tell him outright that nothing can come of this flirtation."

Mrs. Lundy smiled her strange, sad smile again. She lifted her hand and patted Kate's shoulder. "No, my dear, don't do that. Just be careful. Don't let it go too far. And keep what I have said in the back of your mind. Enjoy your flirtation, but don't give away your heart. It will only lead to sorrow." Her voice was that of experience.

With a nod and her chin in the air, Kate strode down the hallway, adopting a casual manner. Cassie, spreading out the evergreens on the now unpeopled table, looked out as Kate passed the servants' hall, but Kate continued toward the back stairs without a word. It was just as well that duty called; it was a distraction. For Mrs. Lundy's words had had a great affect on Kate's perspective . . . and not likely the one the housekeeper had intended.

Kate was now burdened. Yes, burdened with Mrs. Lundy's trust and faith. Had the housekeeper suggested that Kate avoid Matt or accused him of misdeeds, Kate would have been indignant and waved it off. She knew better of herself and of Matt . . . but no, Mrs. Lundy had simply asked her to be prudent. The good woman couldn't have devised a better way to nip her euphoria in the bud.

Kate would have to be sensible. It was a terrible burden.

LATER THAT DAY, as Matt was fine-tuning his boot polish in the stillroom, he heard a commotion in the corridor.

"Lovely," Pippa muttered as she rushed past the open door, and then stopped. She leaned back, looking into the stillroom. "Hello," she said in a studied casual manner. "I know you was hoping that a tinker-of-all-trades would come by. There's one pullin' into the service yard this minute. Teddy saw him from the kitchen window."

"Indeed. Excellent news." Matt smiled, trying to remember where Johnny could be found at this time of day. Had they been at Musson, he would have known in a trice . . . but this wasn't Musson House and—

"We can walk out together, if ya want ta." Pippa stepped backward so that her entire person blocked his path.

"Hmmm?" Matt said absentmindedly. He turned back to his jar of polish, gave it an extra stir, and then reaffixed the lid. He screwed it tight to ensure that none would escape. When he looked up at the door again, Pippa was still there—quietly, patiently waiting. "Hmmm?" he said again and then frowned, hearing her question. "Oh . . . oh no. No need, thank you kindly. I must take this upstairs first." He lifted the precious elixir, holding it aloft for the young maid to admire. Not all valets were adept at the art of making polish, especially at the beginning of their careers. It usually took years of practice—although Mowat, Sir Andrew's man of many, many years, was still complaining that his polish was lumpy.

Clearly not appreciating his talent, Pippa lifted one shoulder and curled up the corner of her mouth. "Suit yerself," she said before flouncing away.

"Oh, Pippa," Matt called, realizing he was losing a useful source of information. "Do you know where—" The outside door slammed shut, and Matt was left to find Johnny on his own.

It wasn't as difficult a job as he had imagined, for Mrs. Lundy knew that Walker was overseeing the decorating of the grand hall entrance. Scaling a ladder would be most undignified for any butler, and yet, under Walker's direction, a ladder had been carried through the corridor not thirty minutes prior. It could only be assumed that a footman or two would be assisting in the process.

And so it was that Matt found Johnny at the top of said ladder, affixing evergreen garlands over the arch to the west gallery. It appeared to be the last of the embellishments as the east arch was already so festooned, the mantel over the fireplace—where the Yule log waited to be lit—was decorated with colorful glass balls, and a string of dried berries had been threaded through the stair rungs all the way up to the first floor.

In the time it took for Matt to cross from the little hall to the two men, Walker, who was positioned near the entrance, had dictated that Johnny move one errant branch up, down, and then back to its original position. Matt could hear his friend's huff of frustration . . . though Walker seemed deaf.

"Ah, capital. Truly impressive," Matt complimented Walker for Johnny's hard work. Then he looked purposefully at the near empty basket at the foot of the ladder. "Might not have enough apples, though, Johnny. This bough will be a tad sparse—have you enough ribbons to make up for it?"

"There be plenty. Never you mind," Johnny said in a grumbling tone, not bothering to look down at Matt or the basket.

Ignoring the voice from overhead, Matt turned to Walker. "I believe Mrs. Lundy said that there *should* be enough, but . . ." Matt hesitated, giving the butler time to be affronted that the housekeeper would offer her opinion regarding the manor's decorations, infringing upon his domain.

Umbrage stormed onto Walker's face, and he stepped forward to offer the basket a deep scowl. "Not enough!

Clearly, we will run short." Walker straightened his shoulders. "Ruined. Ruined entirely. The galleries will be lopsided. Apples will have to be pulled down from the east arch and hung on the . . . Oh, this is quite disastrous."

"Or Johnny could run out to the yard. A general goods peddler has just pulled up."

"I has enough to do without runnin' after more apples, thank you very little." Johnny had finally turned toward Matt and was tendering his friend a significant glare.

"Are you certain? I believe the man has ribbons, as well."

"I'm not goin' trapsin' after apples or ribbons . . ." Johnny blinked, stared at Matt with sudden comprehension, and then quickly slid to the floor. "I'll tell Mrs. Lundy she be wrong while I'm there, shall I, Mr. Walker?" he said, ensuring that the man would not complain about the rush to the service yard.

They scurried—yes, there was no other manner in which their quick, mincing scuffle could be described; it lacked dignity of any kind whatsoever, but it did the trick. They were out of Walker's sight within moments.

Johnny grinned, stepping ahead of Matt in the hallway, jostling him as he passed. "Much obliged," he said over his shoulder.

Outside, the peddler had stopped his horses before the service entrance, where the huge creatures snorted puffs of warm breath into the crisp air, ignoring the gathering staff. It was a tall wagon, with drawers, cubbyholes, and baskets hanging off the sides. Brooms, rope, and kettles cluttered one side, fabric and ribbons the other, sacks of root vegetables and baskets of dried fruit on top. It was a wonder the whole wagon did not topple over.

Johnny scooted to the far side while Matt suggested to Mrs. Lundy, who was gesturing toward a teacup, that a few additional apples were needed for the great hall adornments.

A slight frown puckered her brow. "Thought that might be the case, Mr. Harlow. Didn't believe there were quite enough, but Walker would not hear of it. Though I must say, I'm hard-pressed to understand why *you* might be delivering the message."

Matt shrugged with feigned confusion, and hastened to the far side of the wagon, where Johnny had already set about implementing his grand scheme to woo Camille through her sisters. Staring, fascinated by a drawer full of colorful ribbons of various lengths and widths, he touched a blue one with lacey edges and glanced up at the peddler. "How much for this, then?"

The peddler, well versed in the game, named a most ludicrous amount. Johnny countered, as was expected, and the haggling began. By the time the dickering was complete, Johnny had bargained the man down by half and included a length of red ribbon, as well. Once the deal was struck, goods and coins were exchanged, and Johnny nodded his thanks as the man dropped his change into his waiting palm. Johnny waggled his brows in Matt's direction, apparently well pleased by the outcome. However, before Johnny could even fold the ribbons, they and the change were yanked back out of his hand.

"No, siree. You don't run off wiff my goods 'less'en you pay for 'em!" the peddler shouted, leaning his stubbled gray face into Johnny's.

"Whatcha talkin' about?" Johnny pointed to the shilling still clutched in the man's fist. "What's that, then?"

"Thievery! An' youse lucky I don't reports ya to the magistrate." The peddler threw the shilling at Johnny's feet. "Are ya gunna pay or not?"

With a growing frown and a swallow of discomfort, Johnny reached for the coin that had landed on the toe of his boot. He lifted it to his eyes, and Matt, from where he stood, could see that the silver had been scratched away to reveal a lead plug underneath.

"Lawks," Johnny said quietly, and then his jaw tightened. "Lawks!" he shouted between his teeth. He shook the fake coin as if he were shaking the culprit who gave it to him. "He cheated me! Stole me ring an' I didn't even know it! I been had."

"I'll cover the cost." Matt sighed, motioning to the peddler, hoping he had enough to pay for the ribbons on him.

"No, you will not." Johnny, unreasonably, turned his ire on his friend. "This is my business. I won't have you sticking your nose in it." He lifted his arm as if to toss the coin across the yard, but Matt grabbed it before Johnny could do so.

With a furtive glance at those around them, Matt noted

that the Musson House boys were getting more than their fair share of attention from the Shackleford Park shoppers. The glint of amusement in Pippa's eyes was particularly irksome. "Perhaps we should discuss this inside," Matt suggested, "where it is warmer."

"Warmer? Warmer? I want me bleedin' ring back. Don't care if I be warm!"

Nodding, as if Johnny were being sensible, Matt grabbed his friend's arm in a viselike grip and smiled at the enthralled staff. He marched Johnny back to the door and pushed him inside, almost colliding with the lovely Kate, who was on her way out.

"Oh, most excellent," she said with a buoyant smile. "I hoped that you had heard about the peddler. Did you find—"

Tugging his arm from Matt's grip, Johnny glared at them both. "Can't buy no ribbons with empty pockets, an' I have no ring besides." Straightening, Johnny started down the corridor, marching toward the men's quarters. "I'm goin' into town. I'm goin' ta get me ring back!"

"Excuse me," Kate called. "I don't understand—"

"Don't be a bacon-brain, Johnny. It's not worth it. Let it be. The ring is gone." Matt rushed down the narrow hall after him; he could hear Kate following behind. "You'll never find the rotter."

"It's not right!" the footman shouted over his shoulder.

"That may be so, but you can't run off. Walker won't let you disappear for hours; he'll have your head on a platter. He'll make certain Sir Andrew knows of it, Johnny; you know he will. Don't throw it all away on account of a piece of tin."

The footman turned by the servants' hall door, waiting for Matt and Kate to catch up. "Do you know him, Miss Darby?" Johnny's expression was as thunderous as Matt had ever seen.

"Him?" Kate leaned away from the accusation disguised as a question.

"A red-haired man. He stole me ring at the Gambling Goat. Paid me with a fake coin. You know who he be?"

Shaking her head, Kate lifted her palms. "The man you met in Tishdale . . . when I was not present? Why would you suppose I know this person?"

"You've lived here all your life! He has red hair," Johnny barked.

Matt straightened his shoulders, taking umbrage on Kate's behalf. There was no call for Johnny to take a run at Kate. The girl had done nothing to warrant such rudeness. "Doing it up too brown, Johnny. You'd best swallow your spleen before—"

"There are at least four or five families in Tishdale alone with red hair," Kate interrupted, not appearing to be in the least daunted by the unfair accusation. "Perhaps it is a trait seen rarely around Chotsdown, but that is not the case here. Red hair alone is not enough to identify your thief." Her tone was reasonable, almost bored. It rendered the attack toothless.

"Argh!" Johnny shouted in wordless frustration. He tossed his hands in the air, cast a venomous look at Kate, and again stormed away, but in the direction of the great hall rather than the men's quarters.

About to express his appreciation, Matt shifted his gaze to Kate's profile and found that he no longer had control of his tongue; he was speechless. He certainly hoped it was a temporary condition brought on by . . . by . . . He couldn't even conceive what might have brought on this unlikely condition. Never before had he been so afflicted.

KATE SHOOK HER head in disgust: disgust at Johnny's foul temper, the thieving red-haired man, and even the initiator of this entire charade, Camille. It seemed beyond comprehension that a young woman could be swayed by gifts—such a person was hardly worthy of Johnny's attention. It seemed an unlikely match: the smitten footman and the indifferent lady's maid.

And then Kate turned to find Matt staring at her. It was a rather intense sort of a gaze that sent her pulse racing. Kate decided that the heart was rarely governed by wisdom or logic and that unlikely matches abounded. And so, despite Mrs. Lundy's kind suggestion, Kate was not going to be sensible in regard to Matt Harlow . . . certainly not at this point in time. For, indeed, how often did an excellent opportunity such as this present itself?

The hallway was empty; the staff was either busy with their duties or out of doors admiring the peddler's goods. And Matt had just come to a halt before the entrance to the servants' hall . . . where a kissing bough had been hung earlier that day.

Kate swallowed in exquisite anticipation, barely breathing. If she lifted her hand, applied a slight amount of pressure, and guided him back just a step or two, they would be directly under the mistletoe. Matt could, would . . . *should* kiss her or suffer the consequences of bad luck.

Even as Kate considered this reckless course of action, her hand rose of its own volition. Her fingers splayed, and she gently nudged Matt backward. After glancing up to the kissing bough, he allowed Kate to guide him, his gaze volleying between her eyes and her lips as they stepped across the threshold. Once under the mistletoe, Kate gestured above their heads with theatric surprise.

"Oh dear, look at that. We are directly under the mistletoe," she said. "Whatever shall we do?"

"A kiss is required." Matt paused as if waiting for a protest. "To appease the Rulers of the Evergreens."

Kate snorted in a most unladylike manner. "Rulers of the Evergreens?"

"Indeed. Terrifying creatures, especially when they perceive a missed kiss."

"A *missed* kiss?" she repeated.

"If we do not kiss, bad luck will follow." Matt leaned

closer until their bodies were all but touching. Kate held her breath as he tilted his head, and they bumped noses as he gave her a chaste kiss on her left cheek.

"I don't think that counts," Kate said, shifting, offering him her lips. She clasped her hands together behind her back, then brought them forward, somewhat awkwardly, to his shoulders. Desperate to feel his lips on hers, Kate was hesitant about her role. Having never engaged in such *shenanigans* before, she wasn't sure how much she should encourage before it became brazen—she would *never* want to be considered brazen.

She watched a grin spread across Matt's face; his eyes gleamed with mischief as he brought his face to hers once again. Kate closed her eyes in expectation, but when she felt his lips touch her skin, they were on her right cheek. Frustration shot through her veins; accusations of acute stupidity sat on her tongue, and Kate was about to grab him by his coat and yank him to her when, at last, their lips met.

Suddenly, Kate was lost. Lost in paradise. Every sense was heightened. She could smell his musky soap, feel the warmth of his body pressed against hers, and hear his hum of pleasure. She longed to wrap her arms around his neck and become entwined . . . She wanted the kiss to last forever. But it was not possible, not standing in the middle of the corridor. Kate dropped her heels back to the floor, lifted her eyes to Matt's, and held his gaze for some minutes.

Her smile faded. She swallowed in discomfort.

Matt's countenance was confusing. His expression was not that of an embarrassed young man. Nor was it concerned . . . or nonchalant. Worse yet, his ardor had disappeared entirely. There was something alarming in his eyes as if he were shocked . . . and not pleasantly so. This was not the face or stance of a young man who had enjoyed their close encounter.

Kate was mortified.

With a shake of her head, Kate stepped back. Shrugged her shoulders.

Matt nodded, turned on his heels, and followed Johnny down the corridor.

Kate watched him go, fighting the urge to call after him . . . to ask him what was so terribly amiss. She needed to understand why a kiss, which they had both seemed to enjoy, had caused such a look of dismay.

chapter 7

In which mistletoe becomes a euphemism

Matt was confused, baffled, befogged, and, yes, dismayed. He had just surrendered to the moment—indeed, behaved in a most reckless manner. It wasn't like him. Impetuous behavior was *not* part of his character. He was lighthearted and flirtatious, only serious about his duties. His passion was for neckcloths and twill fabrics, not dark-haired elves with soft, welcoming lips that made him forget his name—made him forget whether he was standing or sitting—made him forget everything but her flowery fragrance and the press of her attributes against his chest.

No, this could not be. This was not the proper conduct of a young valet with years of bachelorhood ahead of him. Flirting and charming the housemaids was one thing; a dalliance with a lady's maid was another. It would not be tolerated, nor should it be. Most unbecoming behavior of a gentleman's gentleman. And yet . . . his heart still raced, and there was nothing Matt wanted more than to rush back to the servants' hall and pull Kate back underneath the mistletoe.

No, no, no. This was terrible.

He had to think of other things . . . get Kate out of his mind. Yes, he needed to concentrate on polish and whether or not he could repair the left cuff of Mr. Ben's second-best shirt. What could be more important than the open seam of the cream pantaloons . . . the stain on the burgundy waistcoat and the look of ardor on Kate's face? Her eyes closed, mouth raised and inviting . . .

No, no, no!

This was inconceivable; never had he been so distracted. With a deep sigh, Matt straightened his shoulders, stretched his chin forward to release the tightness in his throat, and climbed the stairs to the family floor. He was glad to see a pink tinge to the light streaming through the windows. The sun was going down, making it less likely that Johnny would let the bee in his breeches goad him into rash behavior. He couldn't rush into Tishdale looking for the red-haired thief in the dark. By dawn, his friend's pique would have abated and the day could continue as expected with the hustle and bustle of the Steeples' arrival—all great distractions from the lithe and appealing personage of Miss Kate Darby.

Wednesday, December 17, 1817

Sir Andrew, Lady Margaret, and Mr. Ernest were late. It was no great surprise, as Sir Andrew hated to travel beyond Chotsdown; the old gentleman would have resisted boarding the Steeple coach until Lady Margaret became insistent. Then Lady Margaret would have required the carriage to stop every half hour to stretch her legs—the rheumatism would make them ache terribly otherwise—delaying the group even more. Mr. Ernest would have patiently waited, helped when needed, and read the remainder of the time.

It was not a difficult scenario to imagine, and one that proved to be quite accurate when the big, lumbering carriage pulled up in front of Shackleford Park. The vehicle disgorged three travel-weary passengers who had set out on a two-hour journey that had taken twice as long as expected. Twilight was hard on their heels.

Standing with the Beeswanger staff at the end of the men's line, Matt glanced past Johnny toward the waiting maids on the other side of the door. Kate, looking subdued, returned his gaze with a steady, questioning stare. The bitter wind tugged a lock of hair free from her simple upsweep while snowflakes collected on the crown of her head. She looked lovely, though concerned.

Matt winked, but without his usual accompanying grin. He was trying, and had been doing so all day, to maintain a calm, blasé sort of demeanor when around the entrancing Kate Darby. He wanted to ignore that moment under the mistletoe, treat it as an aberration . . . but Kate was not playing the game properly.

She had tried to talk to him privately after the morning meal; then she had tried to draw him out by knocking at his panel door midmorning, to which he had feigned deafness, or that he was not in his room. In truth, he simply had not answered, despite imagining what might occur if he had. In his mind's eye, he threw the door open and pulled Kate into his arms, where they continued to explore the wonders of her lips . . . He would trail kisses down her neck, press their persons tightly together, and . . . Then he heard footsteps passing down the corridor and a few muttered words of greeting, and he was glad that he had resisted temptation.

Fortunately, the midday meal in the servants' hall was not conducive to conversation; what with the entire staff all atwitter about the expected arrivals, Kate's and his stilted conversation was lost in the melee. And now, with the arrival of the Steeples, their duties greatly increased. There would be more gown changes for the young ladies, and Matt would be required to outfit both young gentlemen again. They would be very busy . . . yes, too busy to remember that moment, that ill-advised moment. After a few days of avoidance, Matt was certain that he would be able to look Kate in the eye without longing for what might have been.

"There she is," Johnny said out of the side of his mouth—confusing Matt terribly until he turned and watched Camille LaPierre descend the carriage steps. The young lady's maid shivered and pulled her cloak tightly around her. "An' I have nothin' for her sisters. A cheerful, happy Christmas that will be. What a disappointment."

"Camille was not expecting anything, Johnny. She can hardly be disappointed."

Huffing in derision at Matt's perfectly reasonable comment, Johnny continued to watch the Beeswangers greet the Steeples. Once the introductions and inquiries into the comfort of the traveler's journey had been dealt with, the driver urged his horses forward—guiding the coach to the service entrance, where the baggage could be unloaded. Staff remained in position even as the Steeples ambled toward the double wooden doors. The Beeswangers did not follow but grinned and called for their guests to turn around.

The carriage rolled away to reveal a group of six villagers who had been hidden behind the great lumbering vehicle; they were standing in a semicircle. Four men in greatcoats and caps and two women swathed in cloaks and woolen mittens stood staring at the newcomers. They smiled and waited. As the noise of the rattling equipage faded, it became apparent that they were humming as well . . . until at last they burst into a stirring rendition of "We Wish You a Merry Christmas."

The observers cheered in great surprise and pleasure as the carolers then continued with "Deck the Halls." Sir Andrew called out for "O Come All Ye Faithful" and joined in when they began, singing in an amazingly tuneful bass. The songsters happily obliged the youngest Beeswanger daughters, Miss Pauline and Miss Harriet, when they asked to hear "I Saw Three Ships (Come Sailing In)" and "The First Noel." By the time the last note of "Hark! The Herald Angels Sing" had faded away, the festive atmosphere was established, smiles abounded, and the weariness had all but disappeared from the faces of the travelers.

When the Steeples made their way through the doors, the Beeswangers and Miss Imogene followed. One conversation tumbled on top of another, as all seemed to have so much more to say than minutes earlier. Mrs. Lundy paid the carolers, wished them well, and signaled for the staff to return to their duties.

Before going inside, Livy asked if there were to be any mummers this year, disguised locals going door to door to perform, but the girl was shushed and waved across the threshold. Though Mrs. Lundy winked at the scullery maid as she obeyed, offering the likelihood that mummers would indeed find their way to Shackleford Park.

Filing in with the rest of the servants, Matt, by his very position at the end of his line, met Kate, who was at the end of hers. They paused, allowing the others to cross the threshold without them. Naturally, Kate was the first to speak and, as would be expected, went straight to the heart of the matter.

"It was just a bit of fun, Mr. Harlow. We need make nothing of it."

Matt smiled at her slightly chiding tone. "Ah, but the problem is, Miss Darby, it was much more than a *bit* of fun."

Kate, who had been staring into the manor through the open door, turned her head toward him. Her brows were knit together. "Was it?" she said with a swallow of discomfort.

"Well, yes, it was an all-consuming fire." He maintained a serious demeanor . . . until he ruined the attempt by bobbing his brows up and down.

"Very poetic, Mr. Harlow," Kate said, trying, to no avail, to control her twitching lips—ah, those wondrous lips—from forming into a grin. She made a ceremony out of tucking an errant lock of hair behind her ear. "It sounds rather enticing."

"No, sounds like trouble."

There was no hiding her grin now. "Of the best kind."

"Indeed, the very best kind of trouble . . ." Matt fought to appear staid and in control. "But one can be burnt by fire."

"One can or might it be two?"

"In this case . . . I suspect two."

Swaying from side to side, looking rather pleased with herself, Kate laughed lightly. "What are we to do?"

"I might suggest that we be very careful, Kate . . . and

perhaps not play with fire." It was not Matt's preferred course of action, just one that circumstances were foisting upon him . . . them.

"That's rather disappointing, Matt," she said as she made a show of batting her eyelashes and playfully knocking his shoulder with hers.

"It most certainly is . . . but we would be taking the prudent path, the higher road." His staid expression started to erode.

"Prudent and practical, rational and restrained—all excellent sentiments. Though discreet and careful could be another approach."

"Do you really believe that to be an option? A harmless option? Of no consequence?"

Kate stopped swaying; her eyes met his, and Matt forgot how to breathe. There was no doubting the intensity between them; it was ever present, heat smoldering under the surface. Had it not been for a voice from within the manor berating them for leaving the door open, reckless and rash might very well have been their option—their *only* option.

Instead, Matt gulped a breath and Kate huffed a sigh.

"Lawks. I believe you have the right of it," she said as they stepped into Shackleford. "Our conduct should be rational and restrained—beyond reproach."

With a nod, Matt closed the door, feeling anything but relieved.

"I believe you sighed, Mr. Harlow," she said, looking not at him but at the family making their way through the east gallery to the drawing room. "Are you well?"

"Nothing that a little mistletoe wouldn't cure," Matt said.

Kate's lovely laughter echoed throughout the hall, causing a few heads to turn in their direction, but Matt made a show of heading toward the little hall while Kate set off for the back stairs. They certainly didn't want to attract attention.

HUMMING TO HERSELF, Kate was aware that the door to Miss Emily's room had opened, but she was so deeply involved in *not* thinking about Matt that some time must have passed before she turned around; Marie stood in the middle of the room waiting—impatiently, if Kate used her scowling countenance as a barometer.

"Marie?" Kate had draped the gown Miss Emily wished to wear that evening over her arm. "Is all well?"

"I came to warn you." Marie's expression was profoundly serious, her tone unnaturally deep. "They know," she said with as much melodrama as the entirety of one of Shakespeare's tragedies.

Kate gasped. "They do? Lawks, that's terrible. Whatever shall we do?"

"You must desist immediately."

Leaning again the bedpost, as if her knees had suddenly given way, Kate moaned. "I will. I will." Then she lifted her head, met Marie's sardonic look and stood. "Who knows what?"

"Kate, how can you be so obtuse? Mrs. Beeswanger heard you laughing with Mr. Harlow."

"I do have a tendency to laugh, Marie. It's a part of my nature."

"Yes, true enough . . . but Mrs. Beeswanger heard something different in that laugh. She turned right around, despite the fact that Lady Margaret was speaking to her, and stared after you and Mr. Harlow."

"How do you know? You did not come to hear the carolers."

"She said as much just now, while I was mending her sleeve—it was only a tiny tear and could have been repaired later, but she wanted it taken care of immediately. And then, casual like, Mrs. Beeswanger asked if there was anything between you and Mr. Harlow that she should know about. I assured her that you merely enjoy each other's company, that there is nothing of a romantic nature between you—that it was just a little merriment during the Yuletide—and that you would never do anything to jeopardize your position. Never."

Kate sighed and shook her head. The Shakespearean phrase *the lady doth protest too much* came to mind. "You said all that in my defense?"

"Yes, I did. Though I must say, Mrs. Beeswanger did not look reassured."

"I'm not surprised." Holding Miss Emily's gown up by the shoulders, Kate gave it a little shake and studied a small wrinkle on the hem. "There is nothing to worry about, Marie. All that you said to Mrs. Beeswanger is true."

"But I have seen you look at each other in *that* sort of way—you and Mr. Harlow."

"Indeed?" Kate remained focused on the gown. "And what exactly is 'that' way?"

"Dreamy like, as if all you can see is each other and none of us around you amount to a hill of beans. If you were betrothed, it would be another matter—no one would think anything of your fits of giggles. They wouldn't be unseemly."

Kate felt her ire rise at the description; she had only giggled once or twice and not in Marie's hearing. "That's a huge leap, Marie. To go from strangers to being engaged; how is one supposed to get there without courting?"

"Don't think courting is Mrs. Beeswanger's concern. It's loose behavior an' the results." Marie turned sideways, cupping her dress and lifting it to form an overly large belly.

"You need not be concerned, Marie. *She* need not be concerned."

Kate was quite ready to defend her conduct. Other than a brief moment of passion under the mistletoe, nothing had happened or would happen, and therefore Kate could get up on her high horse and call foul until the cows came home. Which was all terribly muddled, but everything about Matt left her confused . . . and happy. Fire, he thought they were fire together—

"Kate?"

"Yes? Oh, I beg your pardon." Lowering the gown, Kate fixed Marie with a determined stare. "Were you saying something?"

"Yes, I—"

Before Marie could spout any more pointless, meddling directives, the door to the room opened. Miss Emily and Miss Imogene entered in a rustle of skirts and happy chatter. They stopped abruptly upon seeing Marie.

"Oh, Mary." Miss Emily frowned, glancing between the two lady's maids. "Was there something you needed?" She, too, found it difficult to remember the lady's maid's new moniker.

Marie mumbled an inane comment about passing a message and quickly vacated. Kate was not sorry to see her go; she had had enough of her interference.

"Is all well, Kate?" Miss Emily asked.

"Yes, indeed. There's lots of hustle and bustle this close to Christmas, miss, getting ready for the open house tomorrow afternoon and all. Mrs. Lundy's got us coming and going."

"You need not be pressed into service, Kate. You know that."

"Oh yes, miss. I would not neglect my duties to you and Miss Imogene while trying to help Mrs. Lundy."

Miss Emily laughed lightly, giving Kate a quick hug. "Silly goose, we would not have you overburdened. Mrs. Lundy revels in these busy days—she occasionally forgets everything else."

Kate grinned. Miss Emily was all kindness and consideration. It was not thus in many households.

"So, now that is resolved, I have an important question." Miss Emily paused for dramatic effect. "What do you think of beads in my hair? I know the embellishment is a tad elaborate, but this is the Steeples' first night at Shackleford and I would hate to appear . . ." Glancing over her shoulder, she met Miss Imogene's steady gaze. "Oh dear, that was rather thickheaded of me. You haven't seen Ernest since your dispute in the summer. This was your first meeting after our disastrous journey to the coast to visit him. How are you, my dear friend? Truly. Was it difficult?"

With a smile, Miss Imogene shook her head. "No. Ernest is, and always will be, the perfect gentleman. He asked after my health, my art lessons, and if I had found something suitable for a teaching studio in Canterbury." She paused, her eyes taking on a faraway appearance. "He and Ben seemed very happy to see each other. They seem to have settled their differences. Indeed, all is well. Actually, better than expected."

"Excellent. Most excellent. And when is Ben to receive

that huge tome you purchased for him?" Letting her day dress drop to the floor, Miss Emily stepped out of the puddled material and handed it carefully to Kate.

Miss Imogene laughed. "I thought on Christmas, just before we go to church. I dearly hope he doesn't have that particular book yet." She lowered herself onto the bed, hand on the nearest post, waiting for Kate to finish Miss Emily's evening preparations. "Could you thank Mr. Harlow for me, please, Kate?" Then she frowned. "Or perhaps that is not a such a wise idea."

Tossing her pretty brown curls, Miss Emily glanced from Miss Imogene to Kate. "Why not?"

"Best not have Kate in Mr. Harlow's proximity more than necessary."

Miss Emily nodded her thanks as Kate fastened the last button of her evening gown. "Has Mr. Harlow misbehaved?" Even as she preened in front of the full-length mirror, her eyes met Kate's with a worried expression.

Kate shook her head, though Miss Imogene answered, "No, indeed not. His behavior is beyond reproach, as it should be . . . as one would expect of Ernest's valet."

"So there is no problem."

"Indeed not, Miss Emily," Kate said, pulling open the vanity drawer with a snap. She pointed Miss Emily toward the seat and placed the box of beads next to the brush. Being the subject of a conversation but not a part of it was most uncomfortable.

"Oh, I beg your pardon, Kate. I did not mean to talk over your head," Miss Imogene said as if she had read Kate's thoughts. "Mr. Harlow is a handsome young man and . . . well, he might turn any impressionable girl's head."

"Not to worry, miss. It takes more than a handsome face to turn my head."

Focusing on the task at hand, Kate pulled the pins from Miss Emily's simple upsweep, preparing her young lady's tresses for the more elaborate evening style. The girls' conversation became one of anticipation as they discussed the evening's festivities and the melding of different family traditions. It gave Kate the opportunity to smile without censure.

Her mind had wandered toward the excitement of the season as well, especially as it pertained to mistletoe.

THURSDAY, DECEMBER 18, 1817, MARKET DAY

"WHO IS HE?" Johnny asked again and again, indicating various men around the market until, finally catching Kate's eye, he clamped his mouth shut. Johnny was as jumpy as a jackrabbit, pointing out and asking after every red-haired person they saw.

The Tishdale market was not overly large, but it was diverse and crowded with happy, smiling denizens, muffed and covered by shawls. There were kiosks of hand-knit goods, wooden toys, and miscellaneous decorations.

Eventually, Kate refused to answer Johnny's plaguing questions. She gave him a withering look and shared it with Matt—who jabbed Johnny in the ribs and bid him to be silent. With one last glance at Kate—no doubt realizing by her expression that he had pressed well beyond what was seemly—Johnny desisted.

Smiling faces abounded. Kate bobbed curtsies and exchanged greetings with everyone around her, enjoying the atmosphere so much that she took her time wending her way around the stalls. She could see Johnny's impatience, watched as he had pushed others aside, and wondered where Johnny's charm had gone. It was certainly not evident today. Even Johnny's precious Camille had offered him a frown of confusion, likely surprised by his lack of attention. Rather than seeing it as a lesson, it would seem that Johnny was taking the theft of his ring as a personal affront.

Eventually, Kate had greeted all those she knew; she had spent a moment admiring Peggy's overlarge belly, shaken hands with the Reverend, and picked up a trinket or two. Matt—and, unfortunately, Johnny—met her near the church steps.

"Did you see him? The huge brute of a man with the red grizzled beard?" Johnny asked before any niceties could be expressed. "You should have hurried; the man's gone off down the road. He was with a parcel of young ones—six on my count. One in his woman's arms."

Kate sighed and looked at Matt before turning back to

Johnny. "Yes, that would be the butcher. Mr. Kelp. Surely you are not going to tell me that he is the man who cheated you. Mr. Kelp is a well-trusted man of the community. He would *not* have passed you a fake coin."

"No, no, I'm not sayin' it was him . . . but there is somethin' about him that reminds me of the fella what stole my ring."

"I thought you were going to let it be, Johnny. Stop belaboring the loss." Matt hardly glanced in his friend's direction; he was fixated on Kate.

"*You* decided I should let it be," Johnny said, thrusting his chin forward. "I'm wantin' me ring back."

Shaking her head, Kate guided the boys out of Mr. and Mrs. Adkins's way; the apothecary and his wife were trying to step around a collection of children admiring the toys on display. "There is nothing you can do," she said to Johnny while nodding an apology to the older couple.

"Really?" Johnny smiled an odd, challenging sort of smirk. Not in the least appealing. "Think I might visit a butcher."

"There is no time, Johnny." Matt frowned. "We have to get back to the manor. Everyone is needed to help with the open house this afternoon."

"I got time, I got time." Johnny looked toward the road. "I'll see ya back at Shackleford Park before anyone knows I'm gone." So saying, Johnny nodded to Kate and smiled at Camille, who stared at them from the bottom of the hill. He trotted around the enthusiastic shoppers and was soon out of sight.

Kate watched him go. "I have a bad feeling about this," she said, hoping Matt would disagree.

"So do I," he said, in a most disobliging manner.

chapter 8

In which a thunderous expression leads to prevarication

"Katey-bird, who is that young man over there?"

Looking up from where she was cutting the gingerbread cake, Kate glanced in the direction of her mother's pointing finger—despite the impropriety of gesturing in such a vulgar manner. Matt stood at the other end of the crudely set up trestle table dipping into the wassail bowl with a ladle. The entire staff had been pressed into service, helping with the Shackleford Park open house for the laborers and tenants of the estate. Families had been included in the invitation this year, necessitating a move out of the servants' hall and into the hay barn next to the stables—without the hay, of course. Braziers had been lit near the entrance to offer a modicum of heat to those coming and going, but the cavernous barn itself was not cold, likely warmed by the rowdy crowd itself.

Kate dropped her eyes back to the task at hand, passing Mr. Tupper a second slice of rich, warm cake wafting with the aroma of nutmeg and cinnamon. "He is Mr. Harlow, Mam. Mr. Ernest and Mr. Ben Steeple's valet. The gentlemen's gentleman." She glanced around to ensure that there were no Beeswangers or Steeples in the vicinity, not entirely sure why her mother was asking. She noticed that Marie, handing out plum pudding beside her, was leaning in their direction.

"Did you have enough to eat, Mam? Cook has another goose on the spit, and Mr. Murray has only just brought out the second boar's head. Don't want to miss that. Merle appears to be waiting for a second helping."

"Plenty, plenty. Most generous of the family, I must say. They's doing it up proper. Why does he keep lookin' at you, Katey? Impertinent like. Bold. I don't like it. Best be careful o' him. Kinda shifty lookin'. A bad sort."

"Colby is quite pleased with the model horse Mr. Beeswanger gave him, isn't he, Mam?" Kate wiped her fingers absentmindedly across her skirt and then sighed when she realized that she had missed her apron and now sported a brown smear on the hard-to-launder linen of her charcoal skirts. "Very generous of him to remember the young ones."

"Indeed, indeed. There, he did it again. That Mr. Harlow grinned at you. Who does he think he is, carryin' on so? Did you see that?"

"I'm too busy to worry about handsome valets, Mam."

"I didna say he was handsome. Is that what you think?"

"Might I suggest you join Henry for your dessert?" She shoved a slice of cake at her mother, gesturing toward her brother. He was seated with the other Tobarton farmers at the other end of a long line of makeshift tables. "Oh, look, there's Mrs. Nappleberry." Kate named one of her mother's good friends. "Don't want to miss the opportunity to wish her a happy Christmas."

"Already have."

"Ah, excellent," Kate said somewhat sourly. Dropping the rest of the cake in a very generous serving onto Mr. Jordan's waiting plate, Kate ignored his look of surprise. "Oh dear, it seems that I have run out. Excuse me, Mam. I have to get another cake from Cook." She smiled wanly and tried, without success, to leave the barn without looking behind her.

As she walked to the door, Kate looked over her shoulder. Matt was watching; he winked and smiled and Kate grinned . . . until Marie stepped into her line of sight and offered her a scowl. With a shrug, Kate crossed the threshold and made her way to the manor. It wasn't until she was halfway there that she realized she had left her shawl in the barn and that the wind was howling a very bitter tune. It didn't seem to matter, though; her thoughts of Matt Harlow kept her warm.

"What did Johnny learn?" a voice of soft dulcet tones inquired from inside the pantry.

Matt's pulse quickened, and he turned to find, as he knew he would, Kate standing inside the small room lined with shelves of foodstuffs. He had come into the manor and made his way to the kitchen hall for just this purpose: a moment, no matter how brief, with the lovely Kate Darby.

"I have not seen him as yet." Matt smiled as he watched her lips curl up at the corners. "I'm glad to have the opportunity to speak with you."

"Oh?"

How could so short a word sound alluring and cheeky at the same time? "Yes, I wished to inquire about your plans for your half day tomorrow."

"Oh?"

Matt swallowed and tried to concentrate. "Yes . . . I . . . it is . . . do you . . . ?"

The luscious, wondrous, inviting lips curled up even further . . . even as his gaze dropped.

"Matt?"

"Hmmmm."

"Look up. Yes, that's it; my eyes are up here. There we go." Kate's eyes sparkled with mischief. "It is traditional to spend holidays with one's family."

"Yes, indeed. Your family." Matt fought the urge to look down again. "I do not want to interfere, whatsoever . . . but I wondered . . . I thought I might borrow a sled. No, that won't work; there is only a dusting of snow. Skate . . . yes, might we go . . . No, I have not brought blades."

"And the pond has yet to freeze completely."

"Yes, there is that, too. Well, a walk, then. I know that doesn't sound terribly interesting, but—"

"I thought that we were going to be prudent and practical."

"Nothing untoward about a walk," he said, worried that she would heed his unreasonable suggestion. "I'm sure we can be restrained strolling through the woods." And then he smiled. "Mistletoe does not grow in this area."

"I would love to."

"You would?" Matt gulped his relief. Despite all his objections, despite logic, despite wisdom, he could not stop wanting to be near Kate Darby and her extraordinary . . . smile.

"Yes, of course. I will speak to Henry; he is the most sensible of my three brothers. I'll let him know that I will be busy and, if I have time, I will join them later." She shrugged with a slight downward cast to her expression. "I would invite you to join us, but I'm afraid my mother . . . well, we wouldn't want to cause an ill-founded fuss."

"True enough. True enough. Shall we say—" Matt began, when the click of heels in the corridor stilled his tongue.

"Mr. Heathrow?"

Matt tensed, and then lifted his cheeks before pivoting toward Walker. Kate was hidden behind his back. "Harlow, Mr. Walker; the name is Harlow."

"I care not what you are called, sir. I wish, instead, to

know where your truant friend may be. I am short-handed and need Johnny to bring the dishes back into the kitchen. Where is he?"

"I have no idea," Matt said. "The last I saw of him, he was carrying mince pies to the barn with Bernie." The fabrication made Matt vastly uncomfortable, for, in fact, he didn't recall having seen Johnny all afternoon.

Walker, having ascertained exactly nothing, turned, muttering something about incompetence under his breath, and stormed away.

"Matt, *did* Johnny return from Tishdale?" Kate asked.

"I'm starting to wonder the same."

The atmosphere in the pantry, that moments earlier had been sultry, was suddenly chilled and heavy with disquiet. Where was Johnny?

THE LARGE NUMBER of persons milling about the barn and the stable yard was both a hindrance and a boon. While the overcrowding meant that Johnny was not easily spotted, it also meant that Matt and Kate's search was not readily observed, either. By virtue of their positions, they were invisible and under no obligation to assist at the open house. Their absence would not draw comment now after having graciously served at the food table earlier. Fortunately, too, the Beeswangers and the Steeples had already played host—speeches and gifts for the little ones—and retired to their drawing room to await a late dinner; it was unlikely that the family would have cause to noticc Matt and Kate hurrying and scurrying about the manor.

Matt began in the men's quarters, while Kate chased down the other footmen. As suspected, Johnny was not abed with an ailment or tote-and-carrying with Bernie or Charles. He was not helping in the kitchens or jawing with the grooms. The gardener had seen neither hide nor hair of him, and the tittering laundry maids wished that they had encountered him . . . but hadn't.

As the sated tenants and laborers drifted away to return to their own hearths, Matt still had no idea where Johnny might be. News came from a most unexpected source.

"The Gambling Goat—it has card games the week before Christmas," Camille informed them with a sniff of disapproval. They were standing just inside the housekeeper's sitting room, where Camille was darning one of Lady Margaret's stockings as she and Mrs. Lundy chatted over a glass of sherry. "I heard the *grand* footman—you know, the one with the pip of hair on his lip that he calls a mustache. *Oui*, I heard him talking with the other one about it. Johnny must have heard, too. He is a *terrible* one for gaming."

"Oh yes, of course." Kate turned to Matt with a flicker of a smile. "The Gambling Goat. Now, that makes sense. Mr. Kelp would have sent him away . . . and the Goat is where he lost his ring."

"Vraiment?" Camille's brows knit together. "How came

he to lose . . . ? The one with the stag head? *C'est dommage.*" She turned to Mrs. Lundy as if needing to explain. "Johnny, he was so happy with this ring."

She clicked her tongue, leaving Matt to wonder if she did so out of sympathy or disapproval.

"Poor Johnny," Camille said, clearing up Matt's confusion.

"He is a charmer, that one." Mrs. Lundy laughed. "Quickly a favorite with us all."

"*Mais* never the same. One day a charmer, the next day a clown. One day kindness, the next day gambling. Never the same. So hard to know where you stand with him." She sighed as she turned back to her darning.

Matt blinked in surprise. Camille had never shown so much emotion. Granted, in most others that would be little enough, but for Camille . . . well, this boded very well for Johnny. Something worth sharing when he saw his friend next.

Matt nudged Kate out of the room into the corridor. "It would seem that Johnny might be trying to win another chance to give Camille's sisters a gift."

"Indeed. Foolishness," Kate said, giving him a long, intent look. "But the heart is not always sensible." And then she laughed.

Matt shrugged, ruining the aspect of nonchalance by grinning at the same time. "He'd better be back by the time the family sits down to dinner. His absence behind Sir Andrew's chair will certainly be noticed."

KATE LEARNED NO more of Johnny's whereabouts until she was helping the girls prepare for bed that evening. Their exuberance echoed throughout the hall as Kate waited in her room for them to return from dinner. Following the laughter, she made her way to Miss Imogene's room to find the girls together, exclaiming over a length of fabric.

Miss Imogene was the first to notice Kate standing in the doorway. "Look, Kate. Isn't it beautiful? Belgian lace. For my wedding clothes. From Lady Margaret."

Smiling, Kate made the appropriate sounds. Though it wasn't difficult to be enthused; the material was exquisite. Likely worth three of her year's wages.

"It was a lovely evening. Sir Andrew and Lady Margaret could not have been kinder." Miss Imogene sat on the bed beside the lace, petting it like a cat. "I was afraid that it would be uncomfortable; I did so want to have a pleasant evening."

Miss Imogene looked up at Miss Emily. "Did you see Sir Andrew's face when he looked behind his chair for Johnny? Thunderous."

Miss Emily sighed somewhat sadly and then turned to Kate, explaining unnecessarily. "Mr. Ben begged Sir Andrew's pardon for sending Johnny on an errand that has delayed him in town. And then Bernie took care of the Steeples' service throughout dinner. There was no disruption. It allowed for a very pleasant evening." She turned back to

Miss Imogene. "An excellent start, my dearest friend. Lady Margaret seems quite taken with you."

As the girls continued to discuss the evening and all its ramifications, Kate pulled Miss Imogene's nightdress from the wardrobe. She breathed a great sigh of relief, then snorted a silent chuckle at her pointless concern over the footman's welfare. So Johnny was not missing, nor at the Gambling Goat getting himself into trouble.

Were it seemly, Kate would tiptoe to the far corridor and inform Matt that he need not fret . . . no, she was all but certain that Mr. Ben would have mentioned Johnny's errand to Matt . . . and then Kate would have risked her reputation for nothing.

Kate retrieved Miss Imogene's long white cotton nightdress and tried, valiantly, to keep her mind on the task at hand. The girls only asked once or twice why she was smiling in such an enigmatic manner. To which, of course, Kate merely shrugged and tried so very, very hard not to think of Matt Harlow.

FRIDAY, DECEMBER 19, 1817

THE NEXT MORNING, the sun chased away the clouds, though it offered no respite from the bracing wind. The chatter at Mrs. Lundy's breakfast table was lively. As soon as the midday meal was prepared, most of the staff were free to do as they wished. It was one of the few afternoons that families, lovers, and friends were without duties at the same time. The

Beeswangers and Steeples would keep to themselves and serve their own fare from the remains of the cold meal set up in the dining room.

Yes, it was to be a day of frivolity, and all were prepared to enjoy it to the fullest. Which was why Kate was concerned to see that Matt did not have the lighthearted countenance she had expected. There was no mischief in his eyes. In fact, he barely looked up from his plate—a plate that was still laden with bacon and toast when he stood to leave.

Had Mr. Ben not shared the news of Johnny last evening? Had Matt suffered through the night worrying needlessly about his friend? When he signaled a wish to speak with her, Kate immediately met Matt in the corridor, away from prying ears.

"I'm afraid I will no longer be able to enjoy a walk with you today, Kate." He glanced out the hall window. "And on such a lovely day, too. It will have to be some other time."

Kate knew not when that other time might be . . . next Yuletide, perhaps. "Has something occurred?"

"It's Johnny again. I must go find him."

"Oh dear, so Mr. Ben did *not* speak to you. He sent Johnny on an errand yesterday. He . . ." She glanced down the corridor toward the servants' hall. "He will still be breaking his fast with the others." She turned back to see that the apprehension had not faded from Matt's eyes.

"No, he will not." Then he huffed a sigh. "Nor did Mr. Ben send him on an errand."

"But he told Sir Andrew—"

"Yes, and it put him in a great lather to do so. Mr. Ben blames Johnny for forcing him to prevaricate and is quite put out about it. He feels that had he not stepped in, Sir Andrew would have been in a pique all evening, ruining Miss Imogene's first evening with his family since their betrothal. And now that Johnny has not yet returned, I am to go into town, find him, and deliver a message. If he returns now, his pay will be docked; if he doesn't, his position is forfeit and he can find his own way back to the coast." Matt swallowed visibly. "Johnny has truly cooked his goose, and I don't believe Mr. Ben can be charmed out of his displeasure."

"So there was no errand."

"No."

"And Johnny is still missing."

"Indeed."

"Has he done this before?"

Matt huffed. "That is the most troublesome aspect of this entire situation. Johnny had a reputation for just this sort of behavior before he came to Musson House. I have known him for years—from when my father owned a tailor shop in Chotsdown. I recommended Johnny, thought he had settled down and that being a footman would be the making of him. He *seemed* to have given up the wild life—gambling far less than he had been, and even being besotted with Camille kept him from chasing skirts. But . . . no, it would seem that Johnny has not changed after all."

"It isn't your fault." Kate lifted her hand toward him, but

saw Mrs. Lundy peek out her door and glance in their direction. Quickly leaning back, Kate was unsure how they had come to stand so close to each other.

After their having only *just* reestablished a respectful distance, Mrs. Lundy departed her sitting room and nodded as she passed. She was sporting a most bewildering expression, as if she were trying to retain a tight grip on her lips . . . which wanted to curl upward.

"I'll go with you." Kate returned her gaze to Matt once the good woman had disappeared down the kitchen corridor.

"I can hardly ask it of you."

"I don't believe you asked; I believe I offered. You do not know the town."

"I know the Gambling Goat, and I have it on good authority that most stores are along the main road . . . where I will visit your butcher, should I need to."

"Perhaps a guide might be a good idea . . . and someone that the locals know. Someone they would be comfortable speaking with. Now . . . who could help you with this? Oh wait, I know someone who is no longer expected at her brother's house. Knows most . . . though, she will admit, not *all* residents of Tishdale, and had been anticipating a walk on a sunny day. As the destination had not yet been determined, perhaps she will hike into Tishdale regardless of whether she is accompanied or not."

Matt laughed. His expression told Kate that he was as surprised as was she by the outburst. "Kate, Kate, you are so corky. Would you, my girl, enjoy a jaunt of an exploratory nature into the town of Tishdale, where I will ring a fine peal over my friend Johnny Grinstead and hopefully return the contrite fellow into the welcoming arms of Camille LaPierre?"

"Oh yes, that sounds most appealing. Thank you for asking. And who knows, we might meet Johnny on his way back, holding his head and wishing he had not spent the night carousing."

Matt nodded and smiled—although the spark that had been there moments earlier had already faded. "Yes. Well, that would be very handy. I could thump him before we get back to Shackleford Park."

"And then he could regale the household with stories of thuggery and fake coins while sporting a shiner. He would have great sympathy from all the women." Kate nodded.

"Yes, but would it work on Mr. Ben?"

"Time will tell."

"Yes, indeed," Matt said with a deep sigh.

chapter 9

In which there are accusations of an amorous pique

The road into Tishdale had hardened in the cold, making it much easier to leap from one rut to another without sinking into the boot-sucking mud. There were a few occasions that Matt's hand was required to provide Kate with some sort of balance. As such, she tried to be off-kilter as much as possible, though with mitted hands the thrill was in being close rather than the warmth of his touch.

The conversation was sparse, to say the least; Matt was deeply engrossed in his own thoughts—dark thoughts if one could go by his tight jaw and set expression. Still, it was not an uncomfortable silence nor overlong. It offered Kate the opportunity to watch their surrounding without having to participate in a light discourse. As much as she enjoyed their banter, which she did most prodigiously, looking for any telltale sign of the errant footman seemed to be an endeavor of much more import. Unfortunately—or was it fortunately?—there were no signs to note. No green livery in the ditch, in the woods, behind the Gibbs fence, or at the crest of the fields. Certainly not walking toward them. No sign of Johnny whatsoever.

In due time, the spire of St. Bartholomew became visible above the leafless trees, though it was veiled by smoke pouring from the many chimney pots of Tishdale. However, before entering the town proper, the Gambling Goat sat at the crossroad offering a respite to travelers, nuncheons, ale, or the opportunity of company. The gambling was a given—considering the name of the inn—though it was rarely raucous.

Such was clearly not the case on this day as they approached the inn, for the clamor increased considerably in great guffaws of laughter and shouts, and the skipping tune of a fiddle snaking under the door toward them. A typical posting inn, the Tudor stucco-and-beam building housed a public room on the ground floor with bedrooms above. The kitchens were accommodated on one side of the inn with the stables on the other, in a horseshoe shape.

Originally, Tishdale had occupied a quiet corner of Kent. Then, the gates of the Gambling Goat had enclosed the yard, protecting the patrons overnight from would-be thieves and highwaymen. Now, the gates hung unmoving and immovable, their hinges all but rusted in place as coaches arrived at all hours of the day and night. It was no grand surprise to see carts and wagons with ponies and donkeys hitched to posts, waiting in the yard. The Gambling Goat was in great favor, especially near the holidays.

Matt and Kate squeezed inside, making their way around the celebrating patrons. Kate nodded and smiled and was eventually waylaid by the greetings of those she knew. Marching ahead, oblivious to the curious expressions and affronted stares of those around him, Matt pushed his way to the gaming tables in the back of the room.

Watching Matt from where she stood jawing with the surgeon's wife, Kate could see that he was disappointed. Johnny was not at one of the tables, chancing his luck.

Kate was not terribly surprised; she had found no substance to the theory. Johnny had nothing to gamble with, no stake. He was cleaned out. Nothing but the clothes on his back . . . except perhaps the buttons of his livery, though they were tin and of little value.

Turning around, Matt inadvertently jarred a man who had followed on his heels—a man Matt had carelessly pushed aside in his haste to find Johnny. It was unfortunate, for this man wore an overly large apron atop his significant belly and was now glaring at Matt with great animosity.

Mr. Cryer, the publican of the Gambling Goat, had folded his arms across his chest despite leaning forward to hear what Matt had to say, and he kept glancing to the back of the room, where most of the noise emanated from the gaming tables. By the time Kate arrived, Matt's teeth were clenched and the two men were staring at each other with considerable hostility.

"Good day to you, Mr. Cryer," she said. "The best of the Yuletide season to you and your family, though I can see that my wishes are not needed. Quite the crowd you have here."

Tilting sideways so that he might see her while still keeping an eye on Matt, Mr. Cryer smiled, lifting his muttonchop whiskers into the air. "Ah, Miss Kate Darby. What brings you here this fine day? If it's your brother you be looking for, worry not. Ross has not been in here for a month of Sundays."

"Excellent news, Mr. Cryer. Perhaps he is going to settle down after all."

"Don't want them all to settle down, Miss Darby. I'd have no customers if they did."

Laughing, Kate shook her head. "Don't think you have anything to fear, Mr. Cryer."

He grinned, glanced over his shoulder and then back to Kate—completely ignoring Matt, who had not moved out of the way.

"I'm looking for a fella, Mr. Cryer," Kate said, ignoring the rousing chorus of chuckles from the eavesdropping patrons surrounding them.

"Could probably have your pick, my dear." Mr. Cryer tried, without success, to keep a straight face.

"A particular fella, actually, by the name of Johnny

Grinstead." Kate continued when the publican shrugged, "He might have come in here yesterday, wearing green livery. On the thin side, narrow face . . ." Before she had completed her description, Mr. Cryer was nodding.

"Yup, he were here. Thought someone might come lookin' for him sooner or later. Most don't wander around in their livery when they're not doin' someone's biddin'. He said he were looking for someone for his master, but he stayed overlong asking all sorts of questions about red hair and fake coins. Mr. Belcher took him off for a drink and then I saw him talkin' to Mr. Gupta and the apothecary. Fact is, I saw him going around the room talkin' to everyone, even them that came in later like Mr. Niven and Mr. McDonald. Had a doleful story, and was sharin' with everyone."

"What was his doleful story?" Matt asked, but received a glare for the attempt.

"What was his doleful story?" Kate repeated.

"Been taken, he said, made a fool of. All he wanted was to buy his sweetheart a gifty, but this here red-haired man stole his priceless ring—left 'im holdin' a fake coin. Bollocks. Right here, in my yard? I think not! Puts us all in a bad light, don't you think? Still, Mr. Gupta bought him a drink, and so did some others. He were wobbly-kneed when he left."

Kate smiled despite the sinking sensation in her gut. "When did he leave? Did anyone go with him?"

"Them's always comin' and goin', Miss Darby. I don't rightly know. If I were ta guess, late afternoon—gettin' on to dark." His eyes slid over to Matt and then back again. "I'm takin' it that he didn't find his way back to the big house."

"No, no sign of him."

"Some fool likely offered 'im a bed for the night and now the boy's head is hurtin' too much to rise."

"You might be right, Mr. Cryer." She didn't point out that it was already midafternoon and sore head or not, Johnny should have returned to Shackleford Park.

"A stranger in livery shouldna be hard to find, miss."

"Hope you are right, Mr. Cryer." Backing away, Kate nodded for Matt to follow. Walking in silence as they made their way through the patrons, Kate paused at the door to wave farewell to the overly curious.

ONCE KATE AND Matt were in the cold again, the hubbub from inside the Gambling Goat faded as they trudged through the enclosed yard, past the inn's gates, and out onto the main road. Kate gestured toward the town proper as Matt fell into step beside her . . . and quickened the pace. There was something of an unexpressed urging in his posture, like a twitchy, anxious racehorse raring to gallop.

"Where are you, you bacon-brained numbskull?" he muttered half under his breath and then looked up to see Kate staring at him. "Thank you," Matt said with an attempted smile. "If you had not been there, I would have had no answers whatsoever."

Lost in his gaze, Kate felt her foot slip. "Careful," she warned just as Matt slipped on a patch of ice, too. She leaned over to offer him support as his arms windmilled through the air. He would have fallen, had she not grabbed his hand . . . and then it seemed most natural to continue along the road as such: hand in hand. For ice abounded on this particular stretch of road, and it was much safer to support each other. Besides, there were none to see, and they could walk faster this way . . . and find Johnny sooner. Yes, excuses were not necessary.

"Locals are leery of strangers." Kate returned to the subject at hand—before hands had been involved in such a thought-distracting manner. She observed the warmth seeping through her mitt and enjoyed the bumping against each other when their gaits were not in harmony. She could feel a touch of heat on her cheeks and turned to face the road, lest Matt believe she was embarrassed and let go.

Clearing her throat, Kate continued from where she had left off. Which was where exactly? She paused, listening to the echo of her last words. Ah yes. "I would expect an innkeeper to be more obliging to outsiders. Perhaps Johnny used up the man's goodwill yesterday."

"That could well be," Matt said in a doubtful tone. "But it matters not; we know where Johnny spent his afternoon. It is easy to see how he was further delayed. It was either getting dark or was so already—it would have been foolish in the extreme to try for the manor on a moonless night on an unfamiliar road. Especially when he gets turned around easily enough in the daytime."

"We have to find someone who saw him after he left the Goat."

"Or who he was with, for they likely offered him shelter."

Kate tried not to sigh, for if she did, Matt would certainly hear her disquiet. While Matt was ready to throttle Johnny for his wild behavior, Kate hoped that would be the worst of it. Johnny, charming Johnny might have tried to return last night, foolish though it may have been. Young men had a tendency to think themselves impervious to harm—well, at least her brothers and his friends thought so—until life smacked them upside the head. She could imagine Johnny starting out for Shackleford Park with the best of intentions to return as was expected, and then becoming confused—lost, hurt, he could be lying in a snowy ditch or under a tree with a broken leg, or worse.

"It's as likely to be a girl," Matt remarked.

"I beg your pardon?"

"Johnny's spoiling for female company, what with Miss LaPierre not giving him the time of day."

"But . . . I'm . . . I don't entirely understand."

"Even if Johnny was foxed last night, he would have come back this morning—a pounding head or not."

"Yes, my thoughts exactly."

"So what could keep him in town when he knows he should be at the manor? What could be so bewitching as to keep him from his duties? Knowing, yes, *knowing* that he was putting me in a bind by doing so and getting himself into deep trouble."

Kate glanced over to see Matt nodding at the road ahead.

"Yes. That's what happened." His hand tightened on hers, though Kate thought he was unaware of his reaction. "Perhaps we should make a tour of places housing pretty girls."

Kate couldn't help herself; she snorted a laugh. "So you think . . ."

"That Johnny is being spectacularly dimwitted. In an amorous pique—"

"Amorous and in a pique. Quite the feat."

Giving her a side glance, Matt continued as if she had not spoken. "Johnny, grandly out of sorts, justified to himself, somehow, that he need not return to Shackleford Park only to hie off on his half day."

"That would still leave us with a problem."

"And that would be?"

"Tishdale has any number of fair young women within its boundaries," Kate said, dramatically waving her free hand about. "It could take a seven night to ferret them all out."

"The prettiest being a lady's maid at Shackleford Park."

"Shackleford is not actually part of Tishdale, but it is the thought that counts." She nodded as if impressed and then turned to Matt with a grin. "I shall tell Marie that you think her rather fine, as soon as we return."

"I was not thinking of Marie."

"Miss LaPierre?"

"Now you are just being coy."

"It's levity, Mr. Matt Harlow. Not being coy at all." Her grin grew broader until she remembered why they were not returning to Shackleford Park immediately, and her smile disappeared, replaced by a frown. "Mr. Cryer mentioned a great many folks . . . Perhaps we should start with Mr. and Mrs. Adkins; they live over the apothecary and they have a pretty daughter."

MATT WAS RELUCTANT to drop Kate's hand; he quite enjoyed the sensation. And yet he had no choice; the woods had given way to the first few cottages on the outskirts of Tishdale, and then within steps they were strolling down the main street. Too many eyes, judging and finding faults in others—Kate's reputation dictated a polite distance between them. Though most of the denizens of Tishdale were busy in their cozy cottages, there still were windows aplenty—best to be prudent.

Not recalling the location of the apothecary from his earlier visit, Matt followed Kate toward the first block of red-brick stores. Within moments, he could see a sign depicting a mortar and pestle swinging from the overhang. However, it was the sign ahead of it that caught Matt's attention: two crossed axes between a bull's head and pig's head.

"This is Mr. Kelp's store? The butcher Johnny was chasing down?"

Looking up first, Kate nodded and then she glanced into the storefront. "Yes, but Mr. Kelp will be readying for tomorrow . . . The window is empty . . . Oh, I do believe I see light in the back."

"Let's start here, then," Matt said as he rapped on the door.

"There is no need. We already know where Johnny went after talking to Mr. Kelp. It's after the Gambling Goat, not—Ah, Mr. Kelp. So good of you to answer your door."

The red-haired rotund man held the door partially open, looking past Matt and addressing Kate with a congenial smile. "Not at all, my dear. Though I hope you are not here for sausages; as you can see"—he pointed to the empty bins behind him—"my stock is depleted. I'm only now getting ready for tomorrow's opening."

"No, indeed. I . . . We were hoping for a bit of information. We are looking for a fellow of Mr. Harlow, here." She patted Matt's arm as if to prevent confusion, though there were just the three of them standing at the door. "You might have seen him at the market in green livery."

"Tall? Thin? Long hair? Oh yes, saw him for certain. And not just at the market. The cheeky fella called after me before I was halfway home yesterday. Wanted to know if I had any family in the area. Said I looked quite familiar. I told him not familiar enough, as I had no knowledge of him. Told him to be off. Can you imagine, coming up on a stranger like that, asking questions?" Then he turned to face Matt.

"Don't know how they be where you come from, but accosting strangers on the street don't sit well with no one."

Matt nodded with a tense jaw. He found the accusation unjust. The man had not been accosted; Johnny had merely called after him. Really. Folks on the coast were clannish, but nothing compared to this.

Mr. Kelp turned back toward Kate and continued. "I was hardly going to sit down with the Bible and show him my family tree. Next thing you know, the fella would be hounding my sister and her boys. They are like as any to be the ones he were thinking of. Two be working in Tishdale—one at the grocer, the other at the blacksmith. Then, I got a cousin working at the cooperage and three second cousins farming for the squire. Don't know who he meant, don't care. Friend or foe."

"Indeed, thank you, Mr. Kelp." As Kate was stepping away, she turned back as if just remembering a question. "Oh, Mr. Kelp, you don't recall which direction Mr. Harlow's friend took, do you?"

"Course. I watched that fella all the way to the end of the block. He was heading outta town, toward the Gambling Goat." With that and a firm nod, Mr. Kelp closed the door. Matt heard the lock click and the marching steps of the butcher returning to the back of his shop.

"Well, there. I thought we would get no further speaking to Mr. Kelp."

Matt sighed. "Indeed." It would seem that Johnny's thumping would be held off a little longer.

Mr. Adkins's daughter was not to Matt's taste—blond and rather insipid. He was much more drawn to lithe, dark-haired beauties . . . Matt blinked, bringing his mind back to the conversation. Again they were standing in the cold, a door partially open and no information forthcoming.

The apothecary had a comfortable store . . . as much as Matt could see of it while looking over Kate's shoulder and past Mr. Adkins. His daughter peeked curiously from behind the counter—but of Johnny there was no sign.

"No, my dear. I left the inn before that young fella. Couldn't say when or where he went."

Kate thanked the man, waved to the daughter, and started down the stairs that took them out through the back garden and into the mews running behind the line of shops. After a moment of consideration, Kate glanced at the next block of stores where Matt knew the wine merchant and bookseller to be located.

"I doubt Mr. Niven would have taken Johnny in—not the sort at all. A bit stodgy. He served with the Corps of Royal Sappers and Miners in the war, you know. A servant to one of the officers and walks around as if *he* held the rank . . . but neither Mr. Niven nor Mr. Gupta has a daughter. Still, we are here. And Mr. Cryer did say both men were at the Goat; we might as well ask if they noticed which way Johnny went and with whom."

When a knock at the wine merchant's door netted them

no answer, Kate crossed the road to the mews that continued behind the main street shops on the other side. With short fences delineating the yards on one side and associated stables and warehouses on the other, it was no feat to find the staircases they sought. A loud knock at the door to the flat at the top of the wine merchant's stairs brought no answer.

Fortunately, two doors up Mr. Gupta was home and welcoming. He asked them in out of the cold. He offered a cup of tea, apparently his favorite beverage . . . He always had a cup at his elbow. Might be his heritage, the old gentleman believed. Unfortunately, despite his great empathy for the liveried boy, Mr. Gupta had no idea where Johnny had gone. Mr. Gupta had been much occupied by a gathering of his cronies, and they had enjoyed themselves well into the night, long after Johnny had departed.

It was with an ever-increasing sense of frustration that Matt followed Kate down the stairs and they stood once more in the deserted lane. She looked in both directions, shook her head, and sighed. Leaning against the fence, she stared at the opposite wall.

"I'm starting to think two facers might be necessary," Matt said, grumbling. "And I will give him an earful while I'm at it."

"What if Johnny is hurt? Perhaps he has not returned because he can't."

"Can't? What would prevent him? Yes, he has a terrible sense of direction. If he stayed with someone and—"

"What if he attempted to return in the dark, got lost, and then tried to cut through the woods? The Beeswangers do not use mantraps to prevent poaching, but the majority of landowners do."

"I'm not worried about Johnny falling afoul of some terrible device. He knows enough to stay out of the woods, especially at night. As idiotic as my friend might be, he is not stupid. No, it's his temper and temperament that will get him into trouble—always running amok. He leaps before thinking. Indeed, this behavior is the Johnny of old. Something I thought gone . . . Clearly, I was mistaken."

Kate shook her head, still staring at the far wall. Then she blinked, swallowed, and her brows folded together—tighter and tighter until Matt had to ask.

"What is going on in that pretty head of yours that has caused such a look of consternation? You look perplexed and horrified at the same time."

"What am I looking at, Matt?"

Turning his head, Matt squinted and then crossed the lane. He, too, was confused; he saw *nothing* to cause disquiet of any sort. A warped stable door, bits of straw, manure, wagon tracks frozen in the snowy mud. He shifted his gaze slightly to the weathered wall of a warehouse with faded lettering, loose boards, and a rusty ring.

"Not there," Kate said, pointing lower, to a spot on the wall two feet above the ground. "There, on that hook."

Dropping his gaze, Matt immediately saw what had

caused Kate's bewilderment and why. Caught on a protruding nail, a button and bit of cloth hung abandoned. The embossed metal button was attached to a scrap of material that had been snagged and ripped free. It was a green piece of fabric, akin to the Steeple family livery.

Matt pulled off his gloves, swallowed with apprehension, and reached over to free the button. It was filthy and dented; dirt was ground into the crevices of the crest. It took several wipes across his thigh and a bit of spit before Matt cleared it enough to discern a fish on one corner of the crest. The remainder was nearly obliterated by the dent, and he could not read the scratched and worn engraving that surrounded the crest. Still, it was enough to make Matt uneasy. The Steeples had a fish on their family crest, and the material looked remarkably similar to their livery green.

"This remnant might have come from Johnny's coat," Matt said as he glanced up and down the mews. "It's hard to say for certain." But there was nothing untoward in the vicinity: no person-sized lump of green along the wall, no scuffs in the dirt, no broken gates or fences behind the stores. No hint of Johnny whatsoever—past or present.

"This does not bode well, Matt," Kate said in a hesitant voice.

"Not anything to be concerned about, really." Matt shrugged with feigned nonchalance. "Johnny, or someone with a coat similar to his, must have fallen against the wall and the button caught. What surprises me is that this person left it here. Rents are much easier to repair with the original patch."

"Matt?"

"I'm sure all is well, Kate." Matt dropped his gaze to shrug reassuringly at her, though his smile felt forced and likely looked that way, too.

"Matt, look at your fingers."

Doing as he was told, Matt lifted and glanced at his hand. The button sat on his palm swaddled by the green material. His fingers, however, were covered in the dirt that he had rubbed off and out of the button's crest. His body heat and spit had melted the dirt; it no longer looked like rusty earth. No. It trickled down his fingers in a smear of red.

Blood red.

chapter 10

In which Kate is as tense as a twisted corset

"What are we going to do?" Kate asked, sounding considerably more disturbed than moments earlier.

"About what?" Matt stared, enthralled by the mess on his hand. Then he blinked, reached into his coat pocket with his clean hand and drew out a handkerchief.

"About Johnny. He is hurt. We must get help."

Matt frowned as he encased the button and fabric in his crisp white cotton square—pressed only this morning. He wiped the red liquid off his fingers and then folded the collection into his pocket. "Help?" Matt looked down the lane again, willing his pulse to return to a normal pace. "How do we know Johnny is the one hurt? And if he is, where do we bring said help?"

"Matt, there can be no doubt—the button was covered in blood."

"Was it? That, of course, is our first dilemma. Is the red substance blood? I believe it to be true, but if not, what could it be . . . red paint?" Matt puckered the corner of his mouth, considered, and then shook his head. He was finding it easier to breathe now, letting logic take precedence—forcing his emotions away. "So if we decide the button is covered in blood, is it Johnny's? Is the *button* Johnny's? We cannot say yes—"

"But—"

"Definitively. We cannot say yes definitively. The scrap might be from someone else's coat or, even if it is Johnny's, was he wearing it when it acquired the . . . the red substance?"

"Blood. Let's just call it blood."

"Fine. Blood." Matt swallowed, blinked, and then shook his head, trying to clear his eyes. The lane seemed to be getting dark . . . and yet he knew it not to be the case. Closing his eyes, he breathed deeply, looking for calm, but his father's face presented itself to his mind's eye. He refused to allow Johnny to join his ranks.

When he opened his eyes, Kate stood directly in front of him. Her expression was odd to say the least. He couldn't read it, until she spoke.

"I thought Johnny was your friend. I thought you cared about him. But here we stand discussing whether or not the blood is blood." She jabbed him with her finger. "Why are we not running for help?"

Matt nodded and then shook his head. "Because we still have no idea where Johnny is, where to send help. We are no further ahead than we were before, except that now we are disturbed."

"Disturbed? You are disturbed?"

"Yes, of course."

"This expression indicates disturbed?" She waved her hand in front of his face, sounding incredulous.

"Now who is arguing semantics?" Matt cleared his throat. "Let us try to be sensible."

"Must we?"

"For Johnny's sake, I believe we must."

"Very well." Kate nodded. "We have established that Johnny was wearing his livery at the Goat and, being that nothing was said about a hole in his coat or a missing button, this . . . this *accident* must have happened after he left the inn."

"So, Johnny's coat—for we cannot assume it was in his possession—"

"Tishdale does not harbor criminals; I think it safe to assume Johnny was in possession of his own coat. It would not have been stolen from him."

"Indeed," Matt agreed, "but he need not have lost his coat to a thief; he might have draped it over the shoulders of a pretty girl to keep her warm; it was a cold night. If . . . this is from Johnny's coat."

"This is ridiculous. We know next to nothing," Kate huffed.

"Which is why we are not running off in all directions screaming for help. We could make the situation worse."

"How could we possibly make it worse?"

"Unfortunately, many ways: perhaps Johnny sold his coat to get money to use for gambling," Matt said.

"But he can't; the coat is not his to sell. It belongs to the family."

"Indeed. A justice would not look kindly upon such an act. Nor would he be happy if Johnny was in this lane with a young lady in a state of . . . romantic bliss. So caught up in his emotions, he did not notice the rent in his coat. Or perhaps having had too much to drink, Johnny stumbled. So there we have it. We rush to the justice, magistrate, or sheriff—"

"Most legal matters here are put before the squire," Kate clarified.

"Indeed? The squire, then . . . finds Johnny but has him arrested for theft or indecency or public nuisance. So you see, we'd better have some idea what Johnny was up to before we hie off to the law."

Kate sighed very deeply. "But what if he is in trouble and our delay causes him further harm?"

She looked ready to weep, and Matt understood her fear—it was similar to his own, one that he needed to keep on a tight rein, lest it affect their decisions. "Let us away," he said breezily. "We have others to speak with first. No need to worry. Where shall we start?"

"Mr. Cryer mentioned Mr. Belcher and Mr. MacDonald . . . but then, he also said that many others spoke to Johnny last night. It might be faster to ring the church bell and ask everyone who comes running."

"Indeed. An excellent notion. However, it might be best to try Mr. Belcher and Mr. MacDonald before involving the *entire* town." Matt tried to keep the panic out of his voice. Kate glanced at him one last time, concern still written on her face. He lifted his elbow toward Kate as if they were going on an afternoon promenade with no disquiet . . . certainly, no worries.

Kate was as tense as a twisted corset. She was not at all surprised when the blacksmith and grocer could offer them no further information about Johnny, and silently railed at the streak of red in the sky that forced them back to Shackleford Park. It would not be wise to delay; returning in full dark was the very condition that had done Johnny no favor.

"He might have returned in our absence," Matt said with a lift of his cheeks that could *not* be described as a smile. It was clear he did not believe his own words.

They were rushing down the road, all sense of playfulness shattered by their concern. There were no clever attempts to hold hands, and Kate found the ruts easy enough to traverse without the help of the handsome valet. Their discourse was sparse and repetitive.

"We should speak to someone," Kate stated for the umpteenth time. She was trying to find the right words, the ones that would make Matt understand that he had no choice—to ask for help was not throwing his friend under the wheels of a carriage but . . . the words, the sentiments all sounded the same. "We should speak to someone."

"Indeed," Matt replied.

Kate tried to concentrate on the road, the ice, the process of putting one foot in front of the other without tripping over her skirts. She was stymied; her mind had hit a wall of confusion. Everything Matt had said was true; there were plenty of benign reasons for Johnny to have disappeared—though selfish in the extreme—and yet there were a few that cried out for intervention. A bloody button could be fashioned into any one of those circumstances, but—

"Yes, I agree. We should inform the family. Mr. Ben at least, since he is the one who sent me on this fool's errand."

Kate stopped abruptly, turning to face him. "You agree?" She recalled her words; they were unchanged—no added weight to her reasonable summation of the situation.

"Yes, indeed. I have never been one to come to a conclusion without due consideration—"

"I noticed that."

"Thank you," Matt said, mistakenly thinking Kate approved. "And after this due consideration, I can see that our best course forward is to enlist some assistance. I am not yet convinced Johnny is in dire circumstances—unsavory most likely, but not necessarily dire."

"Oh, excellent. I am so relieved." Kate was relieved that she was not going to have to talk to Mrs. Lundy without Matt's endorsement—for she had had every intention of doing just that.

"We'll see if Johnny has returned first . . ." Matt tipped

his head in the direction of Shackleford Park. "What is that?" he asked.

They were standing at the head of the service lane, the color in the sky gone entirely. Kate could see candle lights flickering through the windows of the manor, and drifting on the wind was a sound . . . clashing with their desperation. Music. Cheerful, happy music. A fiddle, if Kate was to hazard a guess—and if that were so, it would be in Mr. Murray's hands. The head gardener was a wizard with a bow.

"There's often a gathering when everyone starts to return on the half day. With no duties to speak of and the sun gone, what better time to hold a dance? All very informal, of course . . . but plenty of fun and frolic."

"Excellent," Matt said, and then surprised Kate by grabbing her hand and leading her in a half run down the rest of the lane. She was starting to think he had taken leave of his senses when he turned to look over his shoulder. "Music is like a siren's call to Johnny. If he is in the manor, he will be at the dance." And then he smiled his charming, gentle smile, and despite knowing otherwise, Kate thought everything was going to be just fine.

THE TABLES OF the servants' hall had been pushed to the walls; the chairs were a haphazard collection in the corners. In the center, most, if not all, of the household staff was leaping and twirling in the loose squares of a country dance. Nothing like an elegant ball of the gentry, this dance was a riot of movement, laughter, and missteps.

As Kate and Matt watched from the threshold, carefully avoiding the mistletoe overhead, the constant movement and confusion made it difficult to determine who was who. Faces leapt out of the throng, only to be swallowed again by the writhing mass.

Finally, Mrs. Lundy made her way through the crowd. "There you be," she said with a broad smile. "Get rid of your coats and cloaks. Quickly now. Mr. Murray is about to play an Irish jig. Don't forget to start on your right foot; it's bad luck to begin a dance on your left foot."

Neither moved.

"Is Johnny here, Mrs. Lundy?" Kate tried to focus on the housekeeper, but her eyes were pulled back to the crowd of dancers. "Johnny, is he here?" she shouted, realizing that her question had been swallowed by the din.

"Don't know, dear." The good woman shrugged, unaware of the importance of her answer, and then she smiled. "I'm sure he's about somewhere. I'm going to help Cook with the cider, make sure that it is stirred clockwise and . . . well, it wouldn't do for anything of an alcoholic nature to find its way into the bowl." Mrs. Lundy winked and then nudged Kate as she left.

Righting herself, Kate found that she was now under great scrutiny from the staff. Loud, boisterous laughter accompanied finger pointing. They were gesturing toward the mistletoe that was now nearly overhead. Quickly, Matt and Kate turned, bowed to the clapping audience, and moved away in opposite directions. Neither was in the mood for frivolity, even one as enticing as a kiss.

Pulling her mittens off as she threaded her way to the back, Kate searched the faces around her. By the time she had slipped off her cloak, she was fairly certain that Johnny was not present. She pivoted to say as much to Matt when she saw that he was talking to Pippa across the room.

The maid's stance was flirtatious—hair twirling, leaning forward, touching Matt on the arm—for no apparent reason *whatsoever.* However, it was the look on Matt's face that captured Kate's attention. She could see the tension in his jaw ease, even as he leaned back from Pippa's grabby hands. He glanced Kate's way and grinned, and then protested when Pippa latched on to his arm and tried to pull him in among the dancers. Matt turned back to Kate, gesturing to his coat and the door. She met him in the hallway.

"Pippa believes Johnny is behind the stables, spitting tobacco with the grooms. A most unsavory pastime," Matt said with no true criticism in his voice. He was grinning, his eyes full of relief. "I'll go speak to him." And so saying, Matt raced to the door. He disappeared with a quick backward wave.

Glancing once more into the servants' hall, Kate met Pippa's gaze. Sour gaze. Hateful gaze. Kate nodded and turned, making her way upstairs to deposit her outerwear in her wardrobe.

"WHY WOULD SHE say such a thing if it was not true?" Matt was masking his concern with anger . . . or at least that was what Kate believed to be his emotional state. He was not as easy to read as she had previously thought.

Kate had returned to the service hallway to find Matt storming down the corridor. It would seem that Johnny was not with the grooms; they had not seen him since the day before.

"She was trying to get you to dance with her and likely could see that you were preoccupied with Johnny. It was self-serving, not diabolical."

"No. That label is reserved for Mr. Walker."

"I beg your pardon?" Clearly, she had taken too long changing into her party gown and primping in front of the looking glass. "What has happened?"

"I requested that Mr. Murray stop fiddling long enough for me to ascertain that no one, *no one*, has seen Johnny since church yesterday. So I asked Walker to tell Mr. Ben that I wish to speak with him, but he refused. Refused. The family is ensconced, and he will not disturb them for something as insignificant as a shirking footman. Said the fool, meaning Johnny, was likely passed out under a chair somewhere, feeling the effects of too much punch." Matt snorted and clenched his fists. "I can hardly burst into the drawing room demanding an audience."

"No, no, you can't . . . but they will retire in a few more hours, and you can speak to Mr. Ben then."

"True enough, but I find it *very* difficult to wait."

Lifting her hand, Kate touched Matt's coat lapel. She wanted to stroke his face, offer creature comfort, and tell him all would be well. But they were empty platitudes, and it would be most unseemly to offer such an intimacy.

"It will be soon enough," she said with a certainty she did not feel.

Matt jerked a nod and stepped past Kate, heading for the back stairs. "You can find me in my room if Johnny suddenly puts in an appearance."

Kate spent the rest of her half day turning down invitations to dance, sipping the spiked cider, and watching the door for either Matt or Johnny to return.

Neither did.

SITTING AND STEWING, Matt waited. Mr. Ben and Mr. Ernest could have tiptoed to their rooms and still Matt would have heard them in the hallway. As it was, the young gentlemen felt no need to contain their jocularity, and so Matt was not put to the test. Rather than knock on Mr. Ernest's door first, as was his routine, Matt made straight for Mr. Ben's room. Unfortunately, Mr. Ben was in a chatty mood, not noticing

Matt's pointed silence until after he had been divested of his coat and waistcoat.

"All right, let's have it. Was your half day disappointing? You seem sullen."

"Sullen? Interesting interpretation, Mr. Ben. It was a busy day what with running all around town." He pulled Mr. Ben's boots off and set them aside to be shined later.

"That seems an odd thing to do on a day off."

Matt turned, giving the gentleman a look of chastisement. "You have, I see, forgotten your heated words of last night."

"Heated words?" Mr. Ernest asked, walking into the room after a quick knock. "Why were you yelling at poor Matt, Ben?"

Matt sighed with relief, glad to have the attention of both brothers. "Not at me per se, Mr. Ernest. It was regarding Johnny."

"Oh yes." Ben nodded, still more absorbed in untangling his neckcloth than in the conversation. "Did you read him the riot act?"

"I couldn't find him, Mr. Ben. Johnny is missing."

"Really?" Mr. Ernest's question was hard-edged.

As concisely as possible, Matt described the whys and wherefores of Johnny's disappearance, starting with the stag ring and ending in the mews.

"Blood? You believe the button to be covered in . . . Can I see it, Matt?" Mr. Ernest asked.

Matt retrieved his handkerchief from his room and

passed it to the older brother, but it was snatched away by Mr. Ben before Mr. Ernest could examine it properly.

"Lawks, it does look like blood. And it does resemble the family crest. And the cloth is definitely our shade of livery, I believe." Mr. Ben returned the button to Matt, grabbed his boots, and dropped onto the window seat. "We should let the sheriff know."

"I was told such matters are handled by the squire here." Matt did not expound on who had said as much. There was no need to bring Kate's name into this mess.

Mr. Ben paused, his left leg in the air, his boot partially on. "The squire?" He turned to his brother. "Isn't . . . Aren't they coming to dinner tomorrow?" He sat back, one boot on, and his neckcloth hanging limp across his chest. "Yes. And . . . how opportune. He is bringing Lord Bobbington and his bride; I believe Mr. Beeswanger said he's with the Home Office." Without waiting for his brother to answer, Mr. Ben continued. "This is most excellent. Squire Fleming and Lord Bobbington will know—"

"We have not met them yet, Ben. We can hardly ask strangers to rush over at this time of night."

"Oh lawks, that's true. Perhaps . . . I'll go over, then. I'll have to borrow a carriage . . . and a guide."

"Has Johnny ever done this before?" Mr. Ernest asked calmly, an antithesis to his brother's sudden energy.

"Which part, sir? The reckless behavior, the gambling, or the disappearing?"

"The reckless behavior."

"Not since he joined the household three months ago, Mr. Ernest."

"I see. But he was a little wild . . . if I recall the story correctly." With a deep sigh, indicating how uncomfortable he was with the situation, Mr. Ernest lifted his palm to his brother. "Settle, Ben. Let's see if Johnny returns by morning. If he doesn't, the squire and his guests are coming for an early dinner tomorrow."

"But the blood?" Mr. Ben argued, not unlike Kate had hours earlier.

"Might mean anything," Mr. Ernest explained. "He could simply have stumbled, cut his hand, and caught his button. There are many, many possibilities."

Hearing an echo of his own sentiments in Mr. Ernest's reassurances, Matt understood why Kate had been incensed. They sounded like a plea for nothing to be wrong rather than an assurance that all was well.

But try as he might, Matt could not convince either brother—for Ben now saw the wisdom of waiting to shout an alarm. Had they been in Chotsdown, Matt was certain a message would have gone out to the sheriff immediately. But the Steeples and their servants were guests at Shackleford Park. Bringing trouble and great inconvenience to their hosts was a most uncomfortable prospect. It would be made worse if it were found that Johnny was simply truant and the young gentlemen had turned Shackleford Park and Tishdale topsy-turvy for nothing.

And so it was that Matt had to assist his young gentlemen

into their nightclothes, wish them pleasant dreams, and then lie awake all night hoping and praying that Johnny was being an idiot and that Matt could give his friend a proper dressing-down in the morning.

SATURDAY, DECEMBER 20, 1817

KATE WAS ON her way to Mrs. Lundy's sitting room to break her fast when Livy pulled at her skirts to let her know that Colby Jordan was at the service door. With a mind full of anxiety about Johnny and Matt, Kate wanted to ask Livy to send Colby away. She knew that he would only be here at her Mam's behest. Kate was about to be informed about another terrible occurrence that required her to drop everything and rush to her mother's cottage.

"Come right away, miss," Colby finished after telling Kate exactly that.

"Is she sick? Hurt? Is the cottage on fire? Has a herd of cows invaded her kitchen?"

Colby chuckled. "No, miss."

With a great sigh, Kate shook her head. "Then, could you please inform my mam that I cannot come right away? I have much to do what with company coming. I will get to Vyse-on-Hill when I can, but I cannot say when that will be."

Colby nodded and raced away. Watching him disappear,

Kate shook her head and pivoted. Mrs. Lundy stood behind her.

"She will understand, my dear." The housekeeper offered a sympathetic look that hardened Kate's resolve.

"No, not likely. But I'm tired of being called away for no purpose. Mam is going to have to come to terms with being alone. I'm not helping her by rushing hither and yon at her bidding."

"Probably not, my dear. As a dutiful daughter, though, it must be difficult to draw that line." She patted Kate's arm. "Come, let us eat before we are worked off our feet."

And with that, Mrs. Lundy disappeared through her sitting room doorway. Kate was about to join her when she saw Matt coming toward her. She waited, needing to hear what was going to be done about Johnny.

Matt's expression was grim.

"No Johnny as yet," she said without preamble. She had asked Bernie and Charles as soon as she had come downstairs.

"No," Matt said. "And we are to await the squire this afternoon before shouting the alarm."

"But . . . but . . ."

Matt nodded solemnly. "Exactly."

chapter 11

In which Lord Bobbington pays a call

Kate found it hard to concentrate that morning. Glancing out every window as often as she could, she prayed to see Johnny sauntering up the lane . . . or Squire Fleming racing up the drive. Again, she waited in vain.

The girls were all atwitter about the arrival of Lady Bobbington, full of curiosity about the young bride who was only a few years older than they. There was much to discuss regarding ribbons, gloves, and which shoe roses would make the best impression. Still, despite their distraction, Kate's woolgathering became apparent.

"Kate?" Gauging by Miss Emily's tone, Kate thought her name might have been called more than once.

With a shake of her head, Kate brought her thoughts back into the room and the process of readying the girls for the day. Blinking, Kate frowned into the looking glass of the vanity. She had been working on Miss Emily's upsweep—an elegant style that swirled artfully in the back with tendrils of brown curls on the sides and a dusting of hair across her forehead.

Well, that had been the intent.

When her eyes met Miss Emily's staring back at her, it was not from underneath a pretty dust of hair . . . for, in fact, Kate had not tucked in the ends of Miss Emily's upsweep. It looked like she had a mop . . . or a thatch of straw sitting on her crown. The style was not elegant in the least; it could not be considered anything other than clownish.

"Oh, oh dear," Kate said, immediately pulling out the pins she had just fixed into place . . . the wrong place. "I am so terribly . . ." She began to apologize and then noticed Miss Emily's shoulders were shaking and that she was trying desperately not to laugh.

But it was no good.

Miss Imogene, sitting on the window seat waiting her turn, was having a hard time staying where she was—laughing so hard that she was near to tumbling from the bench. Miss Emily tried valiantly not to join her friend in her fit of hilarity; Kate could hear Miss Emily gulping at the air and snorting in a Herculean effort to contain her mirth. But eventually, she needed to breathe, and when she did, laughter burst from her. She laughed so hard that the rest of her hair tumbled down her back and she had to hold her sides against a stitch.

Kate waited. She scratched her chin, tidied her pins, shifted her comb, sighed several times in succession, and then waited some more. Just as it would seem that their humor was spent, Miss Emily giggled; caught again, Miss Imogene burst into laughter, and then, of course, Miss Emily did likewise. It was a vicious circle, one calming only to be brought back to gleeful hysterics by the other. It continued forever . . . a good five minutes.

"What, pray tell, has you so distracted, Kate? Would it happen to be a handsome valet?" Miss Imogene eventually asked between gulps of air.

"No, indeed," Kate answered, unreasonably upset by their laughter. They were not to know. "A handsome footman."

Miss Emily's bright smile froze in the mirror. "Footman? I thought that you were . . . partial to Mr. Harlow."

"It has nothing to do with being partial to anyone, Miss Emily. I am concerned, terribly concerned about Johnny Grinstead, the Steeple footman. He has disappeared."

Miss Emily's eyes grew wide, her smile faded away, and her cheeks reddened. "Disappeared?"

"Yes," Kate said, then explained Johnny's story. "And so now we wait," she concluded. "We wait for Johnny to return or for your guests to arrive."

"But they are not due until midafternoon." Miss Emily frowned, clearly no more comfortable with the delay than was Kate. "Who decided that waiting was the wisest choice? Never mind, it is irrelevant. I will speak to Papa. We need to see Squire Fleming right away. It's already been . . ."

"Two days," Kate supplied.

"Indeed, two days. Far too long." With a nod of finality, Miss Emily straightened her shoulders. "Don't concern yourself with the fancy upsweep for now, Kate. A simple style will be faster; we will have more time this afternoon . . . I hope."

Kate nodded, setting to work. Her fingers were faster and deft. Nothing had been resolved, but the dilemma was now in the right hands—the girls'—and Kate felt immensely relieved.

WALKING DOWN THE hallway, her arms lost under swaths of soft mauve and light blue cloth, Kate carried the chosen dinner gowns toward the service door, heading for the laundry house that sat on the other side of the inner yard. She needed to press the ruffled hem of the mauve gown and the elbows of the blue one. Quickly approaching footsteps forced Kate to shift closer to the wall.

Bernie rushed past her. "Off to the squire's place with a message," he said with a jaunty smile of self-importance over his shoulder. He had his coat and mitts on and was tucking a sealed letter into his coat as he pushed through the door. It slammed shut behind him.

Sighing, Kate juggled her load without allowing the gowns to drag on the floor and tried to open the door, but the handle would not turn. She tried several times until the blue gown started to slip and she had to let go in order to save it from a spill. As soon as she did, the handle turned of its own volition and the door flew open. A figure stood on the other side, looking as surprised to see Kate as she was to see him.

"I believe we were trying to open the door at the same time, Mr. Niven," Kate said to the tall, gray-haired wine merchant with a chuckle.

"I believe you are right, Miss Darby," Mr. Niven said with a smile that only quirked up one side of his mouth. He was a stoic-looking man in his later years, perhaps as old as five and forty, with a somewhat nasal tone to his voice. He dressed well, with a finely cut waistcoat of vermilion and an unusual black neckcloth; his coat was tailored.

She could see a wagon through the doorway; it was pulled into the yard and in need of unloading. "I'm surprised you are doing your own deliveries, Mr. Niven. I heard you had taken on a delivery boy."

"I do not trust anyone with my best customers, my dear. Personal service. Always." He stood a little straighter, looking down his nose at her. "What would the Beeswangers think otherwise?"

Kate smiled; she was fairly certain that the Beeswangers were unaware that Mr. Niven delivered their wine himself. "Would you like me to find Walker for you, sir?"

"No, no, no need. I shall have your footmen assist. I'm sure Walker has better things to do than see to the wine." There was a mocking ring to his words; seeing to the wine *was* an important aspect of a butler's job.

"I'm afraid you will only have the help of one footman today, Mr. Niven. Bernie has just left to deliver a message."

"Oh yes, I did see a young man rush by; startled my horse, in fact."

"Did he?" The load of gowns was starting to feel a trifle heavy, and Kate edged to the side of the narrow hallway, hoping Mr. Niven would enter and allow her past. "That's a shame. Well, I must away. I'm off to the laundry house." It was patently obvious, but since Mr. Niven did not seem inclined to move, she did not mind pointing out the patently obvious; she was more worried about her tired arms letting go of the gowns than insulting the wine merchant.

"Where was he going in his rush?" Mr. Niven lowered his head so that he was looking at Kate from a slightly bowed position . . . a subservient position. One could only assume it was due to habit, from when he served in the army perhaps, but it was a habit that did not sit well with Kate Darby. A raised brow on her part encouraged the man to straighten immediately. "I only ask because of the young man . . . the one you came to my door about yesterday." He lifted one shoulder when she frowned and replied to her unasked question. "Neighbors said you had come around and why. Have you found him? The young man?"

"No, not as of yet." She shifted again, but Mr. Niven was treating her to a lovely chat as if it were Yuletide and they had to do the niceties . . . oh, but yes, it was the season of benevolence and charity. Kate hid her impatience, offered a broad, though feigned, smile and an excuse . . . er, reason for her departure. "I must away, Mr. Niven. The Beeswangers are to be honored with a visit this afternoon from Lord Bobbington and his wife, and I must assist the girls. Please. Excuse me."

"Oh." Mr. Niven started as if just seeing the gowns in her arms. "Here, let me help." And with that, he stepped out of the way.

"Charles is in the servants' hall, I believe," Kate said as she strode into the cold—there was a decided cut to the breeze. She shivered as she hurried across the yard into the steaming heat of the laundry house and tried not to think of how long she must wait before learning if Squire Fleming knew how to set about finding Johnny.

AT LAST, MATT was called to the study. He had paced his small bedroom a thousand times—well, at least ten or twenty, upon hearing of Squire Fleming's arrival at the behest of Mr. Beeswanger. He had been helping Mr. Ben with the last of his ablutions when Bernie had knocked on the chamber door and asked for the young gentleman's presence. Mr. Ernest had stuck his head across the threshold and offered to go ahead.

Matt rushed Mr. Ben into his stylish gray coat, smoothing it over his silver threaded waistcoat and dove-gray buckskins, buffed a slight mark from the toe of his right Hessian, and sent him in his brother's wake within ten or so minutes. Quite the feat!

And then Matt had to wait. He was certain that the squire was here about Johnny . . . hoped it meant that the search was on, not that he had been found in an injured state.

With a gulp, Matt tugged at his own more understated and considerably less expensive waistcoat, verified that his boots were mirror shiny, and joined Bernie in the hallway when he had knocked a second time. Matt glanced down the corridor, hoping for a glimpse of Kate's calming countenance, but he was not rewarded. Bernie left him at the bottom of the stairs; Matt could find his way.

He rapped smartly on the study door and was bid to enter.

Happily, the room was generous in size, being that it already housed five souls. It had the aspect of a library: dark book-filled shelves lined three walls, in front of which an inlaid Georgian desk sat catercorner from the door. The fourth wall offered a large carved chimneypiece and the warmth of a glowing fire. In front of it, a group of wingback chairs provided comfort for the Steeple brothers, Mr. Beeswanger, and an older, bespectacled gentleman with muttonchop whiskers and deep-set eyes. He stared at Matt without expression.

Matt stared back, unsure of the protocol.

"Ah, there you are, Matt," Mr. Ernest said, as Mr. Beeswanger would have had no right to summon Matt to the study. "I have been informing Lord Bobbington of Johnny's situation and he has a few questions for you."

Matt glanced at the seated old gentleman, but he had turned toward a tall figure in his early twenties standing beside the mantel.

"Yes, indeed," the sandy-haired gentleman said as he stepped closer; he had a round face and a cleft in his chin. "I am very curious about that coin your friend was given."

With a frown, Matt nodded. "The coin, my lord?"

"Yes, indeed," Lord Bobbington said with a great smile and an echoing nod. "Did you see it? What was the color of the metal plug? Where there any strange markings on it?"

Matt continued to frown. "The coin . . . Well, I don't rightly remember. But I . . ." He patted at his coat. He had dropped the offending object in his pocket when Johnny had tried to pitch it into the yard, and then forgotten about it. "I have it somewhere . . ." His fingers touched cold metal in his right coat pocket. "Ah, there," he said, offering it to Lord Bobbington.

The gentleman took it gingerly, as if it were precious, not a worthless and troublesome item. He turned it back and forth, his nose getting closer and closer, until he reached into his pocket and pulled out a magnifying lens. He carried both to the window, where he stood for several minutes. The fire crackled, the clock ticked, and all were silent, waiting for some sort of pronouncement.

Matt wanted to talk about Johnny, ask what they were going to do to find him, tell them that he had been seen last at the Gambling Goat . . . and yet all faces were turned to the window, watching the silhouette of a man studying a fake coin.

"Aha! Yes, it is the same." Lord Bobbington turned toward the room, not in the least startled that he had everyone's undivided attention. "The same flaw as the coins in Canterbury." He marched over to the squire. "Look at that," he said as he passed over the coin and magnifying lens. "Just under the figure, an irregular join—likely from the mold." He rounded on Matt. "Tell me, Mr. Harlow, what can you say about the man Johnny met?"

"The man?"

"Yes, the red-haired man who gave your friend Johnny this coin—used it to pay for his . . . his . . ."

"His ring, my lord." Matt swallowed in grave discomfort; this was not going as he'd hoped. "Should we not be discussing Johnny? Where he might be?"

Lord Bobbington blinked at Matt for some moments, looked over at Mr. Ben and then back at Matt. "But we . . ."

"Matt has only just arrived, Lord Bobbington. He was not privy to our discussion about Mr. Coombs," Mr. Ben explained.

"Oh, oh, indeed. I apologize, Mr. Harlow. No wonder you look anxious."

Matt bristled. He did not look anxious—he *was* anxious, but he certainly did not look it. He was quite adept at keeping his feelings in check; he had been practicing for months—

"Squire Fleming is going to have Mr. Coombs, Tishdale's

night watchman, look into Johnny's whereabouts." He waved his hand in the general direction of the older gentleman. "Though he has told me that there is nothing to worry about."

"It's been my experience that those who disappear do so by choice," the squire said, returning the fake coin to Lord Bobbington. "Still, I'll get Mr. Coombs to do a look-see, talk to a few people. He'll get to the bottom of it."

"He was last seen at the—"

"Yes, yes, we know. The Gambling Goat." Squire Fleming huffed and settled back in his chair, clearly finished with the conversation.

"This is most opportune, Mr. Harlow," Lord Bobbington said to regain Matt's attention. "I'm on my way to Canterbury, you see. The Home Office has sent me to investigate the sudden flood of counterfeit coins. But there are so many avenues to follow there, it will be hard to trace all the different paths . . . especially in a city. However, here . . . well, we have one coin and a red-haired man. Let's find out where that man got his coin. You can see how finding him is of the utmost importance. *National* importance," he said, standing a little straighter.

"Indeed," Matt said, but only to be agreeable. His mind was still recoiling from the idea that Johnny had disappeared by choice. He would not do that—he would not leave Matt in the lurch. Johnny would expect Matt to be concerned. Granted, they were closer to London, but only marginally, not enough to jump ship. No, Johnny had not disappeared of his own volition.

"Was there more?"

Matt blinked, realizing that he had been staring at a spot on the wall and that the conversation had continued. "More?"

"Yes, did Johnny describe more fully the man who gave him the coin?"

"No." Matt tried valiantly not to glare. "Just that there was something of the butcher, Mr. Kelp, in his looks . . . but it might simply have been the man's red hair. I really don't know." He turned to address Squire Fleming again. "Johnny didn't say anything about wanting to be elsewhere. He didn't take his belongings. He disappeared after the market, not in the middle of the night. I would have known if he had any such thoughts."

Squire Fleming shrugged. "Yes, that's what most say. He's likely hoping to find a better position."

"But he would need a *character*, if that was his intent, and some money . . . He was tapped out and in livery. His button was covered in blood—"

"If it was his."

"Yes, true. But most of us here . . ." Matt glanced first at Mr. Ben and then at Mr. Ernest. "We believe that button to depict the Steeple crest. The green material matches the color of his coat; if that is the case, then why was it covered in blood? None of it says that he purposefully disappeared."

"We will see, Mr. Harlow." The good squire stifled a yawn. "Mr. Coombs will let us know."

Matt prayed that Mr. Coombs had a better understanding of the life of a footman than Squire Fleming seemed to have.

THE DAY PROVED to be every bit as hectic and busy as Kate had expected. So much so, that after having helped the girls prepare for bed, Kate was tired, bordering on exhausted, but edgy enough that she knew sleep would be elusive. So rather than tuck in and then lie awake wishing for sweet oblivion, Kate headed downstairs, where she could warm a brick in the oven. It would provide soothing heat in her bed—a rare commodity at this time of year.

The kitchen was cavernous when it was not filled with the hustle and bustle of meal preparation and maids rushing hither and yon. There was no sign of Cook . . . nor anyone else, for that matter, just the clink and splash of someone in the scullery—Livy, without a doubt—cleaning up the last of the plates and glasses from dinner. That Livy was still washing, this many hours after dinner, was a testament to the quantity the girl had had to deal with.

Kate smiled to herself as she wrapped a brick and then placed it in the oven to absorb the last of its heat. The misses had returned to their rooms after their exciting evening with Lord and Lady Bobbington and Squire Fleming. And while most of their discourse revolved around their very favorable impression of Lady Bobbington, somewhere in their euphoria, Miss Emily made mention of Mr. Coombs and the search for Johnny.

Kate was relieved in the extreme to know that someone was now looking for the footman. To know that Matt and she were no longer alone, that help had arrived and soon Johnny would walk through the door, was a salve to her frazzled mind. She wished she could have assured Matt as they sat at supper, but the table was noisy and the meal was rushed. It was over, and Matt was gone with no more than a few glances, certainly no opportunity to discuss Johnny's disappearance.

"Who's there?" Livy asked in a quavering voice.

"Sorry, Livy. I should have told you I was here. Not to worry, I'm only heating a brick for my bed. Do you want me to do one up for you, too?" Kate remembered her days in the scullery bed all too well; the draft under the door often brought snow with it.

"Would you, miss? That would be ever so kind."

Kate smiled and wrapped another brick—the last of what was usually a pile—and placed it in the oven. Dragging a chair close to the fading embers of the fireplace, Kate felt a welcome sense of weariness. The click of Livy's work offered a rhythmic pattern that lulled her further into that lovely state when tired becomes sleepy. Her eyes were closed when she heard a scrape across the floor, and glanced over to find

Livy seated beside her, head resting on the back of her chair.

"I have a liniment that might help," Kate said, pointing with her chin at Livy's chapped, red hands.

"Oh, no need, miss. They'll be right as rain in the morning," the scullery maid said with the confidence of experience. And then she, too, closed her eyes.

It was peaceful, tranquil. Kate thought she might stay and sleep right there—for a few hours at least—before the early risers arrived to start the process all over again.

"It were a busy day, miss."

"Mmmm. It was indeed."

"Glad Mr. Niven is going to find Johnny. Bernie and Charles need the help, what with all them guests."

Kate sighed, eyes still closed. "Yes, extra hands are always appreciated. But it is Mr. Coombs who will be looking for Johnny, not Mr. Niven."

"No, no, miss. It were Mr. Niven asking all the questions."

Kate opened her eyes, staring sightless at the ceiling for a moment, and then she sat up to look over at the scullery maid. "Mr. Niven was asking questions about Johnny?"

"Yes, miss." Livy seemed unaware of Kate's disquiet.

"About Johnny?"

"Yes, miss. When he brought in the wine with Charles."

"*Before* the squire and Lord Bobbington arrived this morning?"

Livy opened her eyes and sat up straight; she looked over at Kate. "Is something wrong?"

"What did Mr. Niven ask?"

"Just wanted to know if Johnny had come back. Offered to check Johnny's room for clues. Gwen an' I had a giggle over that—clues, like it were a mystery, or some such. He asked everyone where *they* thought Johnny might go. Did he have family? Finally stopped jawing when he asked who would be enjoyin' his wine this evenin'. He hightailed it away then . . . must not like the squire, I suppose. I thought he were just bein' rude 'til I heard that there was going to be a search . . . but you say it be Mr. Coombs who'll find Johnny." With a nod, Livy relaxed back against the chair again. "Now, that makes better sense, him bein' the night watchman an' all."

"Yes, yes . . . it does. Well, I think I will bid you good night." And so saying, Kate rushed out of the kitchen and down the hall. Lost in thought, she reached the bottom of the stairs barely aware of her surroundings. Her mind was a whirl and a muddle at the same time.

Why would Mr. Niven care about Johnny? Could his questions be simply classified as curiosity? It was, without a doubt, odd. Why would he offer to search Johnny's room? Odder still!

When Kate reached the first floor, she took a tentative step toward the family wing and then glanced over her shoulder. The hallway was empty; the manor was quiet . . .

peacefully quiet . . . deceivingly quiet, as if all were well—when it wasn't. Kate swallowed, pivoted slowly as if drawn in the opposite direction, and walked with deliberate soft steps toward the guest wing. She needed to talk to someone, and not just anyone. Marie would not do. Miss Emily nor Miss Imogene . . . Mrs. Lundy . . . No, none of them. She needed to talk to Matt. But it was late and so very, very improper . . . and yet her feet still carried her in the wrong direction. Toward Matt.

And then she was there, standing in front of his door—the hidden panel that she knew so well. Her hand lifted. With a deep breath, Kate tightened her fist, but she did not knock. This was a mistake. She might need Matt's calm thoughts and his soothing presence, but it was near on midnight. It was imprudent, rash, foolish, impulsive, and ill considered.

Kate knocked.

chapter 12

In which Kate is very glad that she disturbed a certain valet

Kate's knuckles barely touched the hard wood; it was more of a caress. The sound it produced was muffled, faint, nothing to draw attention. She sighed, knowing that she had made the right choice but regretting it nonetheless. Matt might not think well of her, arriving at this hour of the night, no matter what the reason. She could talk to him about Mr. Niven before their morning meal, certainly before the Sunday service. That would suffice. The greatest difficulty now would be to sleep away the night; she had left her brick in the kitchen oven.

Leaning her forehead against the panel door, Kate half smiled and wondered how long it would take after the Steeples had gone before her thoughts would stop turning to Matt whenever something felt wrong . . . or strange . . . or ridiculous . . . or nonsensical . . . or silly . . . or pleasant . . . or funny. All would be dull without the shine of his eyes to brighten her day.

Pushing away from the door, Kate shook her head. It was time for bed, even if it meant a sleepless night. And with that thought, the panel began to move. Startled, Kate jumped back to allow for the door to swing open.

"Matt?" she croaked, trying to think clearly, but clearly it was impossible . . . because it was obvious that Matt had been preparing for bed . . . clearly. She swallowed, trying not to notice how *very* fine he looked with tousled hair, his shirt open at the neck, no coat, and no waistcoat. All thoughts of Mr. Niven and his odd questions flew out of her brain and took every word that she had ever learned away with them.

"Kate. Is all well?" He made the mistake of reaching out for her as he spoke.

Kate stared mutely at his hand as it rested on hers and blinked several times in succession. Then, after giving her head a little shake, she frowned, pursed her lips, and tried to recall why she had disturbed the poor young man. "Mr. Niven was asking peculiar questions," she finally said in a voice that sounded almost normal.

"Peculiar?" he asked very softly, then stepped closer so that he might whisper. "In what way?"

His breath caressed her cheek, lifting a few strands of hair that had come free of her chignon and hung over her ears. It tickled and tingled.

"According to Livy, he was asking about Johnny. If he had family in the area. Even suggested that he could help by looking for clues in Johnny's room."

"Clues? Clues of what?" Then he snorted softly and shook his head. "Must think that Johnny disappeared on purpose, too."

"Pardon?"

"That's Squire Fleming's theory."

"But that's nonsense!" In her indignation, Kate shifted closer to offer solidarity, but in doing so, they were now touching—bodice to chest. She could feel his radiating heat through the fabric of their clothes and she tried to think over the clamorous pounding in her ears. It was difficult to form a pertinent, intelligent question.

"Why?" she whispered. It was the best she could devise. She could feel the quickening of his breath and his sudden tension.

His gaze kept dropping to her mouth until, suddenly, he leaned forward, placing his lips on hers. It was not a gentle kiss; it was full of passion and longing, and Kate thought she might melt right then and there. All thoughts, all logic disappeared—the only thing that existed was the sensation of his mouth, his arms now wrapped around her, and her need to get closer. Leaning, pressing, she gulped at the air one moment, held her breath the next. As his mouth trailed down her neck and started back up again, she might have moaned . . . for she was in heaven.

"Oh Lud, this is not wise," she whispered, as she pressed even tighter, tilting her head up.

And then, just as suddenly, Matt stopped.

Kate opened an eye. "Is something wrong?" She had wanted to scream *Keep going*, but that might have been a tad too brazen.

Matt straightened, unwound his arms, and put some distance between them—a terrible six inches. Kate was bereft; she stared at him, bewildered.

"You are right."

"I am? About what?"

Laughing softly, Matt shrugged with little conviction. "It is *not* wise."

"Wisdom is overrated."

"Not in this instance."

"We are too young to be wise. Let's wait another decade or so." Lifting her arms, Kate tried to wrap them around his neck, but he stepped back. She frowned. "But I was quite enjoying myself."

Matt chortled with too much gusto, glancing quickly up and down the hallway. He shook his head even as he reassured. "I was as well."

"Are you being prudent again? I must say, I'm starting to find it a trifle annoying."

"Perhaps we should call it *cautious* or *sensible*."

"I don't think I like those words, either." A loud thump from within one of the chambers nearby, however, served as a reminder of how precarious their situation was, should they be discovered. "I'd best retire," she said with a deep sigh.

"It might be *wise*."

Kate pursed her lips, trying not to smile . . . and then she recalled the purpose of her nocturnal visit. "Shall we speak to Squire Fleming about Mr. Niven? Though to do so . . . well, it seems wrong, as if we are making an accusation when, in fact, I merely want to know . . . to understand why he was interested in Johnny, beyond what is seemly. Perhaps, yes, perhaps it would be better to speak to him ourselves first, at church."

"Yes, indeed. That might be best." Matt nodded.

Pivoting, Kate turned her head to offer Matt a rueful smile and then tiptoed down the hall to the family wing. She felt better about the decision, their next steps toward finding Johnny. It was only after closing the door of her own chamber that Kate realized that Matt had not contributed to that decision, that she had not needed to disturb him, that she had put her position as a lady's maid in peril for no reason.

And then she smiled.

But she was so glad, so *very* glad that she had.

SUNDAY, DECEMBER 21, 1817

THE CHURCH WAS crowded, though not as crowded as the Yuletide service would be. It meant there was space for the male staff of Shackleford to sit together . . . which was somewhat unfortunate, as Kate was with the female staff two pews ahead. It was probably just as well; every time their eyes met, a longing Matt had never experienced before overwhelmed him.

Pulling away from Kate the previous night had been far more difficult than he had revealed. Far more. Wisdom *was* highly overrated. Concern about Johnny kept his mind focused on non-Kate issues—allowing Matt to regain his composure. Otherwise . . . otherwise . . . yes, otherwise he would be looking at Kate instead of glancing around for Mr. Niven.

Though Mr. Niven did not seem to be attending the service. Matt wondered if this was the man's norm and asked Kate just that when the final hymn was sung and the congregation filed outside. Instead of joining the exodus, they walked over to the crèche set up near the baptismal font by a side altar. They pointed at the various statues, nodding and smiling and giving every impression of being caught up in the nativity scene . . . and amused by the portrayed wild eyes of the braying donkey. Their conversation, however, had nothing to do with Christmas.

"Mr. Niven is ordinarily at church . . . though I must own to not paying much attention to his presence. A rather intense but quite forgettable man. I'm not sure we need be worried."

"We will be going right by the wine shop and his apartment on our way back to Shackleford Park; perhaps we should pay him a visit."

"Yes, excellent suggestion. I will let Miss Emily know . . ." She smiled at Matt in an enigmatic manner. "But I know she will not mind, and Marie has already professed a preference to return by coach with the family. Too bitter for her. And the beautiful falling snow? A disaster—she finds winter intolerable. I, on the other hand, believe that in the right company the wind is not as biting, the snow makes everything fresh, and the crunch of ice underfoot can be almost musical."

Matt laughed. "I would like to live in your world."

Staring at him rather intently, taking his words seriously—not the way they were intended—Kate's expression became rather glum. "I wish you did, too."

Matt nodded; he took her meaning.

Outside, Miss Emily made no fuss about Kate walking back to the manor in Matt's company, although Miss Imogene frowned and glanced his way. When Matt doffed his cap, she looked startled, almost as if she hadn't realized she had been staring. The poor girl turned a bright shade of red, and Matt regretted drawing her attention. Miss Imogene was a bashful young lady. However, all was mended when Mr. Ben stepped to her side; a comment brought back her smile. Piling into the carriages, the family and their guests were soon covered with blankets and on their way. The staff huddled together on the outside seats.

Marie was not the only one unimpressed with the bitter chill of the day; the street quickly emptied as the post-service chats were shortened to nods and waves. Within moments,

Kate and Matt were left to make their way past the green and onto the main deserted road.

The wind swirled around them, catching at their breath, making conversation difficult. It was just as well; Matt was finding it challenging to think of much more than Johnny and Kate. Of Johnny, there was nothing more to say until they talked to Mr. Niven. Of Kate, there was too much to say . . . but it would all be futile.

Rather than turn down the street leading to the mews behind the shops right away, they stepped in the lee of the building. They stamped the feeling back into their feet, blew warm breath into their gloves—well, mitts in Kate's case—and were about to step back into the wind when Kate glanced from the sweets store in front of them to Mr. Niven's wine dispensary next door. She paused, frowned, and, despite the cold, pushed back her hood. She walked over to the window and cupped her face, pressing her nose to the glass, trying to see past the shelves in the storefront.

"What is it, Kate?" Matt asked.

"There has been . . . well, I'm not sure what I am seeing."

Matt was beside her before she finished her sentence, with his face pressed to the glass as well.

The shelves in the window, which eight days earlier had displayed port, claret, and various other wines, were empty. Glass littered the floor. A broken bottle sat in the middle of a red puddle—and no attempt had been made to clean it up. Squinting through the shelf slats, Matt could see into the office. All order was gone—everything was gone. The tasting table and chairs no longer sat near the front of the store. The barrels of wine that had been precisely positioned and labeled in the center of the room were missing, and the desk where Mr. Niven had taken and then recorded the Beeswanger order was no longer there. Even the lists that had papered the walls were missing—light spots on dark wood were the only evidence of their placement. Except for one that had been ripped; it curled away from the wall, looking limp and ruined.

"This couldn't be a robbery . . . *everything* is gone," Matt said. "Right down to the stool that Mr. Niven was sitting on the day I placed the Beeswanger order."

Kate stood straight again, staring at Matt with a puckered brow. "I'm confused. No one moves their shop in the Yuletide season and . . . and I saw Mr. Niven yesterday. He said nothing about closing up his business. No. In fact, he talked about his personal service to his best customers. That's not usually the conversation of a man intending to move away."

"Did he relocate? Perhaps . . . maybe?" He glanced at the door. There was no notice. "This is highly suspicious. Of what, I don't know . . . I'm almost afraid to know. Because if this has to do with Johnny's disappearance . . . only something terrible would . . ." Matt swallowed and tried not to show the horror that he was feeling.

Kate stepped closer, placing her hands in his. "Let us not

jump to conclusions. Let us check Mr. Niven's apartment above the store and his warehouse. It's accessed from the mews. No, stop, Matt, stop thinking. Let us just go look."

A strange sort of numbness settled into Matt's mind; not thinking became easier. He needed to act and react. Considering Johnny and his possible demise was not prudent. No. Act and react.

Letting go of Kate's hands, he acted; he pulled her hood up and gave her a quick kiss on the cheek. She reacted by smiling, albeit weakly and with tears welling in her eyes. "It will be all right," she said softly, and then swallowed visibly.

"Of course," Matt said without conviction—glad, so very glad that he was feeling rather numb.

THE WIND HIT full force as they slipped around the corner of the Candy Bowl. Temporarily blinded, Kate pulled her hood down farther and followed the side of the building until they reached the back. Then, looking up at the staircase leading to Mr. Niven's apartment, she stood for a moment undecided.

"Do we check his apartment or his warehouse first?" she asked. "Or divide up and see to both?" Though, even as she suggested it, the idea of separating made her uncomfortable.

But before Matt could answer, a whinny and thump grabbed their attention. They turned to stare past the back fences where the mews ran behind them. They could see two horses and a wagon through the blowing snow. As they watched, a figure standing on the wagon bed jumped down on the far side and started toward a dark smudge—likely the stable or warehouse door. It was difficult to see from where they were which door the figure was walking toward.

"Mr. Niven?" Kate called; she lifted her hand to wave.

The figure stopped and turned, but rather than acknowledge the hail, he rushed to the wagon. By the time he had clamored aboard, Kate had lifted her skirts and was running pell-mell with Matt down the lane to the mews.

Just as they reached the corner, the reins cracked and the horses jerked forward. Matt rushed across the lane to the far side. They would trap the man between them; the wagon was too close to have any momentum. But the driver must have known their intent, for no sooner had the horses started to walk when he flicked the reins again, startling them into a trot even though they were too close to the wall. Dancing sideways, hooves sliced through the air; neither Kate nor Matt could approach until the horses calmed. And they could no longer turn down the mews or reach the wagon.

Looking up, Kate met the eyes of the man standing precariously in front of the bench. The driver was not Mr. Niven; he was a young man with broad, muscled shoulders, freckled cheeks, and a Grecian nose. Kate watched as his thin lips curled up in a sardonic smile, and then he dropped the reins and jumped over the bench and off the back of the bouncing wagon. He landed hard, spilling onto the road, and knocked his tartan cap off. A shock of red hair was exposed, looking bright against the fallen snow.

Kate gasped, causing the young man to turn and look at her over his shoulder. He snickered or chortled. Kate could not hear the sound, but she saw his mouth open and his shoulders move and then he reached, almost lazily, for his cap. Placed it back on his head, nodded in an overly solicitous way and then turned, and ran.

"Matt! The red-haired man is getting away!" she screamed, almost certain Matt had not seen the spill onto the road through the veil of hooves and wagon wheels. "The warehouse!"

Matt blinked at her in confusion and then his brows shot up.

"Run!" she shouted, pointing to the bottom of the lane. "Follow the road around; there's a door on the other side of the warehouse." If she could have, she would have done the job, but the horses were still thrashing. She could not get by them. "Run!" she screamed again, thankful to see him nod. Thankful until he cornered the wall at the bottom of the lane, disappearing from sight. Then she was filled with a terrible sense of foreboding.

After an agonizing minute, perhaps two, the horses tired of fighting their equipage and the weight of the wagon. They lowered their heads, found an odd rhythm—more of a hop and skip—until at last they were back in harmony, walking slowly forward. The hub of the wagon wheel scraped against the wall, gouging a groove into the red paint until Kate grabbed the collar and then the noseband of the nearest horse. She did not have the weight to bring them to a halt, but she did have the voice of authority. And she used it, shouting, "Whoa!" loud enough to wake the dead . . . Though it stopped the horses, no assistance came running.

By the time the horses, the wagon, and Kate had stopped, they were partway across the lane. Rather than try to back them up, Kate guided them around the corner and tied the reins to the far fence. With a quick glance at the wine barrels in the back of the wagon, Kate lifted her skirts almost to her knees and raced after Matt.

When the wind pushed her hood off her head, Kate ignored the sharp bite of snow that was turning into ice pellets. She grabbed at the sidewall to guide her around the corner without slowing down and raced toward the back door of the wine warehouse. But she did not need to cross the threshold. Heading out of the lower door, footprints in the newly fallen snow showed a trail leading across the road and cutting into the field. A second set joined them on an oblique angle and then continued between the stubby stalks of hewn corn. Without hesitation, Kate ran across the road and into the field, adding a third set.

The trail led directly between two cottages and out onto Toller Road on the far side. It turned left, back toward the main road, but then it deviated. Grabbing a gulp of air, Kate bent over, hands on knees, and breathed . . . and stared at the footprints. Cutting across the road once again, the trail led up the drive of a farmhouse—the Closton farm, if Kate was not mistaken. But rather than lead to the house at the top of the hill, the trail curled around back.

Straightening, Kate lifted her skirts and set off again. Behind the house, the trail led in and around the barn. The prints were confusing, one set on top of the other. It was hard to understand, hard to make out which was which. Eventually, a single set ran down the hill on the opposite side of the farmhouse.

About to follow, Kate jumped in surprise, pivoting toward the barn once again. The large red door banged and shuddered. It rattled, and an eerie cry of anger filled the air. The cry formed words that sent Kate rushing to lift the bar that had been wedged against the door.

"Let me out of he—! Oh Lud, Kate! Excellent, did you see him? He led me in here, locked the back door . . . and as I struggled, the villain—"

"Circled around and trapped you inside." So thankful to see that Matt was hale and hearty, Kate wanted to throw herself in his arms . . . but he was in a tear, hardly aware of her intense relief.

"Exactly. Knew just what he was doing, the fiend. Unflappable. Did you see him?"

"No. But—"

"I called after him," Matt said as he scanned the ground and then looked up at Kate, puzzled. "Havey-cavey business—I tell you! He heard me call, looked back twice . . . and smiled. Can you imagine? I'm calling for him to stop, asking if he's seen Johnny . . . and he smiles, as if it's a game. Doesn't even ask me who Johnny is. What kind of person does that?"

"A malicious one," Kate said, glancing up at the sky. The temperature was marginally cooler, and the hail was turning to thick snow. "Hurry, Matt. Before we lose the trail."

But it *was* a losing battle as the weather outflanked them as easily as the red-haired young man. By the time they had raced back down the hill to Toller Road, the snow on the ground was starting to accumulate. They chased after the fading marks until they reached the main road, and there they disappeared entirely. The snow came down in a blanket, concealing the red-haired man's footprints and their hopes of finding Johnny.

chapter 13

In which the day goes from sinking snow to drenching danger

Holding her hood in place, Kate glanced up and down the road. While it was fairly quiet, the neighborhood was not deserted, not like Toller Road had been. A man and child hurried across the street near the circulating library, a clutch of ladies stepped into a carriage waiting in front of the blacksmith's shop, and a couple looked out at the weather from under the overhang of the glove shop. However, there seemed to be no fleeing figure wearing a cap over his red hair.

Snow dripped down from Kate's hood, landing on her nose and then sliding down to her chin in a never-ending stream. She was miserable, and it had nothing to do with the damp conditions.

"Best get inside."

Kate turned to see old Dame Symons standing in her cottage doorway across the street, waving. It was a welcoming gesture, kindly meant on a cold, wet day. The poor lady had no living family in the area anymore—her son having left for London five years earlier—and was known to open her heart and hearth to strangers . . . well, not people from away, but those in the neighborhood that she didn't know overly.

"Thank you, Dame Symons, but I'm afraid we must get back to Shackleford Park." She paused for effect, not wanting her desperation to startle the old lady. "Did you, by any chance, see a young man run by here a few minutes ago? Dressed in browns with a tartan cap?"

Dame Symons stepped back into her cottage, dismissing Kate and her inquiry with a shake of her head.

"Now what?" Matt huffed.

"Back to the mews? The wagon was full of wine barrels. Should we check to see if Mr. Niven . . . well, make sure that he is all right? That he's not in the warehouse . . . The red-haired man was stealing his wine." Kate squinted in the general direction of the wine shop, but the curve of the road prevented a long view. "Though why was the shop furniture gone, too? And what does this have to do with Johnny, if anything? Bother! This makes no sense, no sense at all."

"None." Matt shook his head. "Let us see to the wagon horses, then check the warehouse and then Niven's apartment."

And so saying, they took themselves down the road, walking quickly, trying to appear pushed into such an unseemly pace by the wind and the sleet and not fear for anyone's well-being. As they passed the church and village green, the stitch in Kate's side eased, and she had the capacity to hasten more . . . almost running again.

Finally, turning down the lane by the Candy Bowl again, Kate came to an abrupt halt. The wagon was no longer tied to the fence, no longer tied to anything. "Of course," Kate said, flapping her hand toward the nonexistent vehicle. "The wagon is gone. The horses are gone, and the wine is gone."

"They *were* all together."

Kate gave Matt a withering look as she started running toward the mews. "He must have cut through one of the yards. He is *no* stranger to Tishdale."

By the time they approached the warehouse, the ground was a sodden mess. The deep snow offered no clues by way of footprints. A cursory glance told them the building was empty; a thorough search proved it to be true. The warehouse was entirely devoid of barrels, crates, and any equipment necessary for a wine merchant. Though there was hay in the loft, the stalls were empty. Scattered around were frayed ropes, broken furniture, a split hitching post, manure, and the general sense of a messy and hasty leave-taking. Of Mr. Niven—and Johnny—there was no sign.

Scrubbing at her face, Kate sighed with frustration. She glanced Matt's way, and they nodded to each other. Time to check the apartment above the store. Climbing the stairs with a heavy heart, Kate dreaded what they might find. She no longer expected a simple explanation. The whole situation was fraught with peculiarities and now two missing persons. Hoping for the best had gotten her exactly nowhere.

Not surprisingly, there was no answer to their pounding. The door was locked, and trying to peek under the window curtain proved useless. The room beyond was dark; it was impossible to see if it was still furnished . . . or if a body lay in the middle of the floor. What a morbid thought.

"Mr. Niven has moved!"

Kate and Matt whirled around to see Mr. Gupta leaning out of his apartment, two doors down, with a large umbrella over his head. "Come, come in out of the wet." His gesture was very enthused.

Kate needed little encouragement. A respite, even one of short duration, was quite welcome. "Oh, thank you, Mr. Gupta. It is a bit raw today."

The old gentleman smiled at her significant understatement. "Indeed, my dear." He opened the door wider.

As much as Mr. Gupta assured them that the water did not matter, Kate could not be persuaded to step next to the fireplace; it was on the far wall. She would not drip across the kind man's floor. However, Mr. Gupta would brook no argument about her mittens. They were placed on a rack by the fire and a dry pair offered as a replacement.

"No, no, worry not. I shall get them from you in due

time. They are too small for me, belonged to my late wife. The color is a bit bright; Shanti loved red. I notice most English women wear dark colors on their hands . . . dull grays, browns, and the like. Not cheerful in the least. But these, yes, these make you warm just looking at them."

"Thank you, Mr. Gupta. They are lovely—and, as you say, very warm."

Mr. Gupta nodded with a faraway look in his eye.

"You said that Mr. Niven has moved, Mr. Gupta." Kate glanced briefly at Matt, noting the tension in his jaw. "Do you know his new address?"

"Oh dear, dear. Sorry. I can't tell you. I saw him running about yesterday; seemed to be in a hurry. Too much of a hurry, if you know what I mean."

Kate nodded with what she hoped was an encouraging expression.

"Yuletide and before the new year, rushing to load a wagon with little care if something breaks . . . well, it doesn't speak of a planned removal. Too much haste. I thought to ask if Niven needed any assistance, but I saw that his delivery boy was with him."

Kate swallowed. "The red-haired young man?" she asked casually.

"Yes, oh yes. That's the one. Rolland, I think is his name. Odd fellow. Not sure I like him."

"Oh?" The wordy question was Matt's contribution to the conversation.

"No, no, not . . . no. A month or two ago, I asked Rolland if he might like to do deliveries for me on occasion, too. He said that he wouldn't work for a—well, he was rude. Quite unnecessary—a simple *no* would have been sufficient . . . I haven't talked to Mr. Niven very much since. And now he is gone. Would you like some tea? That would warm you up."

"No, thank you, Mr. Gupta. It is very kind of you, but we must be going. We need to find Mr. Niven . . . or Rolland. We have some questions." Kate could see the curiosity on Mr. Gupta's face but thought it best to leave well enough alone. "Though where we go from here, I really don't know." She sighed very deeply and turned toward the door, ushering Matt ahead of her.

"You might start at the blacksmith, my dear. Rolland works for Mr. Belcher as well. He might know what's about."

Matt stopped and slowly pivoted. "Really?" He glanced down at Kate. "Wasn't Mr. Belcher at the Gambling Goat when Johnny was there?"

Kate nodded. "But how does that signify?"

"I'm not sure, but it does behoove us to pay Mr. Belcher another visit. Though this time if we ask after Rolland instead of Johnny, we might get an answer."

BACK ON THE main road, Kate glanced toward the blacksmith shop, though it was not visible from where she stood, and then swiveled her head to stare in the opposite direction.

"If we rush back to the manor now, there might be a few comments about our delay but no dire consequences. However, even if our conversation with Mr. Belcher is short, we will have taken far too long."

"Yes, but we have very little new information to add to this conundrum. I think we should carry on. I'm sure Mr. Ben will understand, though I'm not as confident about Mr. Ernest."

"Mrs. Beeswanger will not be happy, but I am almost certain the girls will intercede on my behalf."

"Almost?" Matt asked.

"Quite sure . . . nearly." Kate looked up at Matt with a worried frown entrenched on her forehead. "It's like choosing between the devil and the deep blue sea."

"There is no need for you to risk your future. I will visit the blacksmith—"

"I appreciate the thought, Matt, but Mr. Belcher does not know you."

"I was there when you were asking about Johnny. Right by your side."

"As I said, Mr. Belcher does not know you . . . other than as a silent companion of two days ago. That will not be enough to persuade him to discuss Rolland with you."

"Folks are terribly suspicious in this part of Kent."

"You will find it the same everywhere."

"Not on the coast . . . ," Matt started to say, frowned, and then curled his lip up in disgust. "You could be right." Then he sighed. "I leave the decision in your capable hands."

"Did I mention the devil—"

"And the deep blue sea? Yes, I remember something of the sort."

"Are we seeing a connection between Johnny and Mr. Niven's sudden removal because it fits, or are we trying to make it fit because we know not where to look next?"

"There is the red-haired young man."

"But red hair is not as rare in these parts as it is in others." Kate pinched the bridge of her nose for a moment and then looked back up at Matt. "Is Rolland Johnny's red-haired villain . . . or is he an innocent delivery boy?"

"Who ran off as soon as he saw us coming."

"True, but was that about Johnny? Rolland might have thought we were pursuing him because . . ."

"He was stealing wine?" Matt offered.

"Or he was helping Niven avoid a creditor."

"Do I look like a creditor?" Matt asked, spreading his arms wide.

Kate turned to stare. It was not meant to be a serious question, but upon examination there was a possibility, slight possibility, that Matt could be mistaken as a man of means. His greatcoat was well cut and fit properly; it was made from a sturdy material not ruined in the rain. His cap was a shaped tweed, he wore midcalf leather boots, and he walked (and ran) with his shoulders back in a confident manner. He was rather impressive and made Kate want to step closer, much closer. But that was not the question . . . What was the question? Oh yes.

"You do not look like a creditor to me, but Rolland does not know you. He might have decided to run first and ask later. Oh wait, that doesn't work. He saw me before you. I do *not* look like a creditor."

"Indeed not," Matt said with a great deal of warmth that caused Kate to pause in thought and stare back for a moment or two.

"Not. Indeed," Kate repeated, gave her head a shake, and continued. "So Rolland did act strangely, and we need to know why. And if he can tell us of Mr. Niven, so much the better. For in truth, Niven's questions might simply show him to be a nosy sort or genuinely interested in Johnny's well-being." Kate pictured Mr. Niven's pursed mouth and lifted brow. "Though I have not heard Mr. Niven described as kindly or charitable before."

"So do we chase after Rolland—assuming, of course, that Belcher can direct us to him, or do we return to the manor and keep our positions safe?" His tone of voice made it clear that Matt leaned toward the former.

"What I want to do and what I should do are not the same." Kate tried to chuckle, but it was lackluster at best. It was no joking matter. "We could rush back and inform Mr. Beeswanger."

"Who would then send a note to the squire, and who might or might not pursue the matter."

"Even if he did, there would be a considerable time delay. Rolland and Niven could be halfway to London or Canterbury before the squire bestirred himself. And of Johnny . . . well . . ." Kate pivoted so that she no longer faced the way home. "We have to talk to Mr. Belcher and let the cards fall as they may."

Matt nodded solemnly, then offered her the crook of his elbow, and they hastened down the street in as casual a manner as possible.

SUNDAY WAS NOT a day of labor for the blacksmith, and so they did not stop at the entrance to the shop. They continued around the building to a small one-story addition jammed onto the back wall that served as Mr. Belcher's home. It could not be described as cozy, quaint, or charming. Tools of the trade were scattered haphazard about the place. There was a general sense of neglect; the woodpile was tumbling over, paint was peeling from the door, and a fence, likely meant to enclose a garden, listed worse than a drunken sailor. And yet when the smiling giant of a man threw open his door, the room behind him was clean, warm, and inviting.

"Miss Darby, how nice to see you again . . . and so soon after your last visit. Still looking for that cagey young fellow?"

Kate disengaged her arm, glanced thankfully up at the deep overhang that protected them from the weather, and stepped forward with a feigned sincere expression. "Cagey fellow?"

"Yes. Chasing down a footman, weren't you?"

Kate frowned ever so slightly and ever so quickly. Mr. Belcher was doing it up a little too brown. Anything odd in a town this size was discussed nine ways to Sunday—gossipmongers hid behind every bush, around every corner, and in back of every curtain. Mr. Belcher would know that Johnny had not been found. He knew his name as they had talked at the Gambling Goat, and he likely knew that the squire had been to Shackleford Park about the matter.

"No, not this time Mr. Belcher. We were hoping to talk to your delivery boy, Rolland. Do you know where he is? Could you direct us to him?"

Mr. Belcher's smile did not leave his lips, but it certainly left his eyes. "What would you be needing to talk to him for? Has he done something he ought not to have done?"

"No, indeed not," Kate said, backing up into Matt, trying to signal that they should leave. She was vastly uncomfortable. The blacksmith's expression bordered on confrontational, almost threatening. It was not his usual demeanor; he was most often described as affable. His chuckles and funning belied his bulk and strength. "Just wanted to ask Rolland about Mr. Niven," she said, lifting the corners of her mouth.

"Best ask Mr. Niven about Mr. Niven," Mr. Belcher said sharply enough to garner Matt's attention. She could feel the sudden stillness of his body; it fairly radiated alarm.

"Well, we would, but Mr. Niven has moved, though we know not where." Matt shifted slightly toward the door.

"Need a special wine . . . on a Sunday, when you know the store not to be open?" Mr. Belcher's tone dripped with mockery.

"No, we were just going to ask him a few questions," Kate explained.

"Suffering from great quantities of curiosity these days, Miss Darby. Best be careful. Wouldn't want to get yerself into a tight spot, now would you?"

This time Kate stiffened; her discomfort faded, eclipsed by annoyance and frustration. "Why would you say that, Mr. Belcher? Since when has looking for someone warranted a threat?"

"Threat? Not threatening, my girl. Just letting you know how things is. Now, you best run back to Shackleford Park an' forget about askin' any more questions."

"Too late for that, I'm afraid, Belcher."

A nasal voice from behind startled a gasp from Kate, but she turned slowly, trying to exude confidence. Mr. Niven, looking perfectly hale and hearty—though drenched—and Rolland stood behind them, effectively barring their path, their escape.

"They have questions for you, Niven." Mr. Belcher stated the obvious, and Rolland smirked.

"Excellent. Turnabout is fair play. I have questions for *them*. Shall we all get out of this wretched weather?" He gestured toward the inside of the cottage.

"I think not," Matt said, shifting so that his body was in

front of Kate. "Thank you kindly, but we just have a quick question and then we will be on our way."

"Oh?" Mr. Niven glanced at Matt and then to Kate—who was peeking past Matt's shoulder. "If it has anything to do with Johnny, I suggest we step inside, where we might enjoy some privacy." He gestured again, but with a stiff arm, making the request an order.

Kate could feel Matt's uncertainty; she knew he was desperate to know what had happened to Johnny. There was a sense that Mr. Niven could answer that question . . . at least in some part, though whether he would was another matter. And yet to ask that question, to understand why Niven had been inquiring at the manor and why he'd left his shop in a rush, might put *them* in jeopardy.

"Yes, I was hoping that you could make a recommendation," Matt said. "I thought I might give Sir Andrew a distinguished bottle of claret or port for the new year, but I know nothing of the stuff."

Rolland snickered. It grated on Kate's nerves terribly, but she neither looked his way nor changed her expression. This was a situation fraught with peril; they had to get away, and she had no doubt that Matt felt the same way.

"You couldn't afford a distinguished bottle," Mr. Niven sneered.

"Ah well, there you go. I thought as much. Well, please excuse us for disturbing you." Matt reached behind him, forming a cage around Kate with his arms. He shifted as if about to take a step. "We'll be going now."

"No. No, I think not. You'll run back to the manor and speak to your friend Lord Bobbington."

"My friend?" Matt scoffed. "Lord Bobbington? The gentleman who is staying with Squire Fleming? He would hardly give the valet of a Shackleford Park guest the time of day. Though I appreciate the elevation of my status." Looking over his shoulder, Matt smiled, a very strained sort of smile. "Shall we depart?"

"Think word don't get around? We know Bobbington was at Shackleford Park," Mr. Niven said. "An' he be more than a gentleman."

Kate shifted her gaze back to the wine merchant, swallowing at the menace in the man's voice. Mr. Niven stood with his legs apart as if preparing for an onslaught. His greatcoat was open, sheltering a pistol in his right hand. He twirled a substantial knife in his left. And yet, while there was no doubt of immediate danger, it wasn't until Kate's eyes slid to the young man beside Mr. Niven that she felt her blood run cold.

Rolland, too, had a pistol in hand. It, too, was pointed at Matt. But while Mr. Niven's expression could have been defined as angry, wary, or even nervous, Rolland's countenance was that of pleasure. He grinned, with a spark of enjoyment in his eyes, like a child offered a special treat. It was terrifying.

"Be that as it may, it has nothing to do with us," Matt said defiantly.

Behind them, Mr. Belcher muttered something under

his breath and then cleared his throat. "Come in, everyone. Let's not provide a spectacle for the neighbors."

"No one can see back here," Mr. Niven snapped.

"You would be surprised," Mr. Belcher snapped back.

Suddenly, a beefy hand reached up and grabbed Kate's hood, jerking her backward, away from Matt. Losing her balance, she tumbled against a chair that had been propped up against the wall, knocking it over as she landed on the floor with a jarring thump. Matt was immediately by her side, helping her to her feet. But they were not fast enough.

The door was now closed behind Niven and Rolland. Kate and Matt were blocked from the outside world, from freedom . . . from safety.

chapter 14

In which the true nature of a villainous trio comes to the fore

Matt rounded on Mr. Belcher. "How dare you treat Miss Darby in such a rough manner?" He reached for Kate's hand, and then, having secured it, he tugged her behind his back.

At least, he tried.

Kate resisted; she would have been shielded by Matt's body but also blinded. And while she appreciated the chivalry, she would not be protected at Matt's expense. The grim expressions of their antagonists were as much a concern as the weapons aimed at him.

It was odd to think that a simple quest could turn out so badly—in a place such as sleepy Tishdale, where the closest sheriff was two towns away. How could this be? Mr. Belcher was not a violent man, and Mr. Niven a bland sort. Self-preservation must have warped their sensibilities; they looked hostile and resolute . . . but Kate thought she detected a whiff of fear in the air.

"Wouldna had to be rough, if you'd come in on yer own." Mr. Belcher looked at Kate as he answered Matt's question. There was almost an apology in his eyes—almost.

"It's your own bloody fault," Mr. Niven said. "Nosing around."

"You could hardly expect a footman's disappearance to go unnoticed." Matt huffed with great dignity.

Niven looked momentarily confused. He seemed to have forgotten his unseemly interest in the footman and latched on to the subject of Lord Bobbington instead. Still, there was little doubt that the two were linked. And it stood to reason that it was the coin, the fake shilling that Rolland had given Johnny for his ring that pulled it all together in a neat package. They were, after all, standing next to a shop with a forge used for melting metal—the lifeblood of a counterfeit operation.

It also explained the fear: Producing fake coins was seldom a hanging offense, but transportation—exile to the penal colonies of Australia—was a distinct possibility, and it likely weighed heavily on their minds.

"Gentlemen, gentlemen, there is no need to be uncomfortable," Kate said, trying to instill her voice with affability while leaning closer to Matt to present a united front. "We care not what mischief you might be about." She laughed slightly—very slightly. "We care only about the welfare of one Johnny Grinstead, footman to Musson House." It wasn't true—she had every intention of running as fast as her legs could carry her to the squire's manor—but she felt prevarication at this point was advisable.

As she stood with her back pressed to the limestone wall, the tumbled chair on her right side, Matt on her left, Kate casually glanced around the room. A small window and outside door sat on the same wall—behind Niven and Rolland. The fireplace with a poker, and a good, sturdy broom leaned against the wall beside it . . . and a hefty pan—all possible weapons—were beyond reach behind Belcher. There was a bed—a very nice bed, in fact, too nice for the surroundings—pushed up against the far wall and, oh . . . yes, there in the corner was a smaller door. It likely led into the shop, and the shop had a wide front door that led straight out to the street. Yes. A means of escape.

Kate pulled at Matt's hand in the direction of the small door; using her peripheral vision, she saw Matt's head turn slightly and then nod.

"*You* might not care about our other endeavors, but your guest certainly would," Mr. Niven's tone dripped with derision. He straightened his pistol arm, as if bringing the thing closer would increase the intimidation.

It didn't. Dead is dead; it doesn't matter the size of the hole in your chest.

"I assume you are again referring to Lord Bobbington.

Who is, as I have already mentioned, not staying at Shackleford Park. He came for a social visit yesterday with his wife, the squire, and Mrs. Fleming. I don't know what world you live in, but in my world the gentry don't notice the likes of us. Not interested in our lives or our opinions. Whatever quarrel you have with him, we are not involved," Matt said. "So if you could tell us where we will find Johnny, we will all swear to silence. You go your way; we'll go ours. And let bygones be bygones."

Kate felt him shifting his weight as he spoke. She did likewise.

Rolland snorted, glancing first at Kate's lower limbs and then, pointedly, at the small shop door. He shook his head and clicked his tongue in a tsking sound. It was unnerving, and Kate stilled, forcing Matt to do the same.

Glancing over his shoulder, Matt met her eyes, and she shook her head. Now was not the time to break free and run; Rolland was onto them.

And even as the thought passed through her mind, Rolland truly was onto them. He crossed the floor in four large steps, grabbed the front of Kate's cloak, and yanked her over to what had been his side of the room.

"What is wrong with you people? You cannot treat Miss Darby as if she were a sack of potatoes, dragging her hither and yon!" Matt shouted, still rooted to his spot by Mr. Niven's pistol. "What has she done to warrant such deplorable treatment?"

"Not her, you," Mr. Niven said. "Were she not in *your* company, this would not have happened. You are a stranger causing a fuss. People notice. Just like when Johnny wandered into the Goat asking about a red-haired young man *while* going on about a fake coin. People are going to put two and two together—"

"Niven! Watch what yer saying." Belcher gave his cohort a thunderous look.

"It matters not, Belcher," Rolland said with a shrug, letting go of Kate's cloak and dusting off her shoulders as if he were being courteous. Something a gentleman would *never* do. "They'll have to come with us."

Four persons stared at the young man in surprise.

"How do you reckon that?" Niven asked lazily.

"Belcher won't let you kill them—"

"I should say not!" Belcher shouted.

Rolland barely blinked. "Any more than he let us knock off the footman. We can't let them go—"

"You don't need the two of us. Miss Darby can toddle off—" Matt started.

"Toddle off to the authorities? I think not." Niven looked bored with the conversation.

"She won't say anything—"

"Excuse me, but *she* is standing right here. *I* am standing right here. And I say there is nothing to report to the authorities or Lord Bobbington; there is nothing going on here, and so we simply need to grab Johnny"—Kate looked toward the smaller inner door as she spoke—"and we will all go our separate ways."

Rolland snorted in her ear, and Kate swallowed in discomfort. But instead of arguing or belaboring the point, the red-haired villain reached into the pocket of his greatcoat, pulled out a length of rope, and tossed it to Belcher.

As Belcher wrapped the rope around Matt's wrists and tested the knot, Matt shifted in order to catch Kate's eye. He was fairly certain . . . no, entirely certain that Kate was incensed, and planning. She would attempt something before he had time to think it out properly. He needed to think fast.

And then Kate started to scream. It was loud and long and shrill.

Rolland, unperturbed, leaned even closer to her, an intimate distance. It was boorish and repugnant, causing Kate to shudder in distaste. Enraged, Matt leapt across the divide and raised his bound hands. Rolland dodged, using Kate as a shield, hiding—yes, hiding, the coward! Matt swung, but awkwardly. His tied wrists made it impossible to aim—he nearly smacked Kate in the effort—as Rolland bobbed and weaved around her.

"What did you do?" Belcher shouted, yanking Matt out of the way to grab Kate. He clamped his oversized hand across Kate's mouth and dragged her backward, away from Rolland, in an oddly protective maneuver.

"Nothing yet." Rolland shrugged lazily. "Musta heard me thinkin'."

Kate's eyes grew wide with indignation, and she struggled against Belcher.

"Stop!" the man shouted and then gave her a shake when she didn't. It took a few moments, but she eventually tired and Belcher spoke again. "You can't be heard from the street and you are goin' ta deafen us all. I'll lift my hand, if you promise not to scream any more."

With a piercing glare at Rolland, Kate nodded. "Heard him thinking?" she sputtered as soon as she was able. "I did not! I heard him saying. Yes, saying that he was going to cut Matt's heart out and feed it to the pigs a slice at a time—"

For a large man in a small space, Belcher moved fast, and Rolland had nowhere to go. With a great swoop of his arm, Belcher belted Rolland across the face, sending him sprawling—almost landing in the fireplace pit. His pistol clattered to the floor beside him, and Rolland, wisely, did not try to rise.

"I will have none of that. Do you hear me?" Belcher roared, leaning into the face of the young man.

Rolland smiled, but it was a weak attempt and without the edge of mockery. "I was just trying to get a rise out of her. An' I did."

"Really." Niven shook his head and clicked his tongue. He had not moved a muscle, still stood next to the door, pistol still aimed at Matt's chest. "Do neither of you have any self-control? You with your temper. You with your need to create havoc. I have a good mind to wash my hands of you both."

Belcher pivoted and looked at Niven with his mouth curled up in one corner. "Going to make the coins on your own, are you? Going to run into the city delivering them without anyone getting suspicious like?" He laughed without humor. "You are welcome to try."

"Now who's being indiscreet?" Niven muttered under his breath, but Belcher didn't appear to hear him.

"It was you who panicked, my friend," the blacksmith continued. "It was you who had to pack up and get away. It was you who claimed defeat—when I said *nay.* I said *wait.* I said *let's see what it all means.* An' what happens? It's all yer bloody running around that gets us in trouble, not Rolland's idiocy."

"Thanks ever so," Rolland said, his sarcasm back in place . . . though he stayed on the floor.

"If Rolland hadn't given Johnny that coin, none of this would have happened." Niven sneered at Belcher, ignoring Rolland entirely.

"Where *is* Johnny?" Kate asked.

The question had been on Matt's tongue as well . . . but he had wondered if it was wise to interrupt the bickering.

"You tell us." Niven turned his head to stare—glare—at Kate.

Kate frowned, blinked, and looked from Niven to Belcher and then turned her gaze to Matt. “I don’t understand,” she said eventually. Her brow was deeply folded.

Matt swallowed and shook his head, as she turned back to Niven. “Where is he?” she said again. The third time it was more of a shout. “Where is Johnny?”

“He was making such a fuss,” Rolland answered as he struggled to his feet and then brushed himself off. “I can understand him wanting his ring back, but did he have to go around telling everyone about the stranger, the red-haired young man? Eventually, people would realize that he was no stranger, that he was me. Really. Such a fuss.”

Niven slipped his knife into his boot and tossed Belcher another length of rope; he pointed at Kate. “We agreed you would not spend the coins in Tishdale, boy.”

“Yes, but Johnny wasn’t from here.” Rolland’s voice was taking on a smarmy quality. “I didn’t know he was staying in the neighborhood. I didn’t know he would come back into town looking for me.”

“We agreed—” Niven started to say.

“Yes, I know, but we have been lying low for six months. Six months! I have nothing, nothing to show for my efforts.”

Matt’s anger grew as Belcher signaled for Kate to put her wrists together. But as he watched, Matt could see that Belcher had underestimated Kate. He was tying the ropes far looser than he had with Matt, far looser than he ought, far looser than was wise.

"We agreed—" Niven tried again.

"Yes, yes. But it's takin' too long."

"And look what has happened." Niven finally lowered his pistol, placing it on the table by the window, and stepped to the fireplace to warm his hands.

"I got rid of the problem. I were handlin' it. I don't know why you had to pack up. He wouldn't have survived. It's been two days in the freezing cold—"

Kate gasped and swiveled her head to stare at Rolland. "What did you do?"

"Nothin', nothin' at all. Didn't have to do nothin'."

"But where is Johnny?"

"The last time I saw him, he was sittin' in a barn. We grabbed him in the mews, took him out to the old Bidford farm while we was decidin' what to do. When I gets back, he was gone."

"Gone?" Kate clearly did not believe the lout.

"Yup, ropes shredded an' he were gone. Thought we were in the suds, but then nothin' happened. Just you two askin' around."

"But . . . where . . ."

Rolland shrugged. "There's mantraps and wolves in the woods. Or he could have frozen to death."

Matt would not believe it. No. Johnny may have the devil's own luck, but he was like a cat with nine lives—rising again and again . . . or was that a phoenix? "He could have found shelter. A cave, perhaps," Matt said.

"None here that I know of." Rolland looked pleased to disagree.

"He might have *built* a shelter." Matt would not accept Johnny's demise without proof—not just this villain's say-so. "With branches and bushes . . . and the like . . ."

"What's he goin' ta use to start a fire? No. He's a goner fer certain." There was glee in his tone.

Matt was incredulous. "Are you truly that much of a monster that you can find pleasure in some else's suffering?"

With slow, deliberate steps, Rolland crossed the room and drew so close to Matt that Matt could smell the villain's sour breath. Rolland jabbed his finger into Matt's chest. "Don't push it, mate. No one's comin' lookin' for you, and I'd just as soon drop you into Dame Symon's pigsty as look at you."

"Rolland," Niven said wearily. "Leave him alone; you *are* a monster."

Rolland shrugged, moving to the door. He leaned casually against the doorjamb and smiled, a sickening, weasel-like smile. It churned Matt's stomach.

"There are much more interesting subjects," Niven continued, still standing with his back to the room, warming his hands. "Such as Lord Bobbington, and why he is in Tishdale. You see, Lord Bobbington works for the Home Office. I know that. I heard of him in the war. After smugglers then. But those in the Home Office, they go after counterfeiters, too. So I say again, why is he here *now*?"

"You will have to ask Lord Bobbington. I do not know the man."

Scrubbing at his face, Niven huffed in frustration and then turned to face the room. "This is pointless. We have to plan."

"I'm staying. I have my customers, my forge, my shop . . ." Belcher sat with a thump on the newly righted chair.

"Like Australia, do you? 'Cause that's where they'll send you."

"This is your fault for panickin'." Rolland's eyes were pinpoints of anger, and they were trained on Niven.

"It's yours for using a coin so close to where they are made."

"Idiocy abounds!" Belcher shouted, and then he huffed a sigh that almost sounded like resignation. It was a most disconcerting sound . . . for it had a feeling of finality to it. "What about them?" he asked, waving toward Matt, studiously *not* looking at Kate. "They will have to come with," he said, answering his own question.

"We can't take them to—We can't take them with us all the way," Rolland argued. "They will go to the authorities first chance they get."

"I won't have her killed." Belcher shook his head, now staring at the floor. "I did not agree to that. Not now, not ever."

"I'll get the wagon, drive it into the shop." Niven started toward the door. "We'll leave them in the Bidford barn. It will take several trips to get everything to . . . the city. By the time we are done, we will know what to do with them."

Belcher nodded and then shifted to stare into the fire. Rolland watched Niven step back outside, and then he sauntered over to Matt when the door was closed once again. He leaned toward Matt, placing his mouth by his ear. "You will have starved to death by then," he whispered, and then leaned back so that Matt could see his smile.

KATE AND MATT *did* go through the small door at the back of the cottage eventually, but it was not in the manner in which Kate had imagined. They were not rushing to escape, thugs hard on their heels. No, indeed not. *Plodding* would be one way to describe their gait—being dragged might be another. For whatever was demanded of them, they did not do willingly. The fear of mortal danger was tempered whenever Belcher was present. The other two might not agree, but they were not about to argue with the large man. They knew not how to melt lead and make the plugs or plate them to look like silver—their criminal enterprise depended on the blacksmith. For now, they would not upset him.

And so Kate and Matt set out to be contrary as often as possible. Had Rolland wished for them to remain in the cottage, they would have contrived to go to the shop. When it was decided that they should move to the shop, Kate refused to budge from the cottage. Perhaps it wasn't wise to antagonize, but they had so little recourse, so little control over their own fate, it was the only way to protest.

After being hauled across the dirt floor to the far side of the shop, Kate and Matt were unceremoniously dropped beside a pile of broken tools. Whether they were to be repaired or melted, there was no indication. But Kate noticed irregular edges and tried to fall closer to a hole-riddled plow blade. Unfortunately, Belcher snorted in recognition of her attempt, and shifted them nearer a stack of buckets waiting for replacement staves.

"Out of the way, an' outta mischief," Belcher muttered as he turned and hurried back to the wagon.

Kate righted herself, pushed her skirts down her calves, and looked around. The converted barn was cavernous, large enough to house several carts or wagons and their teams within its walls. Across the entire back, tools—rusty, blackened tools of the trade—hung off brackets in chaotic confusion. The hearth still glowed, offering a modicum of heat to those nearby—nothing to those on the far wall. The anvil had been shifted next to the tailboard of the wagon and the bellows, various tongs, farrier snips, and hammers were placed in and around the already loaded wine barrels. It was a strange collection, melding the two incongruous trades. Then, of course, there were the small but excessively heavy chests that jingled as they were shifted.

"I do beg your pardon. I apologize most profusely," Matt said, drawing Kate's gaze for a moment.

Startled, Kate considered why Matt felt the need to ask for forgiveness and could think of nothing. "I'm not sure I understand," she said, shifting her eyes back to the trio packing up their Tishdale lives.

"I nearly hit you when I went after Rolland."

Smiling weakly, Kate shook her head. "I wouldn't have blamed you if you had, and I can hardly hold you to account for something that *didn't* happen." Lifting her cheeks in a better approximation of a smile, she added. "Yell *duck* next time."

"Perhaps *drop*. Then I could swing at will. Or something unexpected . . . such as *look up!* and then you drop." He huffed, a sound more akin to exasperation than a sigh. "I would really appreciate another opportunity to try," he added.

"To hit me?"

"No. Rolland," Matt answered as if Kate's question had been serious.

Kate turned to find Matt staring across the shop. His eyes were locked on one figure, and they followed that figure as he lifted and loaded. Rolland. All of Matt's frustration and anger were engendered in the red-haired young man. It was not surprising, for Kate felt the same way. Rolland was the one enjoying their struggles and their predicament; he alone advocated their untimely end.

As if aware of their scrutiny, Rolland turned, glared back in their direction and then disappeared through the adjoining cottage door. He was back within a moment and, even as

Belcher protested, Rolland tore a pillow cover in two. Marching over to where Matt and Kate sat, he stuffed the ripped cotton strips in their mouths and tied them behind their heads.

Gagged. It was most undignified.

chapter 15

In which Saint George slays a dragon

For all their rushing about, it took an inordinate amount of time to load the wagon. Perhaps the process would have been faster had the villainous trio not continued to argue over every little bit of space and what should be left behind for the next run. There was an underlying possibility that circumstances might prevent a next time—such as a sudden need to flee Lord Bobbington. And so the value of every item had to be weighed and then, horror of horrors, a portion of that precious space had to be given over for the likes of two meddlesome persons. It was the only thing they agreed upon—a general disgust with Kate and Matt for their interference.

Listening to the bickering, hearing their persons likened to goods, and facing an unknown future churned Kate's stomach. Equal parts of fear, loathing, and dread stirred into helplessness. Only Matt's presence offered Kate a modicum of relief. His leg was pressed against hers, their fingers entwined as much as was possible with tied wrists, and the occasional bump of his shoulder reminded her that she was not alone. They would tough this out together.

With a sharp stone digging into her right hip, her mouth dry from working at the gag, and her wrists chafed from tugging at the ropes, Kate was in a sorry state. Listening to the three men, Kate knew beyond a certainty that she and Matt had to get away before they were tossed into the back of the wagon. Mr. Belcher was not going to accompany them; he would meet Rolland and Mr. Niven at the barn. Whether he truly had something to pick up at a neighbor's or he was simply distancing himself from the fate of the prisoners, Kate couldn't say. But Mr. Belcher was their protection from Rolland. Mr. Niven didn't care; he would rather leave the problem in Rolland's hands, and he said so . . . whenever Mr. Belcher ducked back into his cottage.

If they left town, hidden in the back of the wagon, Kate knew they would never arrive at the Bidford barn. And so, while watching the three villains make preparations, Kate and Matt held hands in the guise of offering each other comfort. Matt was, in fact, trying as unobtrusively as possible to untie Kate's bonds. Their hands half-hidden in her skirts, Matt clawed at the rope, and he was making some progress. The knot had proven to be unyielding, but the ropes themselves were fairly loose and Matt had worked one loop up her thumb. Half an inch more and it would be over her nail; with the ropes looser still, they could—

Kate murmured a warning to Matt as Mr. Niven looked their way. Matt stilled; Kate stilled. Both held their breath.

Niven frowned. "Do we have enough rope?" he asked, staring across at them. "For the cargo and our guests." His lack of hostility was nearly as chilling as Rolland's menacing. "We need to tie their feet or they will run away as soon as we get out of the shop." He almost sounded bored.

Rolland glanced their way with a nasty smile. "Indeed. Plenty." Reaching into the wagon, he produced a coil of rope; grabbing a knife from the shaft of his boot, he cut two lengths. Then he dropped his weapon back into his boot and sauntered—yes, *sauntered*—with supreme confidence to where Matt and Kate sat with their hands no longer together.

With a shove, Rolland pushed Matt onto his back and then sat on him. He was not gentle, laughing as Matt kicked and struggled and twisted, trying to delay the inevitable. Scooping a handful of dirt from the floor, Kate threw it in Rolland's face and surged to her feet. She slammed her shoulder into Rolland's chest while he thrashed blindly, knocking him off Matt.

Grabbing Matt's hands, Kate tried to give him the leverage he needed to get to his feet, but just as he found his balance, Rolland—face streaked with filth—grabbed Matt's leg and pulled it out from under him. Matt fell hard, grunting in pain. Furious, Kate pulled her leg back to kick out at the red-headed fiend, but she was suddenly grabbed about the waist and lifted into the air.

"Now, now, Miss Darby, that's not polite," Mr. Belcher said as he held her off the ground.

Kate twisted and turned, but his hold was too tight and too strong; she could not break free. She panted past her gag, trying to drag in the air she needed; her thrashing slowed and then stopped as the shop darkened. When he released her, Kate fell in a heap, still breathless, but her vision started to clear.

In a deft move, Belcher and Rolland bound her feet and then did the same to Matt. In retaliation for what he called their antics, Rolland punched Matt in the ribs as he lay unable to defend himself; Rolland would have struck a second time had Mr. Belcher not barked at him. All Kate could manage was a muffled scream from behind her gag.

When Belcher lifted Kate into the wagon, he placed her on her side, facing away from the center, a wine barrel at her back. Rolland laughed most unpleasantly as he pulled her arms above her head and attached the ropes to a metal ring secured to the side of the wagon; it was usually used to tie down a canvas or cargo . . . but wait, she *was* cargo.

Kate heard grunting and felt the wagon floor bounce slightly as they loaded Matt on the other side of the wine barrel with as much kindness and consideration as they had offered her. She muttered a wordless question. *Are you all right?* He hummed that he was. Or that was how Kate interpreted the sound. It provided some comfort.

After the canvas had been secured over them and the rest of the goods, Niven and Rolland climbed onto the driver's bench while Mr. Belcher opened the wide doors of the blacksmith shop. Kate could hear it all, listening with great concentration to their conversation and movements. As the wagon started to roll, Kate felt sick. They had to get someone's attention before they left town because, after that, Rolland could do his worst with impunity and leave their bodies to rot until someone came across them in the spring.

MATT SAWED HIS hands back and forth across the ring that secured his bindings. He prayed that the ring's roughness—for it caught and pulled as he did so—would fray the ropes to the point that he could break them. He knew it to be a faint hope, but to do nothing would be unconscionable. He had to save Kate.

Kate. Kate. So wonderfully impulsive. The dirt in Rolland's eyes would have worked had Belcher not intervened. It was excessively discouraging; the big man could have looked the other way or reacted slowly. Matt had thought that Kate's charm had worked on him—but apparently not.

Anger fed Matt's frenzy as he sawed his hands back and forth. Focus—he had to remain focused. If allowed to grow,

Matt's rage would cloud his thoughts, and if ever he needed to think, and think clearly, it was now.

Suddenly, Matt felt a stinging smack on his hands through the canvas, likely from a whip.

"Don't do that," Rolland said in an offhanded manner. There was no menace to the tone—which seemed odd until Matt realized there were footsteps nearby.

"Fine evening, Mr. Niven," a male voice called. "Now that the snow has stopped."

Niven grunted and Matt squinted, trying to hear, trying to understand where the voice was coming from. When he thought the man might be beside the wagon, he lifted both his legs, kicking out at the canvas and shouting past his gag.

"Got yerself a live one there."

"Cat. Gone wild on me," Mr. Niven offered. "Taking it out to the woods."

Matt waited with expectation. Surely the person would question the need to take a cat, wild or otherwise, out to the woods as the sun was going down, would puzzle over the size of said cat to move such a large canvas, and he would find Niven's behavior odd.

Nothing happened. The wagon continued to roll up the road at a lazy pace. The equipage rattled and squeaked, the wheels crunched and scraped against the gravel . . . and Matt was forced to admit that his shout had sounded very much like a distressed cat.

A bump against his foot brought Matt's attention back

under the canvas. He lifted his head, then using the metal ring to brace, raised his upper body. In the half-light, Matt could see that Kate had shifted; she was now on her back, legs stretched out. It had been her boot that had knocked against his. He couldn't see her face; it was hidden behind the wine barrel between them, but the contact of their feet, slight though it might be, offered reassurance.

Matt swallowed in distress, discomfort, and disillusionment. He could do nothing other than shake his head and huff a sigh as he returned her tap. Still, even knowing it pointless, Matt tried twice more to capture someone's attention when he heard walking nearby, and yet the wagon continued to roll unimpeded. It turned right sooner than Matt expected; he surmised that they were not heading toward Shackleford Park but taking another way out of town. The soft clink of a bell, buffeted by the wind, might mean they had turned down the road that led past the church, but there was no way to tell.

Occasionally singing could be heard in the distance, as well as cries for Dr. Quack to restore Saint George to health. It would seem that companies of carolers and mummers were taking advantage of the slightly drier conditions to travel about, asking for charity—or as they called it, "contributions from their audience."

And all too soon the sounds of a town of fifteen hundred souls became fewer and far between. They had reached the edge of Tishdale and now would only be passing the occasional cottage. Next stop, old Bidford barn, although who the Bidfords were and why they would allow a wine merchant to use their barn as if it was his own was not even worth contemplating . . . unless, of course, the Bidfords could be worked upon to help free them from their captors. Oh yes, not all was lost; they could look to the—

"Bloody Hell! What are you doing?" Niven shouted as the wagon came to a sudden stop. "You don't step in front of a team like that. What if I hadn't seen you?"

"I'm carrying a lantern and I'm a dressed as a large green dragon, Mr. Niven," a raspy voice answered. "You could hardly miss me." There was amusement in his tone.

Matt felt the wagon bounce and felt Kate hit his foot again. She was jiggling about—perhaps trying to get the mummers' attention.

"Let us perform for you, good sir," another male voice called. "I am Saint George. Ignore my craggy crown; I just had a nasty encounter with a most vicious shrubbery."

"Some other time, perhaps." Niven sounded delightfully irritated.

"Making a delivery?"

"Indeed." There was a shift as if Niven had lifted the reins. "Make way!"

"No, kind sir. The Yuletide season is all about charity and compassion to those less fortunate. And we are most unfortunate, are we not, Dr. Quack? We shall perform for you, gentlemen, and you will offer us a few worthless coins."

"I have none," Niven said, even as Rolland snickered.

"Ah, then you will be generous with a libation. No, no, Mr. Niven, it will not do. Lay your reins aside and enjoy. Ten minutes of your time, fifteen at most. And then you will share a taste of your wine with us—it need not be your finest. We will be quite content with your worst. And now . . . hold the horses, Ned . . . I mean, Father Christmas. Might as well make yourself useful."

There was a scuffling sound, a few cleared throats, and Rolland whispered, presumably to Niven, "Might as well let them perform. It would look far worse to drive off—it would garner too much attention."

Niven's answer was inarticulate, but he did not sound pleased.

And even as the mummers prepared for their presentation, Kate continued to tap Matt's foot—with great enthusiasm. It was almost as if she were trying to send him a message, but about what he had no idea.

IF KATE COULD have jumped for joy, she would have. That voice! She recognized it . . . him! The raspy voice of the *dragon* could be none other than Jeremy Bulfinchwiggins, one of her brother Merle's closest friends. Jeremy used to be a terrible torment when she was growing up, and yet now Kate was overjoyed to think that he stood only a few feet away.

She needed to get Jeremy's attention. She needed him to look under the canvas of the wagon. As soon as he saw her trussed and gagged—well, that would be the end of that. And yet try as she might, Kate could not scream or shout past her gag. The sound she produced was no more than a weak moan, lost in the conversation and now in the opening words of the Fool. As the characters were introduced, Kate bided her time.

"IN COMES SAINT GEORGE / THE NOBLE CHAMPION BOLD
WITH BRIGHT SWORD AND BUCKLE AT HIS SIDE / HE WON THREE CROWNS OF GOLD."

The play was often improvised, and there was no doubting the embellishment of this amateur troupe, for Saint George, in this version, challenged the dragon, not the Turkish knight.

And as they fought, Kate could hear the thud of a blunt sword and pounding steps as they leapt and danced around the wagon. Panting breath came near, raising Kate's hopes, and then faded away again. Twice more, Kate thought the players close enough to hear her moaning, but they were too intent on their own purpose, too caught up in the drama, to notice anything untoward in the wagon. And then the tragedy—Saint George, not the dragon, was slain. A great shout of horror resounded throughout the troupe . . . overriding Niven's sigh of impatience.

"Excellent, well done. We will be go—"

"Wait, Mr. Niven. We can hope for a miracle to restore poor Saint George to life," Father Christmas said . . . or was it the Fool? Kate could no longer tell; they were all moving about too quickly. "Let us call for a doctor. Dr. Quack, are you here?"

"I am here," a voice called from nearby. It sounded as if the man was standing at the back of the wagon.

Kate kicked out and shouted—moaned—again. She felt the wagon shaking as Matt joined her, and yet no one noticed. The play went on without any hesitation until the doctor, the wonderful Dr. Quack, improvised a tiny bit more.

"LAY HIM ON THIS ROLLING BED / FOR IT NEVER SHOULD BE SAID,
THAT I WORKED UPON THE GROUND / TO RAISE A MAN FROM THE DEAD."

And with those words, Kate felt the wonderful burden of a weight added to her discomfort. This time she undulated and braced herself on the ring, pulling her legs up—batting at the weight. She could feel Matt doing the same.

"Ack! What is that?"

"Get off my wagon!" Niven shouted, no doubt realizing the danger of discovery. "I have a wild cat under there."

"That's no cat!" Saint George shouted, miraculously recovered without the aid of Dr. Quack. "It's too big."

Kate could feel scrambling movement, and she tried to kick out again, following it as best she could.

"Ack, it did it again!" the voice shouted. "John, what is that?"

There was a rattling sound at the edge of the canvas, and Kate held her breath. At last, *at last* rescue was at hand.

"Stand away!" Niven shouted.

The rattling abated and then ceased. In a last-ditch effort, Kate raised her legs and shouted as loud as she could. The sound she produced was still an inarticulate moan, but when Matt joined his moan with hers, it reverberated loudly in the silence. And there was nothing catlike about it.

"I think we need to know what you are carrying, Mr. Niven. There is something havey-cavey going on here."

"Nothing that need concern you. This is none of your business. I will be on my way. Move, Father Christmas, or you will be trampled." There was a snap of reins, and the wagon jerked forward, but that was all—only a roll of a few feet and then it stopped again.

"Grab the leathers, Ned," a voice said. "I have the horses' heads."

"Now, that is rather pointless, Mr. Niven," another voice said, sounding eerily calm. "Put the pistol down, sir. You know as well as we do that those things are dreadfully inaccurate and there are five of us to your two—oh, where is . . . ? It would seem that your companion has left you, Mr. Niven. It is now five to one. Well done, Jeremy."

Kate heard and felt a scuffle as the wagon rocked from side to side. Niven shouted in rage, and then there was a loud thud.

"Oh, bother," the raspy voice of Jeremy said. "I hit him a bit harder than I intended."

"Well, there is no doubt he will have a headache when he awakes, but who's to say he didn't deserve it?"

The scratching at the back of the wagon returned and then the canvas was lifted; a lantern was thrust forward. Squinting in the sudden light, Kate stared at the three painted faces. The ash-darkened face of Saint George with his crown askew, the red and yellow stripes of the Fool with a tricorner hat decorated with jingle bells, and the green face of a frowning dragon, Jeremy Bulfinchwiggins.

Kate smiled despite her gag.

"Miss Kate!" Jeremy engendered her name with horror, then grabbed her by the boot, trying to pull her free, not realizing that she was—"She's been tied to the bloody wagon. The rotter! Give him a kick, Ned, while you are standing over him!"

Kate saw Saint George glance aside and subtly negate Jeremy's order with a shake of his head. Then Matt moved, drawing all eyes to the wagon once more.

"What is going on?!" The Fool jumped and Saint George threw the canvas back farther, exposing Matt, trussed and gagged and sporting a grin as goofy as Kate's.

Their eyes met, and Matt winked. Kate laughed soundlessly and laid her head back on the hard wooden floor of the wagon. Exhausted, aware that her trussing ropes were being cut, Kate hardly moved until helping hands pulled the gag from her mouth and slid her to the tailboard. Someone offered her water, which she gulped greedily until, at last, her mouth felt less like a sandpit. And yet when she tried to speak, the sound was more of a croak. Matt beside her was undergoing the same ministrations, and he, too, croaked a thank-you.

Turning toward him, with every intention of saying something ridiculous to lighten the mood, Kate met Matt's gaze and was rendered mute. The tenderness, the caring, the relief, and the regard in his eyes were palpable. Kate smiled and promptly burst into tears.

Matt lifted his arm, offering Kate his shoulder. She slid next to him, turning her face into his coat, and proceeded to vent her pent-up anxiety. The colorful faces around them stepped away, affording them a modicum of privacy. From the corner of her eye, Kate could see that Niven was soon trussed with his own rope. Three members of the troupe stood at the edge of the lanterns' glow, staring into the night, and declared that "the other one" got away.

MATT MARVELED AT Miss Kate Darby. Her clear thinking had saved the day. Batting at Saint George with their legs had done the job. Matt was certain they would never have succeeded in attracting the attention of the mummers otherwise. That this wonderful girl, so determined, so full of spirit, and so charming, could keep fear at bay until all was well left Matt in awe.

He gently kissed the top of her head, felt her grip tighten on his lapel, and decided that he wanted nothing more than to stay exactly as he was. Yes, the wagon was hard, the air bitterly cold, and he was tired beyond reason, but holding Kate in his arms was as near to heaven as he had ever been, and he would be happy if it never ended.

"We should probably explain," Kate said, finally lifting her head—effectively ending their heavenly embrace.

Wiping the tears from her face, Matt sighed and leaned in, kissing her forehead. Had there been no one else around, even if they were studiously looking the other way, Matt would have chosen her lips instead. But the last thing Kate needed was to lose her reputation, and they were already treading the line, sitting as close as they were. Most would understand him consoling Kate after an ordeal such as this . . . when it was explained.

And so Matt did the honors with Kate tucked against his side, watching calmly, no longer visibly upset, no longer crying.

The men were suitably outraged—Saint George had to restrain the dragon, who shouted in fury and wanted to have at Niven again. However, order prevailed and the villain was tossed into the wagon, where Matt had been not twenty minutes earlier. Matt and Kate were helped onto the driver's bench, where they could huddle—supposedly against the cold—while Jeremy took up the reins. With two in front and two at the back, the costumed men accompanied and guarded the wagon as it was turned around. They rode back into Tishdale and then out the east road to Hendred, the squire's manor.

And as the wagon rattled down the road, Matt allowed his thoughts to return to the very question that had plunged them into danger.

Where was Johnny?

chapter 16

In which Kate tries to listen through good solid oak—to no avail

"This is most grievous," Lord Bobbington said, shaking his head after the tale was told. He took Kate's empty teacup from her, placing it on the trolley. Turning his gaze to the study's busy Bokhara carpet, he frowned and shook his head and then frowned again. When he looked up, meeting Kate's questioning gaze, he continued, "It would seem that we have our villains, or at least know who they are. I am sorry that you have had to pay such a cost . . . but I can assure you that I will not rest until we have Belcher and Rolland confined. Niven has been locked in the storage shed for now, and the groom standing guard has been instructed to ignore his claims of innocence, bribery, and threats . . . for I understand all three have been tried."

"And Johnny?" she asked, almost afraid of the answer.

"I pray that it's not truc, but it does not look good for the young footman. We will search, of course. I'm sure Squire Fleming can find us some scent dogs." He glanced in the old gentleman's direction.

They were clustered in the mahogany-lined study of Hendred Manor and, being that it was not an overly large room, only Kate and Squire Fleming were seated. Lord Bobbington paced in front of the window while Matt leaned heavily against the desk across from the fireplace.

The mummers had departed almost as soon as they had delivered Matt and Kate to safety. They hadn't even offered to perform their drama, citing a sudden need to return to their homes. Squire Fleming had sent them away with fruit-cake and mince pies to reward their valor, but the men seemed dazed. Were they upset about devilry in their midst, or had they come to realize that they had saved two people's lives? Kate would have to ask Jeremy—one day.

"Yes, of course, scent dogs," the squire said. "Though it will have to wait until morning." When Kate gasped, he reached out and patted her hand. "It cannot be helped, my dear. The moon is not out to help us. But we shall start at first light at the Bidford farm. Those poor folks—in their eighties, you know. They have become reclusive as they've aged. I am certain they had no idea what was going on in their barn. Cruel to be used thus." And then he blinked as if pulling himself back into the present. "Yes, scent dogs can be arranged to go after Rolland, as well."

"Indeed." Bobbington nodded. "We can't let him get away!"

"But scent dogs need a scent." The squire sat up straighter and looked toward Matt. "A coat—hose, perhaps. Even a cap would do."

Matt drew in a ragged breath and nodded as he did so. "I'm sure I can find something in Johnny's room."

"Excellent, excellent." The squire leaned toward the wall and yanked on the bellpull. "I'll have my driver take you back to Shackleford Park in my coach."

"Call for mine," Lord Bobbington said as he looked toward the door. "I'll explain to the Beeswangers." And then he glanced at Kate with a mouth lifted at the corners—not really a smile, for there was more than a hint of tension in his eyes. "You will have been missed, and I hope my presence will mitigate the consequences. I am so very sorry that you were subject to such uncalled-for behavior—such abominable treatment." He sighed, shook his head at a private thought, and then straightened his shoulders. "I will take the opportunity to enlist some assistance while I am there. We will need as many men as possible combing the woods in the morning—three search parties."

Kate glanced at Matt, noting the red marks where the gag had rubbed across his cheeks; she likely sported the same. And then there were their wrists—raw and covered in dried blood. It was unlikely that the Beeswangers or Steeples would send them packing without being given an opportunity to explain. The marks of imprisonment were too blatant.

Still, she greatly appreciated the company of Lord Bobbington. To be sent home in a coach was more than a kindness. It was a sign of respect, and to be accompanied by a baron at the same time increased the honor tenfold.

Handed into the closed coach, with a warm brick at her feet and a blanket across her knees, Kate marveled at the comfort. Matt sat beside her, cossetted in a like manner. She nodded her appreciation to Lord Bobbington as they headed south along the main road through Tishdale. The coach dipped as it hit a particularly large rut, causing the carriage to bounce with excess enthusiasm. Matt grunted in discomfort.

"Problem?" Lord Bobbington inquired with a frown.

"Bruised ribs, my lord. Another gift from Rolland."

Lord Bobbington shook his head, curled his mouth in undisguised disgust, and turned his eyes to the dark window.

Kate smiled up at Matt, offering him wordless sympathy, but her effort was lost when he lifted her hand to his lips and kissed it gently. Kate was transfixed, forgetting to breathe for a moment. Her heart thrummed; her ears buzzed, and she swallowed with difficulty. Forcing her eyes away, Kate glanced at Lord Bobbington. She was relieved to see that he was still staring out at the night. But then, when she shifted her gaze to the window, she met the gentleman's eyes in the mirrorlike surface, and she knew that he had seen Matt kiss her hand and noted her reaction.

Lord Bobbington was smiling—a broad grin that stretched from ear to ear.

WHEN THE LARGE coach emblazoned with the Bobbington coat of arms came to a halt at the overly illuminated Shackleford Park, it did so at the undistinguished servants' entrance, not the regal front doors. Before the accompanying footmen had jumped to the ground, said door flew open and staff streamed outside wearing neither coats nor scarves.

Kate, watching from the carriage, marveled at the number of lanterns set up in the yard and the clusters of candles sitting on the windowsills of what was normally a dark corner of the manor after dusk. The crowd parted as Mrs. Lundy stepped forward with a most disconcerting frown, tremendous worry in her eyes. Quickly unlatching the window, Kate dropped the glass and waved until the movement caught the housekeeper's gaze. Mrs. Lundy raced to the side of the carriage, tears in her eyes.

"Oh, my dear, my dear. I have been so worried. Thank heavens you are well—but what is this?" she said, reaching up to touch Kate's cheek. Her frown re-formed, and she looked past Kate toward where Matt waited beside her. "And Mr. Harlow, you as well. Have you had an unpleasant adventure?"

"Most unpleasant, Mrs. Lundy. I will explain all in a moment," Kate said softly.

The steps were lowered and the coach door opened to reveal the tall, lanky form of Lord Bobbington. Those gathered shifted back to allow the baron room to descend.

Leaning out, Kate squeezed Mrs. Lundy's hand in reassurance, but in doing so she unintentionally increased the poor woman's anxiety.

"Your . . . your wrist, dearest Kate. It looks . . . well, I won't say what it looks like because it cannot be. You were not bound, were you?"

With a heavy sigh, Kate nodded ever so slightly and watched as tears formed once again in Mrs. Lundy's eyes. "We are fine, Mrs. Lundy. Please don't be distressed."

The woman nodded silently.

"Away, away! Out of the way!" Walker shouted. He elbowed and pushed to the front of those gathered and then bowed before Lord Bobbington. "Welcome, my lord. I—"

"I need to speak with Mr. Beeswanger, Wooker." Lord Bobbington turned to offer Kate a hand out of the carriage, and a wink of conspiracy.

"Walker, my lord."

Lord Bobbington pivoted. "If you say so." And with that he led the procession into the manor, waited until Kate and Matt were comfortably ensconced in the housekeeper's sitting room, and then followed the butler to the front of the house.

Monday, December 22, 1817

Matt awoke with a feeling of dread . . . No, that wasn't entirely true. He had barely slept, and the feeling of dread had not left him since Lord Bobbington had voiced the possibility that Johnny might not have survived three . . . no, four winter nights in the woods.

Camille's reaction upon hearing their story and the part Johnny played in it—entrapped by a fake shilling—was gut-wrenching. She had swooned in a graceful silent collapse, caught at the last moment by Charles, the footman. It would have been less affecting if she had succumbed to hysterics, for when the smelling salts were administered, she sat still, seemingly unaware of the tears streaming down her face. Marie had helped the poor girl from the room while Mrs. Lundy continued to rub marvelous Kate's wrists with some sort of fish-odored ointment. Matt had declined the treatment.

And now, dawn had at last come.

Ignoring the chill and the laid but unlit fire, Matt quickly performed his ablutions and dressed. He thought to tiptoe away before the young gentlemen needed him; they would not rise for some time, and Matt could join the search for the first few hours before his valet duties would call him back to the manor. Though Johnny might have been discovered by then. Matt could but hope.

However, Mr. Ernest and Mr. Ben were *not* still abed.

They were waiting in the hallway, fully dressed, outdoor clothing in arms.

"There he is." Mr. Ben greeted Matt with affection—a slap on the shoulder and a pumped hand. "You had us quite perplexed yesterday. Rode out twice looking for you. So glad that you are well, though I must say, you are not in the best of looks." He glanced at his brother as he said this, moving so that Mr. Ernest could have his turn shaking Matt's hand.

This was their first meeting since Matt's return, for a message had been sent down the previous night—by way of a disgruntled Walker—that Matt and Kate were to have the evening off. Eternally grateful, Matt had spent what remained of the day as near to Kate as was politic. He told himself that it was to ensure that she was not suffering any late effects of their ordeal, but in truth it was a wish, no, a need, to be close to marvelous Kate for as long as practical.

"Bobbington explained, Matt. And we are ready to do our part." Mr. Ernest nodded.

"We're just going to grab a bite in the dining room, Matt, and then we will head out with you," Mr. Ben said as the two gentlemen started toward the front stairs. "The squire is coordinating the searches from Hendred Manor."

With a bob of his head, Matt proceeded to the back stairs, going toward the men's quarters at the bottom of the staircase rather than the servants' hall. He had to ask Charles—or was that Bernie?—where Johnny's room was located, but once there, Matt found a pair of slippers, a scarf, and a vest that could provide a scent for the dogs. Throwing the items into Johnny's satchel, Matt glanced around the small room. His jaw tensed when he noticed a pair of dice sitting near his friend's bedside.

Despite Matt's disinclination to gamble, he knew that the odds were not in Johnny's favor.

IT WAS HARD to eat; nothing was palatable. Matt could see that Kate felt the same way. She was chasing her food around her plate and putting nothing in her mouth. They were standing, plates in hand, in the servants' hall. The breakfast had been set out on the tables, but no one wanted to sit. There was a general rushed feeling despite the very early hour. And a sense that there was not enough time. Well, not enough daylight. It was dark early at Yuletide; the sun would be down by four.

Just as Matt poked at his eggs for a third time, one of the Shackleford grooms leaned across the threshold into the room. "Wagon's ready for them wanting to go to Hendred Manor," he called.

Nearly all the men dropped their plates on the table, most unfinished. They grabbed at coats and hats that had been temporarily set aside and piled out of the room, heading toward the yard door. Matt started to follow until a gentle hand on his arm stayed his steps.

"Good luck," Kate said, meeting his gaze with a steady

look. Her eyes said far more than her mouth, but in a language Matt had yet to learn. While there was no doubting her concern and anxiousness, Matt could see something more, something deeper. But now was not the time to query her about it.

"Thank you," he said, resisting the urge to place his lips on hers . . . for comfort, merely comfort.

Outside, Matt was the last to exit the manor, and he was dismayed to see that the wagon had already started down the drive.

"Here, Matt," Mr. Ernest called from a coach sitting next to the stables. "I sent the wagon ahead. There is room with us."

Matt nodded, turned to see Kate standing with Mrs. Lundy by the servant's entrance. Their eyes locked, and for several moments neither moved . . . until Mr. Ernest called again. Kate lifted her hand as the cold wind whipped against her skirts.

Matt waved back and then joined his two young gentlemen in their coach.

KATE TRIED NOT to dwell on what was or was not happening beyond the grounds of Shackleford Park, but the searches were all she *did* think about. When one of the squire's footmen arrived just after one o'clock to speak to the Beeswangers and Steeples, Kate contrived to be near the drawing room door. To no avail. Good solid English oak prevented any sort of listening, as did Mr. Walker's persistent interference.

"Your young ladies are not in the drawing room, Miss Darby. They are in the library—chatting and sketching and not in *any* need of your assistance that I can tell."

"I will verify that for myself, Walker." And so saying, Kate marched toward the library until out of the butler's sight. Then she sat upon the first chair she came across.

Some time later, Miss Imogene found Kate sitting in the gallery under a painting of a distant Beeswanger relative. Lost in thought, thoughts of what she could not identify, it took a few minutes before Kate became aware of a person standing next to her with a St. John's water dog at her side. It was the movement of Jasper's tail that caught her attention.

"Oh. I beg your pardon, Miss Imogene," Kate said, jumping to her feet.

"Not at all, Kate. Walker looked in the library a moment ago expecting you to be there for some reason, and I offered to find you. There has been a message from Hendred Manor that I thought to share with you."

"Yes." Kate swallowed and stared expectantly at the young lady.

"Mr. Belcher has been found and arrested."

"And Rolland . . . Johnny?"

"No word yet, I'm afraid. Come join us in the library, Kate." Miss Imogene gestured down the hall.

"Is there something I can do for you, Miss Imogene?"

Kate was offered a sad smile. "No, no. Indeed not. I thought you might like some company. Even if you don't wish to talk."

Taking a deep breath, Kate smiled, albeit rather weakly. "Thank you, miss. That is most kind of you." She hesitated for a moment. "But if you have no need of me, I think I will take some mending to Mrs. Lundy's room."

Miss Imogene reached out, encasing Kate's hand in both of hers. "Excellent idea. Sit by the fire and get warm. Your hands are like ice."

Kate nodded, leaving Miss Imogene to her own devices, and retrieved the sewing basket from upstairs before heading to the housekeeper's sitting room. Voices from within floated down the hall toward her, giving Kate pause. She did not feel capable of participating in pleasant conversation at the moment and nearly turned around. But upon realizing that the voices were those of Marie and Camille, Kate continued. It would be cowardly not to be with Camille as they waited to hear about Johnny—for it had become amply clear that the French lady's maid harbored a *tendre* for the young footman.

"*Bonjour*," Marie said brightly as Kate stepped into the room. "Camille has been teaching me some French . . . Well, actually, I've only learned to say hello, but I am doing so with an excellent accent—apparently." She grinned and pointed—indeed, pointed—toward the petite figure next to the fire as if Kate would not know to whom Marie referred. "I'm a natural linguist . . . though I don't rightly know what that means. But I like the sound of it."

Kate smiled at her friend, knowing full well that Marie's

enthusiasm was a ruse. She was doing her best to distract Camille. It was a kindness and an endeavor in which Kate *could* participate.

"Most excellent, indeed. Might I listen in on your lesson?"

"But of course," Camille said, sitting up straighter, though only marginally.

For the better part of an hour, Camille tried to teach Marie how to say *Comment allez-vous* and *merci* correctly, with marginal success. Marginal success in terms of Marie's dubious accent, not as a distraction, for the lesson did, in fact, do that trick. As Camille tried to help Marie roll her *r*s and ignore final consonants, she began to reminisce about her early years in France. It brought out memories of childhood friends, delicacies not available in England, and visits to Paris—*Paree.*

Midafternoon brought a knock at the servants' door loud enough to break through their frivolous chatter. Kate rose to answer it but saw Mrs. Lundy rush down the hall and remained as she was . . . standing . . . listening. There was no reason for a message about Johnny to come to the servants' door. Squire Fleming would notify the master of the house and Sir Andrew first, and yet Kate held her breath. Tilting her head slightly, she strained to hear.

The tonal range of the person who had knocked was high. Was it a woman? Girl? Oh. A young boy. A lad. A voice she recognized.

Today? Bother. Why today?

Kate sighed very heavily, turned to drop her mending on the chair behind her, and walked out of the room with a shake of her head. This was something personal—again. And monumentally frustrating.

By the time Kate got to the door, the message had already been relayed, for it was Mrs. Lundy who turned to deliver it. "I'm afraid it's your mam, Kate. She wants you to come to her cottage—"

"She's quite put out, miss," Colby interrupted, still standing on the stoop. "Thinks that you have forgotten her." His face was pinched as if he shared the insult—perceived insult—as well.

"Did you tell her that things are in a muddle at the big house, Colby? Before it was company and now it is a missing member of the staff." Kate leaned past Mrs. Lundy, feeling the bitterness of the wind drafting through the open door. "I can't rush away as yet."

"She won't be pleased, miss."

"That is unfortunate, but it can't be helped. I will be there as soon as I can. Did she say why she needs me?"

"No, miss. She just told me to say: You should stop dilly-dallying and get yourself over to Vyse."

"I will, Colby. I will as soon as I can." Kate nodded, closed the door, and hit her forehead against the cold wood, making a dull thunk. After a moment, Kate straightened and pivoted to find Mrs. Lundy still behind her.

"You are needed here, Kate," Mrs. Lundy said with an

enigmatic look, then glanced out the window at the mid-afternoon sun. "Besides, it's getting late. And this is one time too many. And your mam has neighbors to help her if need be." She turned back with a deep frown. "Will that do or should I think up something else?"

Lifting the corner of her mouth, Kate snorted. "Yes. Thank you, Mrs. Lundy. That will do quite nicely. There is no question I am required at the manor."

"For now, at least," Mrs. Lundy said kindly, ruining her contrived forceful manner.

"Indeed," Kate said, turning her thoughts from her mam and her back to the door.

"Is that three . . . no, two?" Mrs. Lundy muttered behind her. "Oh dear, it *is* three. But are they ravens?"

Kate looked over her shoulder. "Is all well, Mrs. Lundy?"

The housekeeper was again looking out one of the windows that lined the corridor. Her brow was deeply folded, as she leaned toward the glass. "Yes, yes," she said dismissively without looking in Kate's direction. "There are one, two, three, but . . ." Mrs. Lundy sighed, straightened, and turned toward Kate. "Nothing to worry about, my dear; they are starlings . . . just starlings." She smiled, looking somewhat sheepish. "Thought they were ravens—and you know that three ravens together—"

"Bring bad luck." Kate nodded, trying to hide her grin, and returned to the cozy sitting room and her mending.

The sun dropped below the horizon just after four

and the men returned within the hour. They crossed the threshold with dirty boots, weary frowns, and limited news. All met in the servants' hall before cleaning up to share what was known.

"Belcher was caught first thing this morning," Matt announced. He was sporting a few new scratches on his cheek, and his coat was thoroughly rumpled, his boots caked in mud. "Sitting at his sister's table, wolfing down ham and toast, when the squire's men knocked on her door. I heard he bellowed something fierce, cursing Niven up and down." Matt glanced at Kate as he spoke with a slight curve to his lips.

Then he turned to Camille. "I was with the searchers at the Bidford farm. The dogs found the scent well enough at first but lost it within a quarter mile. It took near on two hours to find it again. And so it went all day. The weather has not been in our favor, burying the trail completely in some places. We will go out again tomorrow to pick up where we left off. We will find him."

Camille nodded, her expression grave.

"And of Rolland," Matt continued. "He was sighted near Wattage Lane but has not been seen since. The search for him will continue tomorrow as well."

Just as Matt finished speaking, Walker rushed into the servants' hall.

"I have news of the search!" he shouted, trying to get everyone's attention. He clapped his hands until those who had been in the process of leaving stopped and turned around.

"Belcher has been arrested," Walker crowed. He looked triumphant, as if he had been there in person.

"Yes, Mr. Walker," Charles said. "We know, but what of Johnny?"

"No news there," Walker said, frowning as en masse the staff turned and filed silently out of room.

"You cannot go alone," Matt protested. "Not with Rolland still on the loose."

Kate pursed her lips. While she appreciated his attempt to protect her, she would visit her mother if she saw fit, and no one could tell her otherwise . . . well, except Mrs. Lundy. And the misses . . . Mrs. Beeswanger. Yes, no one except them . . . and perhaps Mr. Beeswanger. Certainly not a well-intentioned, overly concerned young valet who looked rather fetching when his eyes flashed with anger.

"Really?" Kate stared, daring Matt to say more. In truth, she did not want to leave Shackleford Park until Johnny's fate was known. The thought of a message coming to the manor while she was gone increased her anxiety tenfold, but she had to see her mother. Had to solve whatever problem had gotten her mam's petticoats in a bunch. "I won't be long."

"That's not the point," Matt harrumphed.

They were standing at the top of the back stairs where they had to part: Matt to the guest wing, Kate to the family wing. It had been a subdued and short evening. The family had not dressed for dinner for the first time since Kate had entered service, and they had all retired early. Another long and tiring day was anticipated—a day of waiting for the older generation, a day of searching for the young gentlemen.

"What is the point?"

"Being by yourself for *any* length of time, be it a minute, be it an hour. Rolland is a nasty creature with no qualms about hurting others."

"But you said Rolland was spotted near Wattage. He is likely halfway to London by now."

"It is possible, yes . . . even likely, as you say. But what if the person who saw him was wrong or the lout doubled back to fool the searchers or Rolland has a secret hideaway . . . or stash he needs to retrieve—"

"We will be up all night if you are going to list *all* of the possibilities. Suffice it to say that I will be careful, but I *will* be visiting my mam tomorrow."

"If you go early, I can accompany you and then join the search once you are back at the manor safe and sound."

"No . . ." Kate started to disagree, and then realized that this was a perfectly reasonable suggestion. In fact, Matt could leave her at her mother's; the new search site was nearer to Vyse-on-Hill than it was to Shackleford Park. He would argue about escorting her back, but he would not win. "Actually, that is a good plan," she said, and then couldn't help but tease. "And thought up rather quickly, too."

Matt smiled; it was not a thing of beauty but a display of wearisome relief. "I'm getting better at it. One day I might even do something spontaneous."

Remembering his peck on her cheek, Kate thought Matt might have a more impulsive nature than he supposed. "I look forward to it," she said, trying to sound saucy. She knew she had not pulled it off when Matt nodded, touched her cheek, and said good night.

chapter 17

In which there is a conspiracy of tiny troubles

TUESDAY, DECEMBER 23, 1817

The baying of hounds echoed through the trees as Kate and Matt hurried through the woods. It wasn't early . . . well, not as early as they had intended, though they had neither overslept nor stopped long when breaking their fast. The blame had to be thinly spread. Sluggish, fatigued limbs; a chatty mistress; long, needless warnings from Walker; icy roads; and so forth. It was a conspiracy of tiny troubles.

It created a sense of urgency when Kate had hoped for a respite, a little one, from their worries. But now they rushed while Matt scanned the trees. Ahead, behind, side to side . . . repeat.

Kate watched the path. The hares had been through, leaving their prints in the thin layer of snow, likewise a fox.

But there were no human signs other than the ones they were leaving behind them. It boded well. Who would take a difficult route through the bushes when a path was available? No, she was almost certain the villain was far and away—especially if he could hear the dogs.

And yet Matt was still not convinced that Kate could return to Shackleford Park on her own. They had been discussing it rather heatedly and lapsed into silence a moment earlier—a state that Kate found difficult to maintain.

"Perhaps I could go with you to the search—"

"I should say not!" Matt said forcefully.

Startled, Kate swung around in time to see Matt glance about as if ensuring there were no witnesses to his lack of composure. As if the trees and shrubs would chastise. "I should say not," he repeated in a calmer, quieter tone.

Kate tipped her head, trying to understand the implication and not liking the direction of her thoughts. "You are not expecting a happy conclusion to your search, are you?"

Matt swallowed, pressed his lips together, and then shook his head, as if he didn't trust his voice.

"Four nights is not . . . ," Kate started to say, then amended her statement. "Five nights is not too long to be in the woods."

Matt sighed. It was a weary, sad sound. "Five nights at the start of winter. If he hasn't found shelter as yet . . . well, no, I don't believe Johnny will have survived." He dropped his eyes to the ground and proceeded to stare in silence for some moments.

"Johnny and I have been friends since we were in skirts," he finally said, referring to the loose frocks baby boys wore. "The Grinsteads had a haberdashery two doors down from Harlow Tailor Shop." He snorted a laugh, lifting his head, but his eyes were still focused in the past. "We got into a great deal of mischief . . . Well, at least we did until my father passed away. I hardly saw him after I moved in with my aunt and her family. It was better when I began working at Musson House; I would visit the Grinsteads on my half days. Then he started getting into trouble . . ." Matt snorted again in a poor imitation of a chuckle. "Trouble found him, as Johnny would say. Though he did have a round of bad luck . . . set him back on his heels for bit. But he came around. His position at Musson House was going to see him through. He had already started talking about being an under-butler . . . but I don't imagine . . ." Matt grew silent again; his gaze fixed somewhere over her shoulder.

Stepping toward him, Kate lifted her mitten—Mrs. Gupta's mitten—to his cheek; it was a startling contrast, bright red against his pallor.

Matt blinked, shuddered slightly, and shifted his gaze to her eyes. He shrugged in a vain attempt to seem nonchalant. "But you never know . . . ," he started to say, and then trailed off again. He swallowed visibly.

"Johnny might have found shelter or someone has taken him in or he boarded a coach . . . or—"

"Or he sprouted wings and flew away."

Kate clicked her tongue as if admonishing him for his glib remark, but there was no weight to her reproach.

"If he is fine, then he should have returned to Shackleford Park by now or sent a message," Matt said.

"He might have banged his head and can't remember who he is."

"Is that supposed to make me feel better?" Matt stared at her with a quizzical expression.

It was Kate's turn to snort. "No, indeed not. Still, I can see many a reason why he could be safe and sound but unable to let us know where he is."

"You, my dearest Kate, have an idealistic nature."

"And you, my dearest Matt, should emulate such a worthy attribute. If misfortune must pay us a call, the least we can do is hold it at bay for as long as possible."

"We are now in the realm of fantasy."

"With unicorns and fairies."

"Yes."

"I happen to like unicorns and fairies."

Shaking his head, Matt smiled—a tiny bit. "Why am I not surprised?"

Turning to link her arm with his, Kate playfully bumped his shoulder and stepped forward, pulling Matt along with her. She knew it was easy enough to talk of hope and speculate about a happy outcome when she had only known Johnny for a short period of time. She liked him very much. She prayed that he was hale and hearty . . . but it would be

Matt who would be devastated should this tale turn into a tragedy. It was Matt who would need her support and caring—for, despite her words, Kate knew the chances of finding Johnny were slim, and those of finding him well were slimmer still.

BY THE TIME they climbed up the path that lead out of the woods and into Vyse, Matt had once again lapsed into silence. Kate, too, had run out of frivolous dialogue. The weather could only be discussed in so many ways.

Mam's cottage was tranquil. The chimney pot belched smoke, the curtains were pulled back to allow the gray light to shine in, and the chickens clucked and pecked around the back gate. Nothing seemed amiss—certainly not at first glance. Kate sighed; it sounded more like a growl.

"Trouble?" Matt asked.

"No, none at all," Kate said, lifting her cheeks. "None at all." And that, of course, was the problem.

Leading the way, Kate unlatched the gate, careful not to let the chickens out. They could, if they desired, wander farther afield by flapping up and over the stone wall, but they never seemed inclined to do so. At least, the majority didn't; there was an occasional escapee, chased down by Colby—the antics related to Kate on her next visit.

Without knocking, Kate opened the door and entered, expecting to see her mother standing by the huge fireplace, stirring a pot of porridge. And that was exactly what she saw; however, that was not *all* she saw.

Sitting on the opposite side, her *father's* pipe in his mouth, leg propped up on an overturned bucket, was Johnny Grinstead, errant footman.

Kate screamed. Matt shouted, and they rushed across the room, which, as it was not large, gave Johnny no time to prepare for their onslaught. Kate threw her arms around his shoulders, and Matt grasped his hand, pumping it up and down.

"Here now, here now," Johnny said. "What's all the excitement?" Trying to lean away from the effusive display, he tipped his chair back toward the wall. "Watch the foot." He pointed his chin at the bucket.

Kate straightened, swallowed the lump in her throat, and then jumped to catch the chair as it overbalanced. Matt snatched at the front of Johnny's shirt, and between them they returned Johnny to the chair, the bucket, and his comfort. Though he was rather out of sorts.

"Well, you took long enough," Johnny complained.

Kate produced a staccato gurgle and blinked in astonishment. She glanced up to meet Matt's frown and adopted a similar expression.

"I beg your pardon?" Matt asked. He, too, had straightened and stepped away a pace or two.

"Too much *frivolity* going on to remember your old friend?" Johnny snarked. He glanced significantly between

Matt and Kate. "Two days, I understand . . . even three. But four days to come fetch me. Really!"

"But . . . but . . . ," Kate sputtered.

"We have been looking everywhere for you—" Matt started to say.

"Clearly not *everywhere*."

"We did not know where you were," Kate protested.

Johnny tilted his head slightly. "You didn't?" His tone was far less combative. His frown disappeared; he blinked at Kate and then turned his head. "Mrs. D.?"

"I sent a message three days ago." Mam shook her porridge spoon in Kate's direction, dripping oatmeal on the floor. "And then again yesterday."

Kate shook her head. "Mam, you didn't say anything about Johnny. You just told me to come."

"That should have been enough." Her mother's expression was very disgruntled. She glared at Kate.

"It was *not* enough. Not when I was busy *looking* for Johnny, Mam. Even as we speak, a score of men are scouring the woods—for nothing. Really! Would it have hurt to offer some reason I was to drop everything and run over here? I asked Colby if there was a problem, and he said there wasn't!"

"Well, of course there wasn't a problem. Johnny here is not a problem; good company, a friendly fellow, yes. But a problem, no indeed." She offered Johnny a broad grin. "'E's been tellin' me all about his childhood and his people. Including you, Mr. Harlow." She nodded in Matt's direction. "My, you boys have seen your share of mischief."

Kate lifted her brow at Matt and watched him squirm. "Oh," she said noncommittally.

"Well, we had to talk of something." Mam rebutted Kate's tone. "He needed to be distracted. The poor boy twisted his ankle something fierce crossing a ditch and can't move about."

"Then that would be a problem, wouldn't it?" Kate could not hide her derision and did not want to. She was incensed. All the angst and anxiety, all the suppression of terrible fears, the sleepless nights . . . the peril she and Matt had dealt with! Kate was so enraged that her thoughts were leaping all over themselves with no rhyme or reason, no attempt at logic.

"No—oh yes. I suppose it is. But by the time I sent Colby ta get ya, Johnny were all cleaned up, warm, and napping by the fire."

"Mr. Jordan could have brought Johnny to Shackleford Park in his cart, Mam. There was no need to wait on us to fetch him. Johnny could have been returned to his own room and his own bed, slept in comfort."

"Oh, I was comfortable enough, Kate," Johnny said most unhelpfully. "Your mam put a pallet in front of the fire with blankets . . ." He lapsed into silence, finally recognizing that he was treading on dangerous ground.

"I wouldna ask the Jordans, Kate. You know that. It would set up an obligation. Then that woman could ask anything she wanted of me. No. I will not be beholdin'."

"I find that a rather odd stance given that you have no compunction about sending Colby to the big house with a message."

"Your brothers pay Colby to help out around the house. There is no obligation. He's not doing me a favor; he's doin' a job."

"I see," Kate said in a clipped tone, glaring at her mother. She turned back to Johnny, with a quick glance at Matt before she did so. He was still smiling, though not as broadly as a moment ago; he was still caught up in the euphoria of Johnny's return to life. Kate would be, too, if it hadn't been her family member who had exacerbated the situation. It was dire enough without her mam . . . Kate sighed, shook her head, and lifted her brows.

"Johnny, I cannot tell you how overjoyed I am to discover that you are hale and hearty." Her eyes wandered toward the bucket and then back up to his face. "Well, most parts of you are. And I humbly beg your pardon for the . . . confusion," she said, studiously not glancing in her mother's direction. "And ask your indulgence for a little while longer. There are men out looking for you, and I think it behooves me to inform them of your situation before we arrange a cart or wagon to pick you up. But fear not, you will be back at Shackleford Park before midday."

Johnny nodded formally and then ruined the effect by grinning. "Lawks, I'm glad of it—that I'm not going off right away, that is. Your mam makes excellent oatmeal."

"It's the honey," her mother said, as Kate knew she would.

With a nod and feigned smile, Kate returned to the door,

threw it open without a backward glance, and had every intention of slamming it shut. Unfortunately, something got in the way.

"Not without me, Kate," Matt said, catching the door and closing it behind him.

"I thought you would want to stay with Johnny." Kate knew she was not thinking as clearly as she ought—anger had a tendency to do that. She marched to the gate, scooting a large brown hen out of the way. After stepping back onto the lane, she turned into the hamlet.

"We'd best take the road north first and cut into the woods when we hear the dogs getting closer," she explained even though Matt had not asked. "The men might want to join the search for Rolland or they might want to go home, but there is no need for them to be out in this cold unnecessarily. Really, what if someone had been injured? And for what? Look at you . . . you have scratches. Yes, needless scratches. Scratches that would not be there had we known that—Good morning."

Kate waved at the silhouette visible through the Jordan cottage window and continued to chunter. "Uncalled for. If only we had known. If she had sent a clear message . . ." Kate waved at the remaining two cottages—not that she could see anyone about, but just in case there was and they thought Kate as standoffish as her mother. Really, could the woman be any more exasperating?

"It's not your fault, you know." Matt had remained silent

until they were well away from Vyse-on-Hill, now hidden by a curve and a stand of larches.

"I know that," Kate said, stomping, kicking, and marching down the road, pulling ahead of him. "I blame my mam entirely."

"It's not your fault," he said again, as if she hadn't replied.

Pivoting, Kate rounded on him. "I know that!" she said rather forcefully. She stood akimbo, leaning forward, hands fisted in her mitts.

"No, you don't, but you should." Matt had come to a standstill as well.

"I would appreciate it if you would not stare at me with what appears to be sympathy; it is most irritating."

Matt closed the distance between them, but he left that sympathetic, understanding, kind, irritating expression on his face. "Had you known, you would have acted differently. But think on it this way: While it caused us some . . . um . . . difficulty—"

"Difficulty? We were tied to a wagon, soon to be animal fodder, all because we were trying to find someone who was perfectly safe—far safer than we were."

"True enough. But had we not gone looking for Johnny, we would not have known who our villains were. Belcher and Niven would not have been caught."

"Yes, they would have. Johnny would have told us. They nabbed him, tied him up, and left him in the barn. He knows full well who the culprits are; that, in fact, is the reason they tried to hightail it out of Tishdale."

"Lud, I see what you mean," Matt said dourly as he folded his brow, shook his head, and tut-tutted with gusto. "Indeed, it *is* all your fault." His scowl was entirely ruined by the mischief in his eyes.

A laugh burst from Kate, and she grinned for a moment before the smile slowly faded. "Well, perhaps not. Still, I beg your pardon. While you are right, my mother and I did not willfully obstruct, it amounted to the same thing. Johnny was . . . *is* your friend, and his disappearance was a sore trial to you."

"Apology accepted." Matt bobbed his head and then looked up, tilting his head to listen. "I believe the dogs have turned in our direction."

Kate paused to listen as well. She was surprised by how much closer they were when her inattention could not have lasted more than a minute or two.

"Should we *meander* into the woods and *suggest* an end to this particular search?" Matt said, gesturing with a wide swoop of his arm.

"Excellent notion," Kate said airily, feeling much better for no reason at all. And with that she crossed the ditch and stepped into the woods.

THERE WAS NO doubt that at some time this stand of forest had been cut down. The trees and scrub were not ancient, but they were still old and gnarled and jumbled. There was no path to follow, and so Matt tried to lead, to take the brunt of the hanging skeletal branches. Kate would have none of it, wending among the trees beside him.

She was no longer a bundle of repressed rage, walking instead with a rolling gait and relaxed shoulders; her jaw was no longer taut. Matt could unwind now, as well. He glanced to his side, only to find Kate looking back. They shared a grin that lasted several steps—several blind steps. His heart pounded in his ears; he forgot to breathe, and he decided that one of his favorite pastimes, *ever*, was hiking through the woods with someone who had stolen his heart—one Miss Kate Darby, lady's maid extraordinaire.

Then he walked into a tree, bounced back, and nearly took a tumble.

"I'm fine," he said, correcting his balance, and then dusted the detritus off his shoulders.

Kate laughed lightly—prettily—and grabbed his hand, giving it a squeeze. "Best come this way," she said, tugging him to the right. "There is a fast-moving stream up ahead; it hasn't been quite cold enough to freeze as yet, and I am not enamored with the idea of wet feet. The plank bridge upstream would mean a large detour; better we use the fallen log downstream. It's just over here."

Just over here didn't prove to be as close as it sounded, and yet upon reaching the stream, Matt could see the wisdom of altering their route. The stream was fairly wide and rather deep. The banks had eroded; tree limbs drooped and dragged across the water's surface, and large rocks channeled the water around them in splashing, roaring torrents. Beautiful and dangerous to cross.

And yet Kate made it seem easy. She jumped up on a log that lay diagonally across the stream, resting on the top of the banks a foot above the swirling water. It had been worn flat, no doubt the result of many pounding feet over the years; it was clear that the tree had not fallen recently.

Matt offered his arm as support until she reached the water's edge, where she let go, found her balance, and skipped—not literally—to the other side in lithe, well-practiced strides. Matt's crossing was somewhat slower, but as long as he stared at the log and not Kate, he could think clearly enough. Clearly enough to put one foot in front of the other and not tip into the water.

Once back on terra firma, they stood staring into the woods with hands once again clasped—mitten to glove. Four paths branched out ahead of them . . . well, more like spaces between the trees, because there seemed to be no true path. As the sound of the approaching dogs grew louder, the echoes reverberated from the north and they turned accordingly, slipping through and under the branches until the terrain eventually forced them to unclasp their hands.

Matt sighed deeply . . . but silently.

"I hope the team is being led by someone I know." Kate frowned as she wiggled past a scraggly alder and a beech. She likely realized the upcoming difficulty of convincing a stranger to call off the search for Johnny on their say-so.

"Mr. Snowdon, Squire Fleming's huntsman, knows me well enough, but I believe he is conducting the search for Rolland."

"I'm sure there will be someone that you can—"

A loud twig snap cut Matt's sentence short. He wheeled to the left, just in time to see a figure leap at them from behind a tree. Matt fell hard to the ground, receiving a kick to the ribs as he did so—right where Rolland had hit him not two days earlier. He twisted, reaching out for Kate, knowing that she had fallen, too, trying to cushion her, trying to reach her, to protect her. But his fingers came up empty.

With elbows beneath him, Matt struggled to sit up, but a boot held him in place. About to toss said boot to the devil, Matt stilled. His eyes had gone past the boot, to the figure above him.

Kate had not fallen; she was still upright, being held tight, an arm wrapped around her waist pinching in her cloak. She was being used as a shield, protecting a fiend that held a knife to her throat.

"We meet again, Mr. Harlow," Rolland said with an ugly grin.

chapter 18

In which sacrifices are required

Looking down her nose without moving her head, Kate watched the blood and all expression drain from Matt's face until it resembled a mask—a death mask. She wanted to know if he was all right; he had gone down so fast and hard that she had heard the slap of the force on the ground. But she couldn't ask, couldn't say anything. The blade of Rolland's knife was sharp and pressed against her vocal cords. She didn't doubt for a moment that the villain would do her an injury, gleefully, if she gave him the excuse.

"I'd like to say well met," Matt drawled, no longer straining to sit up. "But I would have preferred to *never* see you again." His cap had been knocked off in the tumble; his hair tangled over his brow.

"You were destined for disappointment."

"So it would seem." Matt continued to stare, barely blinking, hardly moving.

A raucous echo of baying hounds filled the air, preventing any continued conversation—if they had even desired to do so—for several minutes, after which the knife at Kate's throat loosened and she could feel Rolland shift. His voice, when he spoke, seemed to indicate a turned head.

"Those bloody dogs. I have doubled back, hidden in ditches, and jumped a brook, but they just keep coming."

"Such a hardship," Matt said with no inflection whatsoever.

Kate felt Rolland stiffen, and then he huffed into her ear; her hood had fallen when he had leapt at them, and it now hung down her back. It was no protection from the cold or Rolland's proximity. She tried not to shudder, not to swallow in discomfort, not to push away. The blade was still at her throat.

Matt met her gaze, but his expression did not change. Kate watched his brows; his mouth, his chin. Nothing. No secret message. No indication of what he was thinking, or what he was planning . . . if he was planning. The possibilities were rather limited, positioned as they were . . . the first need was to get Matt up off the ground. But how to—

"What now?" Matt asked.

Rolland hummed as if in deep thought—Kate could hear it and feel it. And then he lifted the blade away from her neck—still at the ready but no longer pressed into her skin.

Lifting his foot off Matt, Rolland stepped back a few paces, dragging Kate with him. When he stopped, they were partially behind a tree—another shield between him and Matt. Such a brave person.

"Get up slowly," he said. "Too fast and we will see if Miss Darby's blood matches her mitts."

Swallowing while she had the chance, Kate tried to lean away from Rolland, away from his knife. But he felt the shift and yanked her back against his chest once more. Watching from where he sat, Matt exuded calm as he squatted and then rose to his feet. Kate knew it to be a facade, knew him well enough by now to see the signs of disquiet—but she doubted Rolland would recognize the lifted chin and flared nostrils as anything other than posturing.

"Excellent, excellent," Rolland said, pulling Kate back another few feet. "Now stop. There. You, Mr. Harlow, are going to save the day."

"Oh." Matt glanced at Kate and then back to Rolland.

"Yes. You are going to stop the dogs."

"And how might I do that?"

"You are going to walk in that direction . . ." Kate felt the jerk and movement as Rolland used his shoulder to gesture. "And keep walking until you find them. And then you will tell those . . . those addle-patted fools, that if they do not desist *immediately*, I will use my knife on Miss Darby here. I'll give you five minutes. Go!"

Matt pursed his mouth and shook his head before

answering. "They will not listen to me. I am a stranger and someone of little consequence. They will not end a search for a blackguard such as you on my say-so. Best take *me* hostage and let Miss Darby go. They *will* listen to her; they know her."

Rolland snickered. It was oily and repugnant. "You would like that, wouldn't you?"

"I would, indeed, otherwise I would not have suggested it."

Unable to remain silent, Kate took issue with the proposal. "*I* would not like it." She glared at Matt; it was a terrible idea, fraught with danger and disaster. Matt's life would be forfeit. "Rolland," she said, her voice staccato as she tried to breathe with the viselike grip across her gut. "You have. A better chance. To get away. On your own. If *you* go—now! Run."

"I think not," Rolland said, backing up farther, dragging Kate with him once again. It was most tiresome, being treated as a rag doll.

Matt stepped forward, keeping the distance constant.

"No!" Rolland shouted. "You stay where you are."

Matt smiled. It was a gentle smile, genuine and caring. He was looking at Kate, and she smiled back. She wasn't entirely sure what it meant, but even if it only served to throw Rolland off, it was a lovely sight. Kate swallowed and breathed—tried to breathe . . .

"Rolland, loosen your grip. Allow my feet. Back on the

ground. I will pass out. A dead weight." Kate gasped dramatically. It was more than what was warranted, but it did the trick—Rolland eased his hold. She gulped at the air with great theatre. She could now see the knife out of the corner of her eye, and she wondered if she had the strength and speed to grab his arm—secure it just long enough for Matt—

"The dogs are closer, Rolland," Matt said with undisguised triumph. "Soon you will have far more to contend with. Best—What are you doing?!"

Swiping downward, Rolland slashed his blade across Kate's hand. Mrs. Gupta's lovely warm mitt was rent across the top. Kate felt a sting and glanced down, watching a line of red form and then ooze into the wool. Fortunately, it was not deep and it did not hurt as much as it might—oh, bother, there it was . . . There was the pain.

"That was entirely unnecessary," Matt sputtered, his hand outstretched toward Kate.

"I beg to differ." In a deft move, Rolland released her waist, grabbed the ruined mitt off her fingers, and tossed it at Matt. It fell short, as one might expect of a flying woolen object, but while they watched it drop to the ground, Rolland grabbed Kate about the waist again. "Now," he said, "unravel it."

Kate suppressed a growl. She knew where this was going—but would he bind her or Matt? Kate's answer was not long in coming. By the time Matt had unraveled all but the thumb, Rolland had placed the knife back on her neck and waved Matt closer.

"Tie her wrists," he said, forcing Kate to her tiptoes when he pulled the knife higher.

Matt glanced at Kate, who once again could not speak for fear of a ravaged throat. She offered him an infinitesimally small nod. "I beg your pardon, Kate," Matt said, with a visible swallow.

Kate put the palms of her hands together as if praying, one mitted and the other still bleeding but not as freely as it had been. She offered them to Matt as if it were of no consequence, but she could not control their shaking. He encased her hands with his for a moment, meeting her gaze—until Rolland protested by way of pressing the knife tighter. Kate involuntarily sniffed in distress. Rolland shouted, forcing Matt to bind her wrists *tighter* and to do so *faster.* Kate's heart hammered against her chest; she wanted to scream. Being bound was so much worse than being hauled around.

Just as the job was complete, Rolland swung the knife and brought it down hilt-first onto the side of Matt's head. Matt saw it coming and tried to duck, lifting his arm to ward it off, but the steel connected with his skull in a horrid thunk, and he dropped to his knees. Groaning, Matt shook his head and tried to stand, but Rolland shifted Kate, kicking out at the downed figure. Matt slapped the ground, face-first.

"NO!" Kate screamed and thrashed, kicking back to no

avail. Rolland evaded her every move. "Matt!" She lost sight of her danger, of the knife, in her frenzy of anguish. She dropped her weight, letting gravity pull her out of the fiend's grasp, only to have him recover his balance and snatch her back just as she landed by Matt. In a practiced move, Rolland hoisted her up and over his shoulder, grabbing her flailing legs about the knees and holding them and her skirts tightly.

Had Kate been able to breathe, she might have been able to struggle longer, but the brute's shoulder was pressed into her gut. Kate had barely enough air to survive let alone to fight.

Rolland snorted and started to make his way through the bushes. "Not as much weight as a wine barrel," he said in a half whisper.

Kate dragged at the air, gasping and gulping as the irregular terrain bounced his shoulder deeper into her belly.

"Serves you right, Kate Darby. I would not be in this scrape were it not for you. So now *you* will be my insurance."

Kate pushed her bound hands against Rolland's back and lifted her head to look behind. The figure lying on the ground became smaller and was soon lost behind the snowy trees, but Kate no longer feared for Matt's life. He would recover, would not be lying vulnerable to the elements for long. When Kate had landed beside him, he had croaked, "I'll follow," even as he had moaned in pain.

He was not unconscious, not mortally wounded. She repeated that mantra with every one of the fiend's steps and added another—a truth only just realized. Matt was not unconscious, not mortally wounded, and she loved him. Her abject despair moments earlier had shown her just how much she cared—this was not a flirtation; this was love.

Kate swallowed, almost dazed by the awareness. She would not think beyond that, not now . . . She had to focus, concentrate, plan. She let her head drop, finding it hard to keep her neck arched, and stared at her hands, bound, tied messily, as the ends flapped and bits of wool broke off and floated away on the breeze. Red fluff. Bright and noticeable.

Kate smiled, used her free fingers to pull at the frayed strands of wool, and dropped a wad of bright red fluff onto the ground. And then she did it again, and again. Snow in some places, hard-packed earth in others—it mattered not; there was a trail of red to follow. Matt would find her; they would defeat this brute together.

MATT CURLED ON his side, snorting dirt and leaves from his nose as nausea kept him from jumping to his feet. He lay for a moment staring through the bracken and then shifted to a sitting position. He closed his eyes as dizziness threatened to overwhelm his senses and lifted his hand to gingerly touch the goose egg on the side of his head.

"The blighter!" Matt shouted to the trees, though they likely did not hear him. The forest was being inundated by a cacophony of echoes.

And yet, the baying hounds sounded no closer than they had before, and Matt wondered if the dogs had lost the trail—Rolland's trail. It hardly mattered; they were taking much too long to get here. They would be of no help.

Grabbing at a branch beside him, Matt pulled himself upright and was pleased to find that, after a moment or two, the dizziness passed. Lumbering to the path where Kate had disappeared, he stared down at the footprints. They were clear enough in the thick layer of snow, but where the snow had failed to accumulate, there were no telltale signs of a person passing. Except . . . except . . .

Matt lifted one side of his mouth in a lopsided smile. Except Kate, fast-thinking, marvelous Kate, had left him a trail. Red bits of fluff stood out stark against the monochrome of the winter tableau. No slow, methodical scrutiny required, no fear of losing the path. It was clear and well marked.

Straightening, Matt stepped forward, snapping a twig as he did so. He felt it . . . but did not hear it. The dogs were making too much noise; they would mask his footfalls. With a deep breath and a conscious effort to ignore the throbbing in his head, Matt quickened his pace, following the trail of red, praying that the color was not an omen.

Straining to see into the forest, Kate thought she saw a movement and jerked in her enthusiasm.

"Do that again, an' I'll drop you. Don't think that I won't," Rolland snarled. He was panting now, overexerted . . . or panicked.

Naturally, there was only one answer to such a threat. Kate jerked again. She had the pleasure of feeling Rolland slip, catch himself, and then lose his footing again. However, in his falling, Kate was tossed to the ground as well . . . but lady luck was with her, for Kate landed on a small hazel and then rolled to the side. In a flash, she was on her feet, running back the way they'd come. "Matt!" she screamed until Rolland raced after her; she was yanked backward, nearly strangled by her own cloak.

She landed on Rolland, sending him sprawling and his horrid knife clattering as it dropped under an evergreen. But he held on to her cloak, and Kate was twisted up in the material. She could not get away again. She glared at him as they sat on the ground, chests heaving with effort and anger.

"I don't intend to be caught, Kate Darby. Best you get used to the idea of my company. I'm not liable to set you free anytime soon . . ." And then he added, spittle hitting her face as he shouted, "if ever!"

Kate shrugged—not because she felt nonchalant about the prospect, but to cause as much irritation to this maggoty worm as possible. She had the pleasure of seeing his jaw tighten and his eyes squint. But he was more concerned about the dogs than spewing any more venom, for he glanced back over his shoulder toward the worst of the noise and jumped back to his feet, dragging her with him. And *drag* was the best descriptor, absolutely, for Kate refused to put her legs beneath her.

Undeterred, Rolland grabbed the cheerful red bindings tied around her wrists, lifted her arms above her head, and hauled—heels in the snow, collecting dead leaves and twigs, *towed*—until a particularly loud snap caught his attention. Wheeling around, Rolland stared into the woods for one blink, maybe two, and then he lunged at Kate, hoisting her back over his shoulder.

Had Kate been able, she would have mocked him for being so fearful that he left his knife behind, but as it was to her advantage—and his shoulder kept hitting her in the gut—the words remained unspoken. They had not gone much farther when a new hum was added to the mix, a sound that she was expecting, a noise that she welcomed.

Water. Fast-flowing water.

"Bloody Hell. God's teeth! What now?" Rolland shouted to . . . well, no one in particular. He loosened his grasp on her knees, and she slid over his shoulder, down his front, to the ground . . . much, much too close to his person. Kate leaned back. "What is that?" He pointed behind her.

Kate lifted her brows. "What is what?" she asked as if she couldn't hear the roar.

He grabbed her by the shoulders and turned her around.

They were standing on the bank at a significantly wider and higher spot in the stream than the one that she and Matt had crossed earlier. It looked quite daunting. There was no doubting the danger of crossing here.

"How did you get across?" Rolland shouted into her ear, and then he quickly pivoted, swinging Kate around with him, using her as a shield yet again. "What was that?"

Kate had heard nothing. She shrugged but scanned the woods as she did so, looking for a figure in brown: a handsome figure with a thoughtful character and gentlemanly manner—a very lovable young valet.

"What is that?" the fiend behind her repeated, but this time he pointed at the little bits of red trailing back into the woods.

Kate thought they looked rather pretty, festive even. "Yuletide decorations?" she asked innocently.

"Nothing to worry about, Rolland," a voice called. Its echo masked where the sound originated . . . that and the dogs baying and the water roaring over the streambed rocks. It was not a tranquil place. "Actually, too late to worry, to be more precise."

"Don't come any closer," Rolland warned. He grabbed at her shoulder with one hand, the other patting frantically at his coat, likely searching for the knife left under the evergreen . . . unless he had another knife. That thought sent Kate's heart racing until Matt spoke again.

"Kate, look up!" he shouted.

It took a moment but only a moment for Kate to realize what he was asking her to do; it seemed an age since their discussion in the blacksmith's shop. Kate buckled her knees and dropped like a stone, falling to the ground. A human projectile leapt over her head, slamming into Rolland. Knocked backward, the two young men tumbled down the streambank, rolling and skidding in a jumble of limbs.

Up in an instant, Kate ran to the bank's edge in time to see Rolland punch Matt in the ribs once, and then twice. Matt grunted with the impact and swung at Rolland, giving him a glancing blow on the arm. It served to push the villain back enough that Matt's next fist landed on his nose. As Rolland backed toward the stream, he reached forward, grabbing Matt's coat lapels and pulling Matt with him.

Stumbling down the embankment, Kate scooped up a rock and raced to the water's edge. She dropped to the ground to avoid flailing arms, and smashed the rock onto Rolland's foot just as he dragged Matt into the frigid water. It did not stop him. She swung the rock, connecting with the fiend's ribs, but again he was undeterred.

As the two grappled in the water, the current swirled around them, knocking them off their feet one moment, standing them up the next, and still they fought. It was messy and perilous; blood dripped into the water, and yet Rolland was unstoppable. A creature possessed. He tried again and again to push Matt's head underwater, grabbing his face, clawing at his eyes.

Kate waded into the bitterly cold water, the current tugging at her skirts threatening to drag her under, sweep her away. She screamed Matt's name, and in the instant their eyes met, she tossed the rock. It didn't go far, not nearly far enough, but Matt leapt back and sideways and snatched the crude weapon out of the air. He turned and swung the rock down. Down on Rolland's hand, pounding it into the boulder next to him.

Kate did not hear the snap of broken bones—there was too much noise—but she saw Rolland's face contort with pain. He released Matt's coat to cradle his hand, and in doing so, the current caught him, dragged Roland out to the middle of the stream, and bounced him through the rushing current. He screamed as the water slammed him into and through a cluster of rocks. He grabbed at a fallen branch wedged between them. Catching it with his unbroken hand, Rolland held on, buffeted by the water but no longer tumbling; the roaring current rushed past him.

Wading, fighting his way to the bank, to Kate, Matt slipped. His head disappeared under the torrent. Horrified, Kate rushed forward, bound arms outstretched, an anchor should he need one. There to her right; Kate swung her arms. She felt a touch, but just a touch. Like a scythe, she cut her arms through the water back and forth, searching for his hand, fingers, hair, anything—and then his head came out of the water and he gasped for air and flung his arm forward, latched on to the red wool around Kate's wrists.

The jolt nearly knocked Kate off her feet, but she dug in her heels and hung on. Stayed upright and slowly backed up . . . pulling, towing Matt until he could find his footing again. And when he finally could stand, he splashed to the side of the bank. He flopped onto the ground, his chest heaving; his face was beet red from the cold.

"You're shivering," Kate said, squatting beside him. "You're freezing." She lifted her hands to his cheek. They, too, were burning red from the cold—her sleeves were soaked almost to her shoulders; her cloak and gown were sopping wet from the waist down.

"So are you, Kate dear," he said as his whole body started to shake.

"Use my cloak." Looping her arms over his head, Kate straddled Matt's legs and sat down. There was no other way to get close with her wrists bound as they were. "Stop complaining. I will not desist. Wrap my cloak around your shoulders. Yes, there. Isn't that cozy? We are both using it—a modicum of warmth." She laughed weakly. "It's all relative."

And though they could in no way, shape, or form call themselves comfortable, Matt's violent shaking did subside. He started to breathe easier, and when he rested his chin on her shoulder, his occasional shudders were fewer. Kate did not comment on the fact that the damp was now seeping through her bodice. And then Matt lifted his head, staring behind her. He swallowed audibly. "We can't leave him there."

Kate twisted around to see, her arms and cloak still draped over Matt's shoulders.

Rolland was still in the middle of the stream—for while it seemed that an inordinate amount of time had passed, it had, in fact, been but a few moments. And during that time, Rolland had begun to tire. His hold was faltering; his grip slipped farther down the branch twice, even as they watched.

"If he lets go, his life will be forfeit," Matt said, shaking his head.

Kate stared, thought, and then nodded. In an awkward maneuver that involved great balance and the significant use of her lower limbs, Kate disentangled from Matt's warmth and stood. "If he lets go, he'll be swept toward the log . . . if I can get there first, I can grab him and pull him up—out of the water."

Matt rolled onto his knees and then struggled to his feet, still shaking, though not as violently. "I'll try to hold him until you get there." He glanced downstream, likely trying to estimate the distance to the overturned log.

"You've only just stopped shuddering," Kate said with her eyes still on the figure in the cold water. About to argue for Matt's safety, she watched as Rolland slipped again, nearing the end of his branch.

Without another word, she turned to the streambank. Climbing quickly, grabbing at roots and saplings with her hands still bound, she was atop in a trice and running through the bracken. She ignored the branches as they whipped against her and snatched at her cloak, looking for a path, hole, opening . . . anything that she could race through. She stayed next to the stream; to veer away would add too much time. She had to be across, be at the ready when Rolland let go. With that thought, she pushed harder, added a burst of speed, and, at last, spied the log up ahead looking unnaturally sedate, surrounded as it was by swirling, violent water.

Chancing a glance back, Kate gulped. Matt was knee-deep in the stream, reaching toward Rolland with a long branch. She could see his mouth move, knew him to be yelling, but she could not hear anything above the roar of the water. Could Rolland hear? It was impossible to tell. Turning back, Kate raced to the log, slipped as she stepped on, righted herself, and slowed. It would do no good to fall now.

Two deliberate paces later, a strange movement caught Kate's attention; her eyes shot upstream. Rolland was tumbling toward her. His head was above the water one moment, gone the next. The stream was not deep, but the current was too strong for him to put his feet down, too strong to find a foothold among the rocks, too strong to do anything but sporadically gasp for air.

Watching the water for a moment, Kate dove to where the current funneled beneath the log, throwing herself down, lying across its length. She barely fit in a prone position, but that was not the worst of it; she had nothing to cling to, nothing to brace herself, nothing to prevent her from tumbling into the water when she caught—

Oh no, there he was, feetfirst—but right where she thought he would be.

Kate reached into the water, grabbing and coming up empty over and over. His feet passed, his legs, and then his torso. She was going to lose him!

He flailed, and Kate grabbed his arm. She hooked it over the log and then grabbed the other, doing the same. Kate reached into the water again, closing her hands around the front of his coat, and she tried to lift. She had unconsciously placed her boots on either side of the log, but with every heave, they slipped—slipped until her grip on the log was as tenuous as that of Rolland.

"I won't let go," Kate promised, finally meeting Rolland's gaze—finally taking account of his appearance. He looked battered, exhausted, and surprised. "I won't," she repeated louder, as much to convince herself as to convince Rolland.

And then a heavy weight bumped into her leg, almost knocking her off the log, but a hand came up righting her legs. "Hold on just a moment longer, Kate. I'll grab him from the other side."

The sound of Matt's voice and his proximity gave Kate hope, and hope gave her strength, and she held on. No longer required to heave, Kate could cling and wait and concentrate on not losing her grip, not allowing her numb fingers to release the material that she could no longer feel. Kate was aware that Matt had climbed over her, over to the other side of the log, and yet when he placed his hand on Rolland's coat next to hers, she gasped in surprise. It had seemed fast and slow . . . but it mattered not; they could lift him together.

And so they did. They lifted and dragged . . . well, Kate dragged, Matt pushed. Until, finally, all three were gasping on the side of the streambank. Kate yanked off her cloak and flung it over Rolland while he lay spent, his red hair plastered to his head—looking anything but villainous.

Dropping her arms over Matt's head, she tried to ease his shudders with her own body heat, but it, too, was nearly depleted. And yet they did not move; they sat thus, trying to fight the cold and offering comfort to each other as best they could, until the searchers, their dogs, and their wonderfully dry coats reached them a *very* long five minutes later.

chapter 19

In which an earth-shattering truth is realized

They descended on her mother's cottage en masse. While the dogs had been sent home with their handlers and another two men rushed to call off the other search, the group still arrived with enough souls to fill the cottage's living space and most of the yard. By the time they had carried Kate in and deposited her, Matt, and Rolland in front of the fire, her mother was bustling around, trying not to look pleased with all the company.

Had Kate still been bound and shaking, she was fairly certain, her mother would have been upset and slightly more concerned with her daughter's health. But Kate had a dry coat over her shoulders, the red wool bindings had been cut, and the nasty gouges and abrasions on her wrists were hidden . . . well, Kate hid them as best she could within the folds of her skirts.

And if Kate's mam was glad of the company, Johnny was doubly so, laughing and joking with the men until their numbers started to dwindle. A few were sent to Shackleford Park for a wagon or cart to transport those returning to the manor, another few ran for instructions from the squire regarding Rolland, and still more were sent for medical men: the apothecary and the surgeon.

Within a quarter hour, Kate began to relax. She glared at Rolland—sitting across from her, nursing his hand on his lap—and then turned to gesture Matt closer to her. Strange, he did not argue. His hair was drying, and he appeared less bedraggled; his color was no longer cadaverous. All very good developments. Though there was more than a hint of exhaustion in his expression. Kate smiled wanly, dropped her head onto his shoulder, and there—cuddled together for the world to see—she fell asleep.

WEDNESDAY, DECEMBER 24, 1817—CHRISTMAS EVE

MATT AWOKE THE next morning in his narrow Shackleford Park bed with the well-banked coals in the fireplace still glowing orange. He was surprised that he had slept; his mind had been such a whirl that he had envisioned tossing and turning all night. He snorted, realizing that it had taken him mere minutes to nod off. Struggling to sit up, Matt pushed against two heavy counterpanes and shifted to the side of the bed.

It was not surprising that his first thoughts were of Kate.

How was she? How had she dealt with the emotional and physical turmoil of the day before? And when would he see her again?

Kate had not returned to the manor with Johnny and him. Mrs. Darby had finally recognized the sorry state of her daughter when the apothecary had arrived to prescribe restoratives. Though not usually his job, the man had bandaged Kate's wrists as well, all the while exclaiming with great indignity about the way Kate had been treated.

Mrs. Darby, seeing the damage and then learning the cause, had ordered Rolland from her house. She would not have the monster what hurt her child under her roof. There were not many to disagree—actually, none had disagreed. A blanket was thrown over the villain's shoulders, and he was shunted outside to sit under guard with the chickens. Mrs. Darby cared not a whit about his broken hand—thought it just desserts. Rolland was lucky that Mrs. Darby had no pigsty.

And then, when the wagon from Shackleford Park had pulled into Vyse-on-Hill, Mrs. Darby had refused to allow her daughter to be taken away. Kate was instead transferred to the lumpy bed on the other side of the fireplace and covered in blankets.

It was good to see her cossetted, at last.

Matt was treated to a hero's welcome upon his return to Shackleford, though it paled in comparison to Johnny's greeting. Almost the entire staff streamed out of the door as if they had been waiting, watching, and anticipating their arrival. Camille was at the head of the line and surprised everyone, including Johnny, when she ran to him, ensured that he was steady on his makeshift crutches, and then threw her arms around his neck. She kissed him—long and hard. The staff were laughing and clapping when Camille came up for air; the look of happy astonishment on Johnny's face was priceless.

Matt had spent the rest of the day restoring his dignity with a bath, a change of clothes, and playing honored guest in Mrs. Lundy's warm drawing room. The staff took turns bringing him foodstuffs, dropping by for a chat, or asking questions about the ordeal. Marie was concerned about Kate, not certain that Dame Darby would be able to nurse her good friend through her worst hurts . . . but allowed that there was nothing she could do about it. Though the staff tried to be diplomatic, curiosity was rampant. And yet he had not been expected to work in any way, shape, or form.

THURSDAY, DECEMBER 25, 1817—CHRISTMAS DAY

CHRISTMAS AT SHACKLEFORD was, as usual, an irregular day. The family saw to themselves after church while the staff was busy pursuing fun and frolic most of the afternoon. The weather had cooperated, snowing, rather heavily at times. Big, fat flakes drifted onto leafless branches, collected across the roof ridge of the manor, and quickly covered the grounds.

It was a true white Christmas, and the sense of celebration filled the air with laughter.

Mr. Ernest and Mr. Ben refused Matt's service beyond the rudimentary basics of laying out their clothes for the morning. Charles was asked to bring up the washing water, and Mr. Mowat shaved the young gentlemen before he was required to lather up Sir Andrew.

While Matt appreciated the attempt of all to provide him with another day to recover from his ordeal, it also provided too much time to think. It might have been better had Kate returned to the manor with him—no, it would *definitely* have been better if she had returned . . . although, since he was constantly thinking of her . . . oh bother, he didn't know whether he was coming or going.

Matt was in a quandary, a great quandary of such a large degree that he was nearly beside himself with indecision. There was no doubt of what he *wanted* to do—a vision of racing to Vyse and pulling Kate into his embrace and staying entwined until the end of time came to mind. But what he wanted, what could happen, and what Kate wanted were not necessarily the same thing.

Through the course of the morning, Matt had come to realize a profound and somewhat earth-shattering truth. He was *deeply* in love with Kate Darby. It was of the forevermore variety, he was certain. He could envision no happy future without Kate at his side.

There were, however, great obstacles in his way . . . in their way. First and foremost was the question of how Kate felt. And even if she thought highly of him—which had seemed rather evident the day before—did that mean she wished to continue their . . . flirtation, increase their flirtation, or rearrange their lives in light of this . . . flirtation? All very complex questions when taking into account that Kate worked for a family hours distant from where he worked. Would the Beeswangers and Steeples visit more than once or twice a year? Not likely. Would Matt be content seeing Kate only once or twice a year? Not likely. Could he look forward to occasional holidays in the general vicinity of Tishdale? Not likely.

There were other possibilities, too. Less appealing possibilities: Would Kate think it better to step away, away from these heady but overwhelming emotions? For it would not be an easy courtship—if that was the path they chose. They would spend years apart, saving for the future: Matt for his tailor shop, Kate for her dress shop with her mother. Could they feed and sustain a closeness when they were, in fact, not close? It was all very confusing, and there was only one certainty.

Matt needed to talk to Kate.

And so it was that Mr. Ernest offered little comment when Matt informed him that he was going for a walk out of doors, possibly to ice-skate or take a meander toward Vyse.

"Heading west?" Mr. Ernest asked with studied nonchalance before nodding and returning to his book.

Matt donned his cap and, having no inclination to follow the path through the woods, took the road to Vyse-on-Hill—which, oddly enough, was west of Shackleford as Mr. Ernest had suggested. Despite beginning with a staid and steady pace, Matt was near to running as he approached the turnoff toward the hamlet. His need to see Kate became desperate, to see that she had truly fared well, that her recovery was as profound as his.

And then, the Fates produced a miracle. Coming toward him, looking hale, hearty, and lithe, was none other than the love of his life.

KATE ALMOST TRIPPED when she recognized the figure up ahead. A smudge lost in the curtain of falling snow on the horizon of the road at first, the shape soon formed into a tall, broad-shouldered young man with entrancing eyes . . . though she could not see his eyes as yet. The basket of linens that she was carrying became lighter, her steps faster, and the cold snap of the wind felt positively balmy.

As they rushed toward each other, Kate could think of nothing she wanted more than to wrap her arms around his neck and feel his lips on hers. It was all she could think about, to the extent that she disregarded all else around her . . . including Matt's sudden hesitance. His expression was that of a young man not entirely sure of his reception, but Kate had every intention of making it clear. And so, when they were finally at touching distance, Kate dropped her basket on the ground and threw himself in his arms.

Matt was not hesitant then. She felt his arms go around her, heard his sharp intake of breath, smelled his musky, manly scent, but she could not see him . . . because her eyes were closed. Closed so that she could wallow in this glorious moment to its fullest, revel in the sensations as Matt kissed her until her toes curled and then trailed his lips down her neck, back up to her mouth, and started all over again.

In heaven, yes, most certainly. There was no other way to describe a place of such delightful emotion and sensation. Her entire body thrummed, and she forgot to breathe—momentarily. The weather, where they were, who might see them, all aspects of anything not Matt, dwindled into the background until Kate was lost. A future of moments such as these would be nothing short of paradise—and then Matt ruined it all.

"We should probably stop," he said, leaning back a full inch, though they were still blissfully entangled.

"No, I don't think so," Kate argued. Her hand slid up to the back of his head, and she pulled it forward to where her lips were waiting, welcoming, anticipating . . .

"We need to talk," he said, breaking her concentration yet again.

"I'm somewhat occupied, Matt. Could we talk later?" It was a rhetorical question, for her lips were already on his.

The proceedings proceeded in a great procedure—that of a tighter clasp and lips wandering past the collar of her cloak until he pulled away again, this time a full *two* inches. He was in earnest, frustratingly so.

"We *need* to talk."

"Really, Mr. Harlow, I don't know what there is to talk about! You are leaving with the Steeples next week; we need to kiss as much as possible before we are faced with a dearth of embraces."

"That is exactly what I wish to talk about."

"Oh. I thought you wanted to talk about Rolland or our watery adventure . . . or some such."

"Not at all. I wanted assurance that you are well . . . but I can see and feel that you are." He squeezed as he spoke, smiling either at the knowledge that she was fine or the recollection of her demonstration of . . . fineness. "Squire Fleming has the counterfeiters well in hand, and it is no longer our concern."

"Excellent. So let us return to our former activity." Kate leaned forward, pressing her lips to his. But he did not press back. "Matt! Kiss me." He did not comply. It was most inconsiderate, positively rude. "Fine. What, my dear sir, would you like to discuss about your far-too-early departure? Will I write? Most certainly . . . Perhaps the most pertinent question would be will *you* write?"

"I don't wish to discuss writing when we have not established where our relationship is going."

Kate grinned. "I thought that patently obvious." She wiggled in his arms, trying to get closer, but it was not possible without kissing again, which she was all for . . . but it would seem that Matt was still in a talking mood.

"Kate, we have barely had time to get to know each other. Our living arrangements have forced us to rush. While there is no doubt that we are attracted to each other, where does it go from here? Our positions—"

Laying a finger across Matt's lips, she shushed him. "It will be difficult seeing each other irregularly, relying on letters or news from others to maintain contact, and it will be thus for years. We are young, and we have a long time to wait . . . to save for our future, but really the only question should be about love. Do you love me?" She watched his face become excessively still and plunged on before she lost her nerve. "I love you. I think it patently obvious."

She stared expectantly, anticipating the glow of rapture to shine through his eyes. Words echoing her own would not be out of place . . . and yet. It was rather disconcerting when Matt's brow puckered and he huffed a sigh. A sigh? Kate swallowed in discomfort, shifting slightly away.

"There is no doubt of how we feel right now." Matt nodded as if what he was saying made any sense. "We survived an ordeal together, with each other and helping each other, but in the days to come, will this euphoria fade? Will you come to wonder why you threw yourself into my arms?"

Kate frowned. Her euphoria was already starting to fade,

and it had nothing to do with the ordeal or *her* feelings—why was Matt not declaring undying devotion . . . ? Wasn't that the way this was supposed to proceed?

"Do you have doubts about how *you* feel? For I have none. I can see a future for us—a happy future that involves living above a tailor shop or ladies' dress shop—"

"Or both. We could divide the space." Matt lifted one side of his mouth in a quirky smile—at last.

"Exactly." Kate nodded emphatically. "Clearly, you have been thinking on this as well. I am greatly relieved. I was starting to wonder—"

"This is no easy path to walk. We are choosing a long, winding road full of pitfalls."

"No, indeed not. It is a long road of anticipation and glorious moments like these. Although I would much rather be kissing than talking."

Taking her at her word, Matt leaned forward, but Kate stopped him this time.

"Excuse me, kind sir, but I believe you have something to say before we continue."

Matt grinned, lifting his hand to her cheek and caressing it. He shifted his gaze from her lips to her eyes. "Will you marry me?" he said in a solemn tone.

Kate shook her head. "No. That's not it."

Matt's brow shot up, and he stared at her with an expression of confusion. "You won't marry me?"

"Goose. No, that is not what you need to say." Young

men could be so thickheaded at times. "You have to state how you feel."

"But you know how I feel."

Kate snorted in a most unladylike fashion, but it *was* warranted. "You still have to say it."

"I love you, Miss Kate Darby?"

"Is that a question or a statement?"

"A statement. I love you, Kate Darby. Completely. Now and forever."

With a sigh of contentment, Kate nodded. "Wonderful. I love you, too, Matt Harlow." Balancing on her tiptoes, Kate leaned forward, puckered and ready to seal the moment in a kiss, but Matt was *still* not finished talking.

"Excellent. Yes, most excellent, for I thought that might be the case. I gave Mr. Ernest my resignation this morning."

Kate was dumbfounded, flabbergasted, and horrified; she stared at Matt, wordless for a second or two before expressing her disapproval. "Pardon! Matt, you can't do that. I know we will not see each other nearly enough, but there are no valet positions available in Tishdale, certainly not at this time of year. I will not let you work in the field . . . No, no, you must go back to Mr. Ernest—"

"I could be a blacksmith; there seems to be a sudden lack at present. Or, perhaps, a wine merchant?"

"That is not in the least amusing, Mr. Harlow. No, no, this is terrible. I won't have you give up your livelihood, a position of which you are rightfully proud, for me. Oh dear, what shall we do? You could claim to have been confused, not in your right mind . . . anything. Really, Matt, I will not let you sacrifice your very identity so that we can be together more often. I will not do it. I would much rather see you rarely than to have you think less and less of me because of what you gave up. Please, Matt, you will learn to hate me. I couldn't take that; I couldn't deal with that. Please—"

"Kate, no, it's fine. All is well. I already have another position." He touched her cheek again. "I apologize most profoundly. I did not realize how much the idea would upset you or I would have immediately added that I will be Mr. Ben's man. When I spoke to him about the prospect, I found that he and Mr. Ernest had already discussed the possibility at Miss Imogene's behest. Not perfect, I grant you . . . but Mr. Ben contrives to see Miss Imogene at least every month . . . and I can do that . . . we can be satisfied with that. Every month, not every year. Much better . . . don't you think?"

Throwing her arms around Matt's neck, Kate rested her chin on his shoulder. "Yes," she said, though it sounded muffled.

"Was that yes, we can do it . . . or yes, you'll marry me?"

Kate suppressed a giggle; now was not the time to be frivolous. She lifted her head and answered clearly and precisely, so there would be no doubt or misunderstanding. "Yes, Matt, my love, I can survive on monthly visits, and yes, I will marry you."

She started to grin, but Matt's reaction prevented her from doing so as her mouth was otherwise occupied.

IT TOOK AN extraordinary amount of time to stroll back to Shackleford Park; they could only walk about three steps before feeling an overwhelming urge to be in each other's arms again. Since none expected them to be timely, they weren't.

Marie greeted them as they stepped across the threshold. She clasped Kate tightly, tears welling in her eyes. When she pulled away, she glanced toward Matt, back at Kate, and then again at Matt. Almost certain, almost, that their newly forged relationship was not written across their foreheads, Matt was a trifle confused. However, Marie laughed, kissed his cheek, and hugged Kate again. Apparently, Marie was a mind reader.

Kate had to have a private talk with Mrs. Lundy, about which Kate was excessively mysterious. Matt found it alluring . . . though, truth be told, he found everything about Kate alluring. The way she walked, turned her head, blinked, smiled . . . yes, every move she made drew Matt's attention. He thought he was hiding this finely honed interest, but he caught several side glances going from him to Kate, followed by a wide grin. Perhaps he wasn't being as discreet as he thought.

The servants' hall was bustling and noisy until Kate and

Matt strolled in and then the staff, as one, turned toward them expectantly. Matt's discomfort grew as he recognized the eager expressions. They were anticipating an announcement, something Matt wasn't yet ready to do. If nothing else, he had to talk to Kate's mother first. Looking for an escape route, Matt's eyes wandered to the window and the frozen pond beside the stables.

"Can you skate?" he asked, leaning toward Kate.

"Not my forte," she said quietly. "But I'm sure you would not mind catching me, if I fell."

Matt turned toward Kate. "I would love to catch you." He shifted dangerously close, within kissing distance.

"I'll be at the pond, if you have need of me, Mrs. Lundy," she said over his shoulder. And then in a whisper she added, "I'll borrow Marie's skates. She's not inclined to spend any time in the cold."

"I'll see if Charles has any blades I can strap to my boots." He leaned closer, garnering a collective gasp from their onlookers.

Rather than supply the expected kiss, they smiled at each other and then set off in opposite directions, ignoring the groans of frustration behind them.

BY THE TIME they were once again in the frigid outdoors, the snow had stopped and the sun had come out. The air was still frosty. Puffs of their steamy breath led the way to the deserted pond. Kate slipped a few times; it was near impossible to watch her footing when Matt was so near. She didn't think he minded catching her, as he had not let go of her arm the last time.

Strapping on their skates took longer than normal, as there seemed to be a great need to stare wordlessly at each other for inordinate amounts of time. But eventually, they made it to the ice, which was far from smooth.

Kate, showing off, glided out ahead of her beau . . . only to stumble. Matt caught her as promised, but they both went down in a tumble anyway. Laughing, Matt reached over to help Kate up, but rather than cooperate, she pulled him down onto the ice beside her. He rewarded her, as expected, with a long, lingering kiss.

"We are already reaping the benefits of my changed employ, Kate, my love," Matt whispered, as if his words were sweet nothings.

"How so?" She knew the ice was cold, but her body tingled with heat from her toes to her head.

"Mr. Ben has decided that he no longer wants to rush back to Canterbury. We will be staying until Twelfth Night."

Kate gasped . . . quietly. "Another seven days. Oh, Matt, that is tremendous."

"This does *not* mean we should limit our kisses."

"Of course not." Kate giggled. "We have to practice as much as possible."

Matt smiled, lifted her hand to his lips, and pressed a

soft, gentle kiss on her palm. He watched Kate flush, her gaze intensified, and she was suddenly breathless. It was a mirror of his reaction.

"You and me," he said softly, swallowing, thinking of the future—until reality smacked him upside the head. "You and me . . . and your mam makes three," he said with a grin. Kate had to know that her mam was not only included in their plans but welcome; he would not be the cause of a rift.

Kate's smile grew. "I am very touched by your readiness to accommodate my mam, and I am happy to say that it will not be necessary. Our future is ours and ours alone." She attempted to sit up and was very glad of Matt's supporting hand.

"I don't understand." He pulled Kate to her feet.

"I had a good long talk with Mam when I overnighted in Vyse. She does not want to move into town or be part of a dress shop after all; she wants to stay near her boys and allows that she will get used to the solitude. She even complimented Mrs. Jordan . . . Though it was backhanded, it was the first time I have heard Mam speak with any kindness about the good woman. It bodes well. I believe Mam will settle quite happily . . . eventually. But I have come up with a splendid arrangement to speed up the process. I spoke to Mrs. Lundy about Mam doing the mending in the servants' hall instead of her cottage. She could come over two days a week and enjoy the chaos of the household—more than enough activity for anyone. Mrs. Lundy thought it a most excellent idea."

Matt smiled broadly and started to lift Kate's hand to his lips again, but paused. A fairly large group of people were approaching the pond, skates in hand. It would seem the staff, almost in its entirety, had felt a burning need to skate. They huddled together at the far end of the pond—watching, trying to appear disinterested in the two persons on the opposite side.

Pippa watched them rather intently. Matt bowed in acknowledgment of her interest, and the girl huffed and turned away. He returned his gaze to the most marvelous person on the pond. "You are really quite amazing."

"It was Johnny who brought about the change . . . well, encouraged Mam to admit that she did not want to have a dress shop."

"Johnny?"

"Yes, he extolled your virtues almost the entire time he was in Vyse and convinced Mam that you were a worthy young man and that you would be able to care for me in grand style."

"But you don't need me to set up your business."

"Yes, I know that. But it would seem that my mam was going to open the dress shop with me because she thought that I would not do it otherwise."

"Silly Mrs. Darby."

"Indeed." Kate smiled again, glancing at the overly curious staff watching from the other side of the pond. "Shall we give them something to talk about?"

"I thought you'd never ask." Matt placed one hand on each of her cheeks, looking deeply into her eyes. "I love you, Kate."

"I love you, too," she said just before his lips touched hers . . . and the crowd at the end of the pond hooted and hollered and generally made a great nuisance of themselves.

Matt and Kate ignored them—completely.

Glossary

CHIMNEYPIECE: a fireplace mantel, mantelpiece

COTTAGE: in the Regency period, a small house with living space on the ground floor and one or more bedrooms under the eaves

DICKED IN THE NOB: silly, crazy

ELUCIDATE: explain, make clear

EWER: large jug with a wide mouth

LADY DAY: March 25; feast of the Annunciation

MARKER POST: road or mileage indicator

MUMPERS: beggars

STIR-UP DAY: day associated with the making of Christmas pudding

TETCHY: bad-tempered

RESPITE: short rest, postpone

Acknowledgments

Practically everyone that a writer meets influences her perception of the world. This, in turn, impacts her characters, helps flesh them out, and allows them to live and breathe with all their odd quirks and stellar qualities. So thank you, one and all!

More specifically, I would like to express my great appreciation to everyone at Swoon Reads. Emily is a patient and thorough editor whose enthusiasm is a great inspiration. Thank you, Rich and KB, for the amazing cover. It shouts *historical Christmas* and hints at the content perfectly. Thank you, fellow Swoon writers Danika and Kelly, for your advice and friendship.

To my family: I cannot tell you how much your support has meant to me, especially these past few months. To my husband, Mike: There are not enough words to describe how much I appreciate your care as we deal with new challenges. Deb and Christine: This book would not have made it to print without your help reading and rereading—updating and catching inconsistencies. Dan, Mom, Steve, Trudy, Dillan, Matthew, and Stew: Thank you for your encouragement.

And to my readers: Thank you for your eagerness and interest in my characters and the dilemmas they face. I hope you enjoyed *Carols and Chaos*.

Merry Christmas!

Cindy

Fall in love with Ben and Imogene in

Shy aspiring artist Imogene Chively has just had a successful Season in London, complete with a suitor of her father's approval. Imogene is ambivalent about the young gentleman until he comes to visit her at the Chively estate with his younger brother in tow. When her interest is piqued, however, it is for the wrong brother . . .

Turn the page for a glimpse at a summer full of secrets, scandal, and, of course, sabotage.

chapter 1

In which Miss Imogene Chively prays for a sudden rainstorm or a stampede of goats

GRACEBRIDGE MANOR, FOTHERINGHAM, KENT—EARLY JULY 1817

"Jasper!" Imogene Chively shouted as she jumped to her feet, flinging her sketch into the grass. "Don't move! Stay. Stay exactly where you are!" Grabbing her skirts ankle-height with one hand and desperately waving the other, she raced across the courtyard of the old castle. "Emily, help!" she shouted over her shoulder without a backward glance.

She couldn't look away; Imogene's eyes were glued to those of Jasper. If she looked away, he might try to leap off the crumbling wall. And he couldn't. . . . Shouldn't. It was too high. There was no doubt of an injury—a broken leg or, worse yet, a snapped neck or a blow to the head. "Stay," she said again but in a softer, crooning tone, almost a prayer.

Having reached the wall, Imogene found Jasper two feet above her reach—even on tip-tip toes. He stared down at her, pleased with all the attention, tail wagging, tongue lolling.

"Oh, Jasper," Emily Beeswanger said behind her. "You silly dog, what have you done now?" Emily, Imogene's fast friend for all their eighteen years, was well versed in Jasper's antics.

The St. John's water dog continued to wag.

"Can you keep him from jumping, Emily? Yes, hold your hands up like a barrier. Exactly. I will go around behind him."

"You can't climb the wall, Imogene. It's too fragile. It will fall down, taking you with it."

"Yes, I know. But I need to get higher. I have to encourage him to back up—he doesn't have room to turn," she said, looking up at the narrow ledge of the ruins. Frowning, she glanced across the courtyard to where they had lain a coverlet on the grass beside the moat. "Or," she said, her eyes settling on the basket atop the blanket. "I have a better idea; I know what always encourages obedience."

"Food," Emily said knowingly.

"Indeed." Imogene turned and sauntered back across the cobblestone. She would have preferred to run, but doing so would have fueled Jasper's excitable nature and encouraged him to leap over Emily's outstretched arms to join her. She had just reached into the basket when a nearby voice startled her. Spinning around, Imogene locked eyes with a young gentleman standing on the arch of the moat bridge.

Imogene gasped in dismay. Ernest Steeple? Surely not. Her suitor was not due until the next day.

"Can I help?" he asked again when Imogene did not answer.

Gulping, Imogene tried to calm her panicked thoughts. She could feel the burn of embarrassment flaring up her cheeks as soon as she realized that the stranger was not Ernest but Benjamin Steeple, her suitor's younger brother.

Suddenly the air was filled with a cacophony of barking, whining, and yipping. Imogene turned to see Jasper's body undulating in serpentine waves as his excitement grew to a fevered pitch. He was staring at the new arrival.

"No!" Imogene shouted as the dog crouched. "Stay!"

Even as she called out, Mr. Steeple moved. In a flash, he was across the courtyard and almost to the wall when Jasper launched himself into the air. Emily jumped up to catch him, but Jasper sailed over her head with ease.

Imogene screamed as time slowed to a crawl. Jasper seemed to fall forever, but in those seconds, Mr. Steeple must have known he would not reach the dog. He flung himself under the dog's path in a spectacular sprawl, sliding across the ground on his back. The dog landed with a heavy thump on the poor gentleman's gut, eliciting a sharp gasp as they tumbled together. The tangled mess of dog and man finally came to a rest at the base of the wall.

Naturally, Jasper was the first on his feet. Bouncing with excitement, showing no injury or awareness of his peril, the dog licked Mr. Steeple's face with abandon. The poor gentleman tried to fend off the affection to no avail; he finally succumbed to the wash and laughed as he struggled to his feet.

Imogene wanted to ask if he was hurt, but her tongue would not cooperate.

"Are you all right?" Emily asked in an easy manner that Imogene wished she could emulate.

"Oh yes, indeed. Just a little dirt here and there," he said as he swiped pointlessly at the ingrained dirt on the elbows of his well-cut coat. "Nothing that can't be fixed."

"That was quite impressive. I'm certain Jasper would have done himself an injury had you not caught him."

Mr. Steeple laughed again. "I'm not certain I would call that a catch."

"It was impressive nonetheless." Emily smiled up at him as he smiled down.

It was a charming tableau: Emily, with her pretty, round face framed by cascades of brown curls peeking out from her bonnet, staring up at the handsome visage of Benjamin Steeple, with the old castle ruins behind them. The smell of flora wafted through the air while cattle lowed in the nearby fields. Yes, indeed, a lovely tableau.

Imogene huffed a sigh. This was dreadful.

Mr. Benjamin's presence had only one possible meaning—

disaster was about to befall them. Mr. Ernest Steeple had arrived early. There would be no meandering through the estate, sketching and chatting with Emily about their London Season. No relaxing at the old castle, chasing butterflies or picking wildflowers today. Guests were about to descend upon Gracebridge Manor *en masse.*

Imogene sighed again. It was a long-suffering sigh, not that of eager anticipation.

Benjamin Steeple bent to accept Jasper's continued attention. It was the respite Imogene needed, and it gave her time to take a few deep breaths, release the tension in her shoulders, and lift her cheeks into the semblance of a smile. As the mutual enthusiasm continued for some minutes, Imogene had an opportunity to observe Mr. Benjamin without reserve.

They had met once before, at a soiree in Mayfair. Though her glance of Ernest's younger brother had been for a short duration—and she had spent the entire length of the conversation staring at his shoes—she had seen the likeness immediately.

There was no doubting that Ernest and Benjamin were brothers, and being so close in age, at twenty and nineteen, it would be difficult for anyone without the knowledge to say who was the elder.

Similar in build, the Steeple boys were tall, loose-limbed, and broad-shouldered. They both had dark brown hair, but Ernest wore his longer, brushed back from a widow's peak.

Ernest's face was slightly broader; Benjamin's chin was slightly sharper. And while Ernest had an open smile, Benjamin's smile was wider, getting wider and wider—as Imogene continued to examine his face without speaking.

Oh Lud! She was *staring.*

© Christine Anstey

CINDY ANSTEY spends her days painting with words, flowers, threads, and watercolors. Whenever not sitting at the computer, she can be found—or rather, not found—traveling near and far. After many years living as an expat in Singapore, Memphis, and Belgium, Cindy now resides with her husband and energetic chocolate Labrador, Chester, in Nova Scotia, Canada.

CINDYANSTEY.COM

Check out more books chosen for publication by readers like you.